LIGHTNING WOLVES

A Novel of the Clockwork Legion

DAVID LEE SUMMERS

Hadrosaur Productions, Mesilla Park, NM

Lightning Wolves
Hadrosaur Productions
Second Edition: December 2021
First date of publication: July 2014

ISBN-10: 1-885093-98-5
ISBN-13: 978-1-885093-98-1

Other Books by David Lee Summers

The Solar Sea
The Astronomer's Crypt

The Space Pirates' Legacy Series
Firebrandt's Legacy
The Pirates of Sufiro
Children of the Old Stars
Heirs of the New Earth

The Clockwork Legion Series
Owl Dance
Lightning Wolves
The Brazen Shark
Owl Riders

The Scarlet Order Vampires Series
Dragon's Fall: Rise of the Scarlet Order
Vampires of the Scarlet Order

To
Gary Every
A valued companion on many literary adventures who encouraged me to explore the wilds of Cochise County and discover little known gems of Arizona history.

ACKNOWLEDGEMENTS

Although much of the experience of writing a novel is sitting alone behind a computer, it also provides exciting opportunities for engagement with people as I've worked through different parts of the writing process.

This novel had its start in thinking about stories of early Arizona settlement. Two people who really engaged me on the subject were Les Reese and Gary Every. Sadly, Les passed away a few years ago, but he first told me about Presidio Santa Cruz de Terrenate, an abandoned Spanish outpost near Tombstone, which I thought would make a fantastic setting for a story and appears in this novel. Gary Every, to whom this work is dedicated, is not only a good friend, but a talented author. His collection of travel essays, *Shadow of the OhshaD*, was invaluable in my early research. Rebecca Petithory-Hayes and Gary Hayes also gave me great insights and pointed me to numerous books and resources about the Clantons and the Shieffelins.

Whether they be in the hands of swashbuckling pirates, samurai warriors, or medieval knights, swords have long fascinated me. Thanks to Doug Williams for a fascinating afternoon's lesson in swordsmanship.

Thanks to Verity Summers for coming up with the name Lyssa Crimson and for a pleasant walk along the Rio Grande imagining the chile farms of days gone by.

Susan Voss, Stephen Ormsby, Kumie Wise, and Myranda Summers all read early drafts of this manuscript and provided useful critiques and suggestions. Laura Givens began working on the cover long before the book was complete. Her early renderings helped me visualize some of the characters and machines better and endow them with more life on the page.

Finally, thanks to Phyllis Irene Radford for her patience working with me to polish this manuscript. I have learned new things from each editor I've worked with, but I particularly value the time and care Phyllis took working with me on this volume.

LIGHTNING WOLVES

CHAPTER ONE
PEER REVIEW

Larissa Crimson dreamed a memory of flight.

She sat aboard a mechanical owl in a chair of light-weight wooden slats. She gripped levers and adjusted pedals while her heart beat a fierce accompaniment. Green hills fell away. Ahead, two impossibly large, silver-gray, cigar-shaped objects floated over Denver, Colorado. Like menacing thunderheads, these ships of the air hung against a backdrop of cloud-streaked blue sky. White, blue and red horizontal bars—the Russian Empire's distinctive markings—decorated the airship tails. Below her, Americans marched through the streets on their way to dislodge the Russian forces. Something small and black dropped from the closest vessel's belly. A moment later a sickening thud sounded and a cloud of black and gray soot rose from the street. Hovering out of artillery range, the dirigibles dropped more bombs on the troops below.

Looking around, she saw eleven other owl-like craft. The occupants knew they were the only people who could put an end to the invasion. Professor M.K. Maravilla, an inventor from Mexico, had built the owls he called ornithopters. Fatemeh Karimi, a healer from Persia, led the small group. She swept her hand forward and Larissa eased the largest lever toward the front panel. The tiny chemical-reaction steam engine under the seat chugged harder, the wings flapped faster, and the mechanical owl shot toward its target, slamming Larissa back into the seat.

Cold, mountain air whipped by and threatened to carry away her coachman's hat, even though she had carefully pinned it to her hair. Despite the chill, sweat beaded around the edges of her goggles and made her face twitch.

As the ornithopters closed the distance, Larissa saw a smoke

1

poof erupt from the nearest airship's flank. A moment later, a whining projectile whizzed underneath her. She caught her breath and fought to steady her hand. Seeing a second, third, and fourth puff, she pushed one of the pedals and moved the control rod to the side, sending the ornithopter into a wide, upward arc. Seconds later, an owl below her burst apart. She slammed her eyes shut. The rider was dead, whether smashed by cannonball or splattered against the earth.

Opening her eyes a moment later, she glanced through the haze of unshed tears. Onofre Cisneros, the dashing pirate captain, waved at her. It was time to begin their assault on the far airship. She completed a circle, faced the target, and opened up the throttle again. With a new burst of speed, she followed Cisneros. As they got closer, ports opened in the sides of the airships' envelopes and men leaned out, firing at them. Bullets whistled through the air. She gritted her teeth, knowing she needed to focus. She pulled back the control lever, lifting the ornithopter higher. The seat's slats cut into her back and legs. A moment later, she was over the airship. Again, she sent the owl into a wide arc, so she approached from the bow. Slightly ahead of her and below, Cisneros's owl canted over. One of its metallic claws gripped the airship's skin and the other missed. The ornithopter spun and Larissa's heart skipped a beat as she thought it would topple off with the captain.

Cisneros leapt from his seat and grabbed the airship's cloth skin. His owl came to a stop right in her path. She slowed her craft as much as she could and banked to the side. She extended the owl's talons, but they only grabbed empty air. She leapt from the seat, toward Cisneros and began to slide past him. She jerked to a stop and nearly choked as the captain caught her collar. Her owl skidded along the spine until it smashed into the tail. The airship lurched and listed to one side. As bile rose in her throat, Larissa became aware of the buildings, streets, and people below, looking small, like some child's elaborate plaything. Her eyes shut and she fell.

Breathing rapidly, she flailed about until her eyes flew open again, revealing a new scene entirely. Firm ground pressed against her back through a thin bedroll. A dagger of light came in through the cave entrance and shone across her face. She rolled over and snuggled further down into her blankets.

Larissa gulped deeply several times and reminded herself she had not fallen. She had survived the Battle of Denver. Onofre Cisneros had pulled her up until she could grab on to the airship's skin. Then he cut a hole into the envelope and climbed down through the girders, past the internal gasbags. Inside didn't feel a lot safer than outside, but at least Larissa couldn't see the ground. They found the unconscious crew in the gondola, tumbling about the floor as the vessel bucked like an unbroken horse. She knelt beside one of the crewmen and checked his pulse, surprised to discover he still lived. Cisneros gained control of the airship and brought it to the ground. They escaped just moments before an artillery shell flew into the vessel and ignited its load of hydrogen. Larissa shuddered.

The enticing aroma of coffee finally lured her from the blankets' warmth. Her muscles ached, protesting the fact that she'd slept on the rocky ground every night for the last two months. She would give good money for a nice soft bed. After checking her boots for varmints, she pulled them on, then did a quick check to make sure she was buttoned up and reasonably covered before stumbling over to the cook stove Professor Maravilla had set up at the back of the cave. A long pipe ran from the stove to the cave's mouth to carry the smoke away. The back part of the cave trapped the stove's heat and made it comfortable—except, of course, for the lack of a mattress.

The professor was nowhere in sight. Larissa knew that most people who encountered a young woman alone with a middle-aged man would make assumptions of a most unsavory nature. However, Professor Maravilla wasn't like that at all. His only concern was science. That suited Larissa just fine. She poured a cup of coffee, took a sip, and walked toward the cave's entrance.

Sunlight gleamed from a bird-shaped framework of saber-thin steel. A spruce seat faced dials and gauges set in a panel. This was the first of a new generation of ornithopters—craft that flapped their wings to fly. The professor hoped to build more. None of the originals had survived the Battle of Denver.

Strips of metal, boxes of gauges, and spools of metal cable littered the cave entrance. Plans held down by rocks carpeted the cave floor. Blue lines scribbled over the papers indicated improvements. Larissa knelt down and traced lines that showed the lift as air flowed both under and over the wings. She sipped the coffee and considered how much she had learned about mathematics, physics, and engineering. Looking up, she sighed. Despite all the clutter, they were missing gears, fabric, and chemicals needed to finish and fly the owl. The few coins jingling in her pants pockets, wouldn't begin to buy the parts needed.

Before joining up with the professor, Larissa had been a bounty hunter. She actually had wanted to be a sheriff or a marshal, but as a woman, her prospects of finding a job in law enforcement were minimal. Being a bounty hunter allowed her to control her destiny. The more she learned about science, though, the more she realized the potential to understand and possibly control the world itself.

Larissa stepped from the cave onto a rock ledge just outside the entrance. Groggy and unsettled by the dream as she was, the sight still took her breath away. Sunlight washed over the Grand Canyon's walls, bringing out vivid shades of rust, ochre and green. As the sun rose in the sky, shadows withdrew from the rocks. Birds called and soared overhead. Despite the frightening memories of battle, she would do anything to join the birds again.

Professor Maravilla crouched on the ledge, apparently absorbed by the view. He looked immaculate despite camping out in this remote cave for two months. He wore pressed trousers and a red silk vest. His boots were polished to a bright shine. Even his mustache was trimmed to a fine line. He cradled a mug of coffee and whispered to himself. Unlike most people who had the habit, the professor would say something, then wait a few minutes as though listening for an answer. Larissa only heard one side of a conversation. She found it more than a little spooky at times.

She cleared her throat.

The professor jumped, splashing a little coffee from his mug onto the ground. "Good morning, Miss Crimson, I didn't hear you come out."

"I didn't mean to sneak up on you."

The professor held up his hand and stood. "No worries. I was just absorbed in ... thought."

Larissa nodded. "I've been thinking, too." She took a sip of coffee. "I'm thinking I might ride into Flagstaff today, go check at the sheriff's office; see if there are any bounties I could collect."

Maravilla sighed. "It's a dangerous way to raise money for this project and there are no guarantees of success."

Larissa pursed her lips. "Do you have any better suggestions?"

"There are industrialists who would pay to develop such a project. Perhaps they would give us better facilities and tools ... more permanent accommodations." The professor's gaze drifted off over the canyon. "Perhaps I might write to the Lowells in Massachusetts."

"They're textile manufacturers, aren't they? What interest would they have in mechanical owls?"

"The owls are covered in fabric, perhaps they could see this as a market they could develop. I've heard their son Percival has an interest in mathematics and engineering. The family might see it as a project to garner his interest."

Larissa narrowed her gaze. "It sounds like wishful thinking." She took another sip of coffee. "It seems like the military would have the most interest in funding your owl research."

The professor shook his head sadly. "They already have my plans. I have no desire to continue their development as weapons. The ornithopters were meant as a way to understand the behavior of wildlife."

"They could be so much more," said Larissa. "We're at war with the Russians."

The professor nodded. "Tell you what, why don't we both ride in to Flagstaff? I can write some letters and send them out. You can see what bounties there are. Between the two of us, we should be able to find a way to continue building the owl. Besides, we could use some more food and supplies."

Larissa smiled. "I think we might just have enough money left for a few nights at a hotel."

Maravilla frowned. "Don't you think it would be better to save our money?"

"What? Try to ride all the way to Flagstaff and back in a day? No thanks!"

The professor shrugged. "Very well, we could use a holiday, but if we're going to leave for a few days, we should make sure the cave is secure."

With that, Larissa and the professor made a hasty breakfast of hot cakes and preserves. Afterward, they doused the cook stove's fire and packed what they needed for a few days in town. Finally they moved the mechanical owl to the back of the cave where it wouldn't be visible to any curiosity seekers who visited the canyon.

Once that job was complete, Larissa wiped out their tracks and did her best to obscure the path to the cave with branches, rocks, and bits and pieces of scrub brush. Such masking wouldn't fool a professional tracker or a bounty hunter, but a casual eye was unlikely to see the trail as anything out of the ordinary.

Satisfied they had secured everything to the best of their ability, Larissa and Maravilla readied their horses, packed up their saddlebags and began the ride south to Flagstaff.

Ramon Morales awoke in a small room of his mother's homestead just outside of Estancia, a little farming town almost dead center in the New Mexico Territory. He and his fiancée Fatemeh Karimi had been there for just over two weeks. After driving the Russian army out of Denver with the help of Professor Maravilla and his clockwork owls, Ramon and Fatemeh wanted a place to rest and they wanted to ask Ramon's mother for permission to marry.

In the two weeks since they'd arrived at the homestead, Ramon had been hesitant to raise the subject. Fatemeh was Persian and belonged to a religion called Bahá'í. Instead of discussing marriage, Ramon and Fatemeh helped out where they could. Ramon tended the animals and Fatemeh looked after the small grove of fruit trees. He found he enjoyed the routine. Better yet, he enjoyed the fact that Randolph Dalton, a mine owner in Socorro, New Mexico, no longer sent bounty hunters like Larissa Crimson after him.

After Ramon and Fatemeh thwarted the Russian airships, they found they had powerful friends in the United States Army. General Phillip Sheridan himself assured Ramon's safety.

Ramon climbed out of bed, dressed, then put on his little round glasses and went out to the kitchen. His mother sat at the table, doing cross-stitch. She wore her salt-and-pepper hair in a bun and blue veins stood out in her thin hands. Setting her work aside, she went to the stove and ladled atole—a thin porridge of cornmeal spiced with cinnamon—from a pot into an earthenware bowl, then poured coffee into a mug for him.

"Good morning, Búho." She used the Spanish word for owl, given to him because of his glasses.

"Where's Fatemeh?" he asked.

"She woke up early," said Sofia Morales, returning to her place at the table. "She went out for a walk."

Ramon took a deep breath and savored the fragrance of the cinnamon-spiced atole. "I've missed your cooking."

"Fatemeh made breakfast this morning."

Ramon looked up and smiled. "So, what do you think of her?"

"I like her." Sofia examined the cross-stitch.

Ramon took a sip of coffee and then took a few bites of the atole. Emboldened by his mother's declaration, he spit out a question before he could stop himself. "Does it bother you that Fatemeh isn't Catholic?"

Sofia pushed the needle through the cloth. "Not terribly," she said after a moment.

"I thought you would want me to marry a Catholic girl."

Sofia pulled the needle and thread, then pushed it into the cloth again. "Ramon, I've known Christians who care less about Jesus and God than she does. She prays. She helps others. She's a good woman. I don't really care whether she calls herself Bahá'í or Catholic as long as she believes in God, and it's clear to me she actually believes more than some people I see at Mass every week."

Ramon sighed relief, then took another bite of atole. As the silence wore on, he sensed there was something else, something unspoken. "So, you don't have any problem if I marry Fatemeh?"

"I have no problem with Fatemeh." Sofia looked up into Ramon's eyes. "What I'm worried about is you."

Ramon sat back, stunned. "Me?" He placed his hand on his chest. "I believe in God."

"That's not what I'm talking about." Sofia sat her cross-stitch on the table and folded her hands. "How long are you going to sit around here? What are you going to do with the rest of your life?"

"Why *can't* we stay here? This is good land. The trees and the animals would support us."

"They might, at least for a while," agreed his mother. "But would the trees support your spirit?"

Ramon's brow creased. "I don't know what you mean."

"You used to be a sheriff. You did that job because you had a desire to help people. You're a man of action. You will grow restless. Fatemeh doesn't deserve a man who will always be looking to the horizon, wishing he was somewhere else. You're a good man, my son, but you're not a farmer."

Ramon laughed, then turned his attention to the atole and coffee. Finally, he looked up again. "I've been enjoying it here … the peace and quiet."

"That's because you've had a difficult year, being chased by Dalton and his bounty hunters. You were tired and you needed a rest. But before you marry Fatemeh, you need to decide what you're going to do with the rest of your life."

Ramon took a deep breath and let it out slowly. He stood and looked out the window. "I wasn't happy being a sheriff, you know."

"Why was that?"

He shook his head. "Everyone I knew left Socorro. I was sheriff in a town of strangers."

Sofia narrowed her gaze. "That doesn't ring true to me."

"Why not?" Ramon looked out over the plains toward the Manzano Mountains. Snow from a late spring storm still capped the summits.

"Fatemeh was a stranger … at least until you got to know her."

Ramon turned around and faced his mother. "If it wasn't strangers making me uncomfortable in Socorro, what was it?"

Sofia Morales stood and took her son's hands. "Ramon, you were growing bored and restless there, just as you will grow bored and restless here if you stay."

"I was happy being a clerk in California. I was happy being a ranch hand in Las Cruces," he protested.

She shook her head. "How long were you in either of those places? Not as long as Socorro, eh?"

Ramon sighed. "No, mama." He squeezed her hands, then sat down again. His shoulders slumped. "So, if I grow bored and restless in one place, how am I ever going to make a living?"

"That's for you to figure out," said Sofia. "When you do figure it out, I will give my permission for you and Fatemeh to marry. I think you'll find the two of you are more alike than you realize."

Ramon pursed his lips, feeling like his mother knew something she wasn't saying. If she knew what would make him happy, why didn't she just tell him? He shook his head and sighed. After a moment, he finished the atole and coffee, helped her with the dishes, then shuffled out to tend the animals.

Billy McCarty rode into Lincoln, New Mexico with a nearly empty wallet, but a head full of possibilities. He still wasn't sure how he had let himself get talked into riding to the Grand Canyon to join up with a force flying mechanical owls against enormous airships that hovered over Denver like storm clouds. Still, he had done it, and what's more, the owl riders had won.

"I flew." The memory left Billy breathless. "I actually flew like a bird."

Billy's horse wiggled her ears as though she had heard the words far too many times already.

Looking to his left, Billy noticed Lawrence Murphy's store. With a scowl, he snapped the reins, encouraging the horse to move on by. Murphy wanted to be the sole supplier for every ranch in Lincoln County. Billy's former boss, John Tunstall, not only started a ranch, but decided he didn't want to pay Murphy's prices, so he opened his own feed store. The two men had been feuding ever since.

When he left Denver just about two months ago, Billy thought he would continue down the Rio Grande to Mesilla and ignore the Lincoln County feuds altogether. Working for John Tunstall, he had been little more than a hired gun. He began to think it might be worth learning a trade that could sustain him as he watched the future unfold—maybe he could even help it unfold. Unfortunately, he'd already spent most of his money just returning to New Mexico. Of course, it didn't help that he'd reach a town, spend a few days gambling and enjoying the company of the local saloon girls before moving on. By the time he reached Lincoln, he needed more money.

He knew John Tunstall would have work for him. He would pay well and he would be interested in hearing about Billy's exploits over Denver. Once he raised a little money, Billy could ride on to Mesilla as he originally planned.

As Billy looked around the town, it seemed emptier than the last time he'd been through. It wasn't quite like a ghost town. A few people ambled along the boardwalks in front of the buildings, but it seemed too quiet for such a nice spring day, as though the town's energy had drained away. His brow creased as he tried to count the days since he'd last seen a calendar. Maybe it was Sunday and people were at church.

Billy smiled when he saw Tunstall's store, down the road from Murphy's. He dismounted and looped the horse's reins around the hitching post in front. As he walked through the door, a bell jangled. He blinked as his eyes adjusted to the relative gloom.

"Well I'll be." Charlie Bowdre, a man with wavy hair and a long, thick mustache, eyed Billy with suspicion. "I never thought I'd see you again."

"Charlie." Billy tipped his hat, then looked around the strangely empty store. No customers milled about within, or waited at the counter. The shelves were not as full as the last time he'd been there. "Town seems quiet today? What's goin' on?"

"Town's been quiet for the last three weeks," said Bowdre.

Billy stepped toward the counter. Bowdre had a lean, gaunt face, but he seemed to have lost weight and a hungry look gleamed in his eye. "I thought business would be booming. What about the army?"

"The army ain't been any help." Bowdre leaned over the counter. "Business has been dead since they packed up and went north."

"Yeah, but shouldn't they be back in the territory by now? They sorted out that business in Denver."

"Then they got sent to Washington Territory." Charlie made the statement as though it was common knowledge. Confused, Billy rubbed the stubble on his chin and realized he hadn't seen any soldiers on the ride south.

"Washington? Why'd they go there?"

"The army may have blown up them airships over Denver, but there's still troops crawling all over Seattle. Denver was just the beginning."

"Oh." Billy frowned. He remembered General Gorloff, the Russian leader and how he spoke with a strange otherworldly voice. Some kind of spirit from the stars that called itself Legion controlled the Russians and made them invade. Before that, there had never been a history of animosity between the Russian Empire and the United States. As the invasion progressed, Legion reconsidered its plans and decided it had made a mistake. Billy thought the invasion had ended. "I was there in Denver and I thought the two big airships were their hold card. With those destroyed, why did the Russians stay? How are they even being supplied?"

"You know, some people got more pride than sense," said Bowdre. "Once the Russians got that territory, they were probably more apt to fight and hold onto it than tuck tail and run."

"I see what you mean." Billy snorted, then looked around. "So, where can I find Mr. Tunstall?"

"He's out at the ranch." Bowdre waved his hand that direction.

Billy tipped his hat and turned to leave.

"Don't expect a warm welcome, Billy."

He continued through the door, unhitched his horse and climbed into the saddle. He ground his teeth and debated whether or not to continue on to Tunstall's ranch or just ride on to Mesilla as he'd originally planned. He decided he wanted to know what happened since he'd last been in Lincoln. Besides, Charlie Bowdre was always something of a grump who often blew things out of proportion.

The sun was high in the sky as Billy reached John Tunstall's place. He climbed out of the saddle and led his horse to a water trough near a patch of grass. After tending the horse, he strode over to the house and knocked, figuring Tunstall would be there. By this time of day, he had typically finished the morning chores and took a break for lunch while reviewing the store's paperwork.

A few minutes later, the door swung open, revealing a man just a little older than Billy. His hair was combed back and he wore a neatly trimmed mustache and goatee. "Well, well, if it isn't Billy McCarty."

"Howdy, John." Billy held out his hand.

Tunstall looked at Billy's hand for a moment, then with a hint of a shrug, reached out and shook it. "What brings you out this way, Billy? When you rode off a few weeks ago, I thought we'd seen the last of you."

"What gave you that idea?"

"Well, you talked me into stopping the raids on Murphy's cattle because the Russians were on their way to Denver." Tunstall shrugged. "I thought it sounded like a good idea, help the country and all. You told me there might be a way to get the army to buy more of our beef, but soon after that, the whole damned army rode out of New Mexico Territory and you weren't far behind them."

Billy's brow furrowed. "Surely you don't blame me for that, John. I didn't tell the Russians to invade America."

Tunstall snorted. "No, and to tell the truth, business has been bad for everyone, including Murphy."

"It can't stay that way forever," said Billy.

Tunstall gazed off into the distance for a moment, then looked back into Billy's eyes. "No, I don't suppose it can, but it doesn't help things right now."

Billy slumped as he nodded. "I suppose this wouldn't be the best time to ask if you had any work, then."

Tunstall shook his head. "I'm trying to figure out how to make payroll for my men as it is. Frenchy, Tom, and several other men went off to join the army, figuring it's a better prospect."

Billy removed his hat and rubbed fingers through his hair. "I'm sorry, John. If I'd known…"

"What difference would it have made? As you say, you didn't tell the Russians to invade." His expression softened and he reached out and put his hand on Billy's arm. "Look, there's room in the bunkhouse. If you want to spend a night or two, catch up on some rest … that would be fine. I can probably spare a little change to help you get down the road a little further."

Billy smiled. "Thanks, John. I appreciate it."

The lack of wanted posters hanging in front of the sheriff's office in Flagstaff caused Larissa to turn her eyes heavenward and hold her hands out to her sides, imploring. There were only three posters. One showed a horse thief wanted in Prescott, another was for a stagecoach robbery in California. The third showed a curly-haired desperado wanted for stealing guns in Texas. The values attached to the bandits were low, each under $500. It certainly wasn't worth the time and effort to ride out after the men in question. She hoped Professor Maravilla would have better luck with his letter-writing campaign.

She continued down the boardwalk to the general store. A man behind the counter placed cans on a shelf. "Good afternoon, ma'am," he said, with a glance over his shoulder. "What can I help you find?"

"Right now, I'm just looking for a newspaper," she said.

The clerk turned around and checked a shelf below the counter. "I don't have much. Just a couple of papers the train brought in from Topeka four days ago. I also have a paper from Tucson that's about a week and a half old."

"I'll take the Tucson paper."

The clerk named a price and Larissa dug out a coin from a satchel on her belt. She tipped her coachman's hat, then took the paper back to her room at the boarding house. She sat by the window to take advantage of the light.

The first page carried news about the war with Russia. Larissa frowned as she read. She assumed the war would have ended when the owl riders destroyed the Russian airships over Denver. However, the Russians were still entrenched in Alaska and Washington and showed no signs of leaving. What's more, it sounded as though the Russians were expanding their hold on the territories and taking more cities. America had sent troops to the Northwest.

Larissa couldn't help but notice that the Russian airships had not left troops in the Canadian provinces and they showed no signs of going there. She sniffed as she considered that the Russians were willing to invade the United States, but hesitated attacking the British Commonwealth. She wondered about that and suspected military strategists were trying to understand the situation as well.

Turning the page, Larissa learned that many soldiers had been pulled out of Arizona and New Mexico. As a result, ranches and mining camps had been left unprotected. There were reports of Indian raids on the mining camps outside of Tucson.

Page three mentioned a notable exception to the rise in Indian raids. Apaches and miners alike stayed away from the area between the San Pedro River and the Mule Mountains. According to the article, miners had reported seeing a camel with a spectral rider in the area. Larissa laughed to herself. "The miners have been out in the sun too long."

She continued reading the paper. Once she reached the end, she tossed it down beside the chair with a snort. The only way she saw to put her expertise to work would be to hire herself out to a mine owner as a guard. That seemed more suicidal than lucrative.

Larissa looked up at the clock and realized it was almost suppertime. She went downstairs to the boarding house kitchen. Although Professor Maravilla knew how to cook, his repertoire was a bit limited and he had a taste for hot spices. She looked forward to giving her tongue a rest.

Arriving downstairs, she found the professor already at the table. "How was your day?" she asked.

"I posted a dozen letters to potential supporters. Four have given me money before, so I'm hopeful we'll be able to continue the owl's construction in a week or two."

"It sounds like you had better luck than I did." She told the professor about the lack of wanted posters at the sheriff's office and the dearth of news in the paper. "At least I got a laugh out of the story about the ghost camel."

"Ghost camel?" Professor Maravilla leaned forward. "Tell me more."

"You can't be serious." Larissa sat back and folded her arms.

"Of course I am. All mysteries are interesting to me." The professor's eyebrows rose.

"Apparently Apaches and miners down near Tucson have been seeing some kind of ghost riding a camel," said Larissa.

"Apaches *and* miners?" pressed Maravilla. "Why would Apaches make up such a story?"

Larissa shrugged. "It didn't make a lot of sense to me. I just figured it was some kind of spook story put in to help sell papers."

The landlady interrupted their conversation when she entered carrying plates loaded with roast pork and potatoes. Larissa took a generous helping of meat and three potatoes. The professor sniffed at the food, then served himself.

"It seems to me," said Maravilla, "that news of the Russian invasion would sell lots of papers. They don't need 'spook stories' to do the job for them."

Larissa's eyebrows came together. "So you've heard the Russians are still in Washington Territory?"

"I've … had my suspicions." The professor nodded.

Larissa leaned forward. "I thought the invasion would have ended when we destroyed the airships. Why are the Russians still there?"

The professor's eyes darted back and forth for a moment as though he listened to two people converse. He did that sometimes when he thought.

"The Russians were motivated by a desire to help their kinsmen with land claims in California and for Alaskan resources."

"Land claims in California?" Larissa shook her head, not understanding how the professor knew something that eluded even the newspapers. "What resources are there in Alaska? I gather we bought it more as a favor to the Russians than anything else."

Maravilla nodded thoughtfully. "Alaska is rich with oil and in a world of machines, oil is very valuable indeed. Just because we stopped them at Denver doesn't mean they'll leave the territories they already control." The professor's voice sounded distant, almost like he was reciting something he'd heard somewhere else. He looked down, blinked at his food, then took a bite. His face betrayed disappointment as he reached for the salt and pepper shakers and doused his food liberally.

"So, what's next?" asked Larissa. "Back to the canyon tomorrow while we wait to see if anyone sends us money?"

"Why not go to Tucson? We could investigate this spectral camel rider."

"We could and we wouldn't find anything," said Larissa. "I tell you, it's just stories made up by miners."

"And Apaches, you said."

"So?" Larissa shrugged.

"Apaches fear the dead. They would not make up such a story unless they had a good reason."

"The other problem is our lack of funds."

"That situation won't change sitting in Flagstaff or at the Grand Canyon, my dear." The professor flashed a disarmingly innocent smile. "Besides, I've noticed that opportunities sometimes present themselves while on the road."

Larissa took another bite of supper as she considered the professor's statement. The food grew bitter in her mouth. The Russians were still in America. She wanted to help, but knew there was little a Mexican expatriate and a woman bounty hunter could do to help the war effort. "All right, then," she grumbled at last. "Let's go ghost hunting. What have we got to lose?"

CHAPTER TWO
BAGGAGE

When Professor Maravilla suggested riding down to Tucson, Larissa thought they would go directly there from Flagstaff. Instead, they returned to the Grand Canyon and Larissa retrieved a hansom cab she had hidden in the woods. She sighed as she pulled off the pine branches. The cab's once-shiny black paint was dulled and scratched after a couple of years on the road.

She had purchased the cab from a driver in San Antonio when she realized how good it would be for transporting prisoners. Like most hansoms built since the Civil War, it had doors that would close in front of the passenger's legs. She had also added doors to the top half of the passenger compartment so that anyone seated there would be completely enclosed.

They didn't retrieve the hansom to transport prisoners, but to carry Professor Maravilla's photographic equipment, a tool kit, and some food, which they placed on the passenger seat. With those items packed, he returned to the cave and emerged some minutes later dragging a wooden crate. He heaved it up the trail from the cave, leaving a deep gouge in the dirt, undoing Larissa's work concealing the entrance. He set one end on the cab's step, then lifted the back end and shoved it into position at the base of the seat, his muscles bulging with the effort. Taking a deep breath, he retrieved a handkerchief from his pocket and wiped his brow.

"What's in the crate?" she asked.

"An experiment I started a long time ago," he explained. "It's how I first met Señorita Karimi and Señor Morales. I was studying wolves at the time."

Before she could ask anything more about his studies, the professor moved on to another task. She looked at the trunk and considered picking the lock, but decided the mystery could wait.

Although Larissa's hansom afforded her room to carry more changes of clothes than she could fit in her saddlebags, her bag proved modest compared to the professor's wardrobe. By the time they were ready to depart, the cab sagged on its axle. She hitched up her horse, gave him a pat, then climbed into the seat and flicked the reins. The animal was a good solid draft horse and he pulled the load easily, but she winced each time a wheel bounced over a rock or the axle creaked, afraid it would snap.

It took a week to travel from Flagstaff to Tucson. After the first day, Larissa relaxed and enjoyed the first part of the journey through Oak Creek Canyon. Spring brought fresh, green leaves to the trees and water was easy to find. The hansom, designed to traverse narrow cobblestone streets, was pleasant enough to drive through the mountainous country. Its spring-loaded seat and large wheels helped to cushion the worst bumps even if the axle creaked ominously.

Once they reached Prescott and turned south, the country-side became much more barren. They took on as much water as they could carry at Lake Pleasant, then made their way south-ward through a veritable forest of Saguaro Cacti that towered as high as fifty feet above the ground. Sweet smelling blossoms sprouted at the top of the cacti, opening at night to perfume their rough campsites.

Each morning and evening, the professor made notes about the animals and plants he saw. One night, his eyes brightened and his smile widened as he pulled out his telescope. He aimed it at some animals snuffling the ground near a palo verde tree in the distance. He handed the instrument to Larissa, then grabbed his notepad. Looking through magnifying lenses, she saw a small herd of humpbacked animals with coarse hair and noses to the ground. "They're javelinas." Larissa shrugged. "What's so exciting about a bunch of wild pigs?"

"Ah, but they're not pigs." The professor's words tumbled forth as though he couldn't get them out fast enough. "They're peccaries. A pig's tusk is long and curled. A peccary's tusk is short and straight. They can chop right into a cactus, hunt small animals, and even burrow into the ground." After scratching out some notes, he went to Larissa's cab and retrieved his camera. Although he almost vibrated with enthusiasm, he took his time approaching the javelina herd.

Larissa was impressed by how quietly the professor stepped and how close he could approach without startling the pig-like javelinas. She'd joined him to learn about science and engineering, but she realized she could learn a few tricks that would help in her trade as a bounty hunter. He took two photographic plates of the small herd before it grew too dark to see.

"What I'd really like to see is a family of wolves," declared the professor as they sat around the campfire that evening, cooking supper.

"No thank you," said Larissa. "I'd just as soon keep my distance from any animal that might want to eat me for supper."

The professor barked out a laugh. "Oh, a lobo would hardly see you as supper. You're much too big."

Larissa glared at the professor.

Unfazed, he continued. "You would only be in danger if the lobo saw you as a threat, encroaching on its territory."

"And how do I know if I've trespassed on a wolf's territory? Do they post signs?"

"In a way, they do." He sat up straight, and Larissa could suddenly visualize him in front of a classroom filled with students. "They urinate and defecate to mark their territory. They scratch the ground in characteristic ways."

"Well, you be sure to let me know if you see any signs that a wolf has used one of these cacti as an outhouse, won't you?"

The professor laughed again. "I will definitely let you know."

"So, you told me you were studying wolves when you first met Ramon and Fatemeh."

Maravilla nodded. "I have developed a special camera disguised as a wolf. It gets much closer to wolves than I can to take photos."

"Is that what's in the trunk?" asked Larissa.

"Very perceptive of you." The professor reached out and stirred the stew.

Larissa narrowed her gaze. "Why in the world did you bring it along?"

"Although I designed my clockwork creation to approach wolves, it could be used in other situations requiring stealth. Maybe we could use it to understand the mystery of the spectral camel near Tucson."

Larissa pursed her lips and nodded as her stomach rumbled. She ate heartily when the professor ladled stew into their bowls, and soon afterward fell into a sound sleep.

The next day, the professor and Larissa arrived in Tucson. As they rode in along Toole Avenue, they saw warehouses, an iron works, and an icehouse. Professor Maravilla pointed out an office for John Rockefeller's Standard Oil. "I should write to the Rockefellers, too. They may be interested in funding my experiments."

At the point where Toole intersected Congress Street, they came upon the largest hotel that Larissa had ever seen, the three-story tall San Xavier. Across the way, masons built a rail depot and a short distance beyond that, Chinese workers hammered railroad spikes into wooden ties. Uncertain whether they could afford the palatial San Xavier, the professor and Larissa turned down Congress Street. They passed saloons, billiard halls, restaurants and an opera house, but no other hotels.

They returned to the San Xavier. The clerk's eyes widened and he smiled as they entered. Immodestly, he wore no coat and he'd rolled his sleeves up past his elbows. A thin sheen of sweat brightened his forehead.

Professor Maravilla cleared his throat and asked the price of a room.

The clerk quoted a price that Larissa found reasonable, then looked down at the counter. "It is pretty noisy because of the construction across the way."

"Is that why the rooms are so inexpensive?" asked the professor.

The clerk looked up and tugged on his suspenders. "That, and the fact that there isn't much of a call for rooms yet. Once the depot gets finished, I'm sure prices will go up. Right now, we only get a train through every few days."

"Well, we have no cause to complain," said Larissa as she lay down money for two rooms. "A new bed at a good price suits me just fine."

Ramon Morales knelt by the windmill's water pump a short distance from his mother's homestead. He cleaned out dust and grime that had found its way into the gears, then applied some fresh lubricating oil to the mechanism. He stood and engaged the windmill's clutch. No wind blew, so he reached out and turned the windmill shaft by hand. Satisfied the mechanism operated as it should, he went to disengage the clutch again, but stopped when something hindered his movement. Looking around, he saw that his shirttail had come untucked and one of his mother's goats had clamped on, chewing contentedly.

"Ay, get out of here, you stupid goat!" he shouted and waved his arms.

Startled, the goat jumped backward, ripping the shirt from Ramon's body.

He tried grabbing the shirt, but the goat ran further away. He looked around for something he could use to get the pesky animal to drop its prize. Although tempted to grab a wrench and brain the creature, he realized goats just chewed whatever they pleased.

Someone laughed at him. Ramon looked up and saw Fatemeh standing nearby holding some wildflowers from the field. Her green eyes sparkled as she approached. She held the flowers under the goat's nose and enticed it away from the shirt.

Ramon bent down and picked it up. He examined the tattered cloth and tried to knock off the mud as best he could, then slipped the shirt on again but the buttons were gone, scattered on the ground. He heaved a deep sigh, then stepped over to Fatemeh and brought her close. She leaned in, but he could feel her muscles tense slightly. She wanted to be near, but felt guilty because of her religion's teachings. "Thank you, corazón."

"It looked like you needed rescuing," she said with a wry, half-smile.

He snorted. "That goat was no match for me."

She took a half step backward and cocked her head. "I saw

you looking at that wrench. Were you going to try to feed it to him?"

"Through the top of his skull," grumbled Ramon.

"Really?" Fatameh grinned mischievously.

"Hey, I was a sheriff. I'm prepared to take a life when necessary."

Fatemeh laughed again. "That's what I love about you, Ramon. You take that very seriously. So, seriously, in fact, that I have never actually seen you *take* a life."

Ramon narrowed his gaze in mock anger. "Do you doubt that I would?"

Fatemeh shook her head. "Not at all." She continued to smile as she stepped back and looked him up and down. "What you are, is a peacekeeper, Ramon Morales."

Ramon's brow furrowed. "Isn't that what being a sheriff is?"

"Are all the sheriffs you know peacekeepers?"

Ramon considered that. Some lawmen ran gambling establishments and brothels on the side. Some did their best to control the towns they were elected to protect. Finally, he shook his head. "No, corazón, not at all." He turned around, disengaged the windmill's clutch, then reinstalled the gearbox housing. "So, I'm a peacekeeper," he said as he worked. "My mom thinks I need to figure out what I'm going to do with the rest of my life. Maybe you can tell her."

Fatemeh sighed and stepped around the tools on the ground and knelt, facing Ramon. "Your mother has a point. You're a peacekeeper, but how are you going to turn that into a living?"

"I was thinking we could buy a farm and I could keep the peace by living a nice quiet life."

"And all the while, goats will be eating your shirts." She chuckled again.

Ramon found her good humor at his expense annoying. "So, what do you suggest?"

She looked down at the ground. "I can't tell you that."

Ramon finished screwing down the gearbox housing and picked up his tools. "Can't or won't?"

"Honestly can't," said Fatemeh. "You need to figure out

how you can be a peacekeeper. You weren't happy being a sheriff…"

He stood and picked up the toolbox. "I'm not sure how else to be a peacekeeper."

Fatemeh stood, following him. "Ambassadors help broker peace. Lawyers and judges keep the peace as well."

Ramon shrugged. "I don't have the education for something like that."

Fatemeh put her hand on his arm. "But you could."

Ramon stopped and looked at her for a long time. He hadn't considered that. He looked around at the grassy plain surrounding the homestead. A gentle breeze rustled the grass. The sky overhead was a brilliant blue. "I like the wide-open spaces. I'm not sure how well I'd do in a classroom. Besides, that kind of education would take a lot of money."

"We can figure out money," said Fatemeh. "The rest, you have to work out on your own. There's no doubt in my mind that you're a peacekeeper. The part you need to figure out is how that manifests in your life."

Ramon nodded and smiled. "Thank you, corazón. At least that's a step in the right direction." He bent down and kissed her on the cheek.

Billy McCarty rode over San Augustin Pass on his way toward Mesilla. He'd worked for John Tunstall for a few days, long enough to earn money for supplies to continue his journey. As he rode down from the pass, he saw tall, spindly ocotillos with tiny green leaves hiding thorns and red flowers along the top of the skyward-facing branches. The vibrant desert plants gave him hope he would find a new beginning at the end of this trail.

Ahead, the Rio Grande wound its way through the valley. Cottonwood trees and farms lined its banks. Two towns faced each other across the river. On the near side was Las Cruces, a small village of a few houses and businesses.

The road made its way through the dusty main street of Las Cruces, then over a bridge into Mesilla. There, the road veered to the left into the Mesilla Park. Horses weren't allowed on the streets of the town itself, so Billy had to find a stable at the horse park. In one respect, Billy liked the law. It meant you could walk the streets without stepping into horse manure. Despite that, it was a damned nuisance having to walk everywhere and his budget was limited. He could think of better ways to spend money than stabling his horse.

As he rode along the row of livery stables and blacksmiths, he spotted a sign that advertised stables for fifty cents per day. After stabling the horse, he walked into town.

A few minutes later, Billy entered the offices of the *Mesilla News*. Behind the wooden rail dividing the room, two men with sleeves rolled up past their elbows worked at a printing press and a woman set type. Billy cleared his throat. "Can you tell me where I might find a reporter named Luther Duncan?"

The woman inclined her head toward a door. Billy opened the rail, stepped through, then knocked on the door. Hearing the muffled greeting from the other side, he entered the small office. Luther Duncan sat at a desk and pushed keys on a mechanical device. He wore a striped shirt and a bow tie. His bowler hat and jacket hung from a coat tree beside the door.

"Howdy," said Billy, "I'm not sure you remember me…"

Duncan looked up from the device, his face blank. After a moment, his eyes widened. "Why you're that kid we met in Silver City. You helped us rescue Ramon Morales from the mine in Socorro." A look similar to a man who stepped in a cow pie crossed Duncan's face. True, Billy had killed a man in cold blood that night, but it was clear the man meant to do the same to Ramon.

"I also went to Denver and helped Miss Fatemeh fight off those Russian airships."

Duncan's expression changed from one of disgust to curiosity in a heartbeat. "You were at the Battle of Denver?"

Billy smiled. "Yes sir, I was! I flew in one of Professor Maravilla's mechanical owls and helped bring down those floating arsenals."

"Well, well," said Duncan. He stood and indicated the chair across from the desk. "Would you be willing to grant me an interview?"

Billy sat down. "An interview?"

"Yeah, tell me your story. I've interviewed a few soldiers from Fort Bliss who were in Denver during the battle. They told me about the mechanical owls, but a firsthand account from an actual owl rider..." Duncan rubbed his hands together as he sat down. "Imagine how many papers that could sell!"

Billy tipped his hat back on his head. "That sounds great, Mr. Duncan and I'd be pleased to help you out if—" Billy sat back and folded his arms. "—you can help me out."

Duncan narrowed his gaze, studied Billy, then nodded. "All right, tell me what you need."

"I'm not lookin' for anything special. Just a place to stay and a job."

"What are you good at?"

"Last few months I've been workin' on John Tunstall's ranch outta Lincoln."

Duncan pursed his lips and sat back. "I'm afraid ranch work has been drying up around here."

"I heard that from Mr. Tunstall," said Billy. "I ain't too particular about it being a ranch. I just need to earn some money if I'm gonna hang around here and tell you my story."

Duncan thought for a minute and finally leaned forward again. "Any problem with farm work? I know some ranchers don't care to associate with sod busters."

Billy considered it for a minute. His first reaction was to decline, but he wasn't in a position to be picky. "Tell me whatcha got."

"There's a fellow who moved to town a few weeks ago. He has a story almost as interesting as yours. His name is Masuda Hoshi and he's trying to get a farm started up north a couple miles."

Billy leaned forward. "What kind of name is ... Masuda Hoshi?"

"He's from Japan," explained Duncan. "I gather he used to own a farm there, but he had to move to America suddenly after some ... trouble."

"What kinda trouble?" Billy grinned.

"Let's just say I think you two might get along just fine."

Duncan gave Billy directions to Hoshi's farm and they

agreed to meet again the next day so Duncan could interview him for the newspaper. Billy returned to the Mesilla Park and retrieved his horse. He considered some other stops before following up on Luther Duncan's lead—like a bottle of good whisky or a night at a high-end cathouse—but those could wait until he knew he had a job.

He skirted Mesilla and rode two miles north until he came to a small farm crouched along the riverbank. A horse path cut through the fields to an adobe house and a weathered barn. An overhang shaded the house's door. Hanging from it, on either side, were two brightly colored paper balls. Billy was used to seeing strings of chilies drying near doors, but he found this a strange sight.

He turned down the path. "Hello, the house!" he called as he approached. Not hearing a response, he climbed from the saddle and led his horse to a water trough.

Just as he was about to turn around, something poked him in the back.

"Who are you and what do you want here?" came a deep, gravelly voice.

Billy lifted his hands where the person behind could see he was unarmed. Then, fast as he could, he spun on his heel and grabbed for what he thought was a gun. Instead, it proved to be some kind of sword. He yelped in pain and pulled his hand away, blood dripping from his fingers.

The man behind him wore a flowery dressing gown. What hair he had was tied back from his balding pate in a ponytail. His long, thin mustache drooped past his mouth, enhancing his scowl. The man pushed the sword at Billy again. "Who are you and what do you want?"

Billy swallowed as he examined his bleeding hand. "Are you Mr. Hoshi?"

The man gave the briefest of nods. "Mr. Masuda would be more accurate."

"My name's Billy McCarty. Luther Duncan said you might have work."

The man sheathed his sword in a scabbard that hung from the sash around his waist. He gave another curt nod. "Come inside and let's talk."

Professor Maravilla and Larissa met in the San Xavier's lobby after they had cleaned up so they could get some supper and see if they could learn anything about the mystery of the phantom camel rider. The sun had just gone down and a man ignited the gaslights that lined the street. Two doors down from the hotel was a brightly lit, smoke-filled saloon containing a mix of cowboys, miners and businessmen.

"This looks acceptable," said the professor as he strode through the doors. She watched him, still not quite sure what to make of the man who dressed like a dandy, but was equally comfortable out in the desert photographing javelinas as he was building machinery in a hidden cave at the Grand Canyon.

No one turned to look at the professor as he entered the bar. Larissa wondered if that stemmed from the professor's self-confidence or because Tucson was big enough with a sufficient mix of businessmen and working-class people that no one took notice of his clothes. She followed the professor in, aware that some heads had turned her direction. She patted the gun at her hip and projected the air of someone who would blow the head off anyone who tried to make an unwelcome advance.

The professor sat at a little round table and scanned the room until his eyes fell on a chalkboard near the bar. He scowled as he read, even though there were a couple of choices.

A few minutes later, a barmaid approached. She cast a brief glance at Larissa, then gave Professor Maravilla a knowing look. Oblivious to her expression, the professor ordered one of the house specials and a brandy. "What would your … daughter like?" asked the barmaid.

"I'm perfectly capable of ordering for myself." Larissa's voice carried further than she expected and she became aware of people looking her direction. She swallowed and composed herself, then ordered one of the house specials. She then beckoned the barmaid a little closer. "Do you have ginger beer?"

"We have sarsaparilla."

Larissa gave a curt nod. "I'll have that … in a beer mug."

The barmaid winked. "Right away, sweetie."

The bounty hunter rolled her eyes. She didn't like to cloud her mind with alcohol, but she didn't want it to be too obvious that she refrained from drinking beer. As she looked around, it seemed as though some of the other patrons were drinking a darker stout in addition to a lighter summer ale. Her father had brewed beer when she was younger and she was familiar with different types of beer even if she didn't like them.

Professor Maravilla leaned forward. "Did that young woman really think you were my daughter?"

Larissa removed her coachman's hat and sat it on the table next to her. "No … I think she thought you were entertaining a … much younger lady friend."

The professor's eyes widened and he sat back, mirth and confusion both in his expression. "You are a friend and a lady," he said after a moment's pause. "Although I can assure you I have no other intentions."

Larissa patted her six-gun again. "And we're going to keep it that way." The shocked look on his face made her realize she'd made her point stronger than necessary.

The barmaid returned and delivered the drinks. Professor Maravilla removed his bowler and sipped the brandy. Larissa left her drink untouched and studied him. "So Professor, do you have a family? You've never talked about them."

Another series of expressions crossed Maravilla's face. "It's complicated," he said at last, "but, of all people, I'd think you would understand."

"Why me of all people?"

"I presume Crimson isn't your real surname…"

Larissa's eyebrows came together. "Why do you ask?"

"Maravilla means marvelous or miraculous."

"Oh." Larissa sat back and formed more questions. It was natural enough for a bounty hunter to travel under an assumed name. After all, someone she apprehended might decide to seek out her family for revenge. She was less certain why a professor would take on an assumed name.

Before she could pursue that line of thought, dinner arrived. She took a drink of the sarsaparilla. It was refreshingly cold. The saloon must keep an icehouse in the back.

The meal was a simple affair of beef, beans and spring

vegetables. She dug in. The professor eyed his own plate with suspicion before sampling the food.

As she ate, Larissa caught snippets of conversation. She thought the miners near the bar mentioned something about Apaches and the Mule Mountains. She drank down her sarsaparilla in one gulp, then excused herself and moved toward the bar.

"It's a shame, too. I've seen traces of silver as well as copper down there," said one of the miners as Larissa approached.

She set her mug on the bar and turned to face the miners. "You boys hear tell of that spook story about the spectral camel rider?"

One of the miners looked around. "Ain't no spook story, little lady. I seen it. It's a man ... or what's left of a man ... all rotted and decayed on the back of a camel. He turned and looked right at me. I tell you, I about soiled my britches."

A shiver went down Larissa's spine despite her skepticism. "Whereabouts did you see that?"

"North end of the Mule Mountains, about five, six miles east of the San Pedro River."

"What about the camel? Was he all skeletal and decayed, too?"

The miner pondered the question for a moment. "No, he was just a plain ol' camel, right out of Araby."

"Why a camel?" asked Larissa. "Why not a horse or a mule?"

Another miner spoke up. "Well, they brought over some camels during the war between the states to use out in the desert. They finally let 'em go 'cuz the beasts were damned near impossible to train." He narrowed his gaze. "Why are you so interested, anyway? You ain't thinkin' o' goin' there are you?"

Larissa shook her head. She reached back and grabbed her mug, which had been refilled. "Just interested in spook stories, is all." She took a sip and had to force herself to swallow and keep the surprise from her features. The bartender had replaced her sarsaparilla with dark ale. She lifted her mug to the miners, then returned to the table, light headed from both the news about the spectral camel rider and the ale. She sighed and took another sip. At least she would sleep well that night.

CHAPTER THREE
REVISING HYPOTHESES

Larissa dreamed about Christmas.

The aroma of roasting goose wafted through the homestead. Her young cousin, Alethea, sat on a wooden chair cradling a porcelain doll in a beautiful red dress.

"What's her name?" asked Larissa.

"Her name is Lyssa. I named her after you." Alethea never quite managed all the syllables in Larissa's name. "I call her Lyssa Crimson because of her crimson dress."

The next thing Larissa knew, Alethea and the chair had vanished. The doll wafted toward the floor like a feather. Larissa tried to catch it, but the air around her was like molasses. When the doll reached the floor, it shattered. Porcelain shards rose through the air in slow motion. Larissa sank to her hands and knees, desperate to repair the doll, but knew there was nothing she could do. The crash and tinkling continued to ring in her head until her eyes flew open and she realized she was hearing the alarm clock next to her bed at the Hotel San Xavier in Tucson.

She reached over and shut off the clock, then took several deep breaths to still her heart and calm her trembling.

The sun had not yet risen. Professor Maravilla wanted to get an early start. He planned to make some changes to his mechanical wolf, then start their ride to the last place the phantom camel rider had been seen. Reaching for a match, she lit a candle by her bedside.

Larissa stepped over to the pitcher and basin that sat atop the room's dresser. She washed her face and ran water over her hair before brushing it out. The routine actions calmed her after the unsettling dream. The night before, she'd availed herself of the hotel's bathhouse. For the first time in several weeks, she felt truly clean.

After dressing, she straightened her bed, then went next door to the professor's room. When she tapped on the door, it fell ajar. From the glow, Larissa could tell the professor had already lit the room's gas lamps. Tools and mechanical parts clattered. She also heard the professor speaking.

"This would be so much easier if you could just persuade someone to give me the money for my research." There was a pause, as though someone responded in a voice too quiet to hear. "I thought you said you influenced the minds of the Russians." After another pause, Maravilla continued. "Yes, it's true I gave my ornithopter design over to the military, but I didn't feel I had a choice. I don't dare return to Mexico."

Larissa's brow furrowed as she listened to what seemed like one half of an exchange. She knocked louder. The professor fell silent. A moment later, he appeared at the door and smiled. "Good morning, Miss Crimson. I trust you slept well."

"Aside from a bad dream, yes. Thank you."

The professor stepped aside and allowed Larissa to enter. She gasped and reached for her pistol when she saw the wolf in the middle of the room. The professor put his hand on her elbow and she looked closer. The wolf stood absolutely still with a hatch open on its side. She walked around the animal and saw gears, rods and a strange, spherical whirligig inside. The clockwork mechanism had been removed and now sat on the writing desk. On the floor sat a steam engine from one of the professor's ornithopters.

Larissa crouched down next to the engine parts and peered around the room, paying particular attention to the curtains and the bed.

"Are you looking for something, Miss Crimson?" asked the professor as he crouched down beside her.

She shook her head. "No. I just thought I heard something is all."

The professor gave a curt nod, then turned his attention to the engine. "I suspect you recognize this. I plan to replace the clockwork spring mechanism with the steam engine. It should increase the lobo's range of travel."

Larissa nodded, fascinated by the wolf as much as the

professor's earlier one-sided conversation perplexed her. She looked at the engine, then peered into the wolf itself. She stood and examined the clockwork mechanism on the writing desk. "It looks like we need to move the transfer coupling from the clockworks to the steam engine."

"Very good," said the professor with a smile. "We also need an exhaust port so the lobo won't build up too much pressure and explode." He peered into the wolf. "I was just trying to figure out how to make it all fit when you knocked."

Larissa looked into the wolf again. "We could run a small pipe down through the center, so it exhausted out the back." She picked up the engine. "It would help if this were mounted in a smaller housing."

"That's what I thought, but I'm not sure we can afford the parts."

She cast a glance toward the writing desk. "Why not strip the gears out of the clockwork mechanism and use that housing? It's designed to fit in the space."

The professor nodded slowly. "Brilliant. Why didn't I think of that?" The professor's usual cheer sounded strained, as though he was rather annoyed with himself. "Let's get to work on the engine." He stood and walked to the window. The sky was brightening. "By the time we get that done, we should be able to find an open mercantile store where we can get the pipe."

"And someplace to get breakfast, I hope."

"Indeed."

The two set to work on the engine. The professor donned spectacles with a series of lenses that he could flip into position for varying degrees of magnification. He skillfully connected the delicate engine parts one after the other. Larissa knew he was well practiced, but it seemed as though some external force guided his hands.

Within the hour, the engine had been mounted in its new housing. The professor checked his supply bag and found a handful of fuel rods—chemical bars that, when brought together, would heat the water, producing steam which, in turn, would push a piston within the engine. That motion would then cause the rotary transfer coupling to spin, driving the attached gears.

Satisfied with their work, the professor and Larissa went downstairs and ate a hasty breakfast in the hotel's dining room, then asked directions to the nearest mercantile store. A short time later they returned to the room with a satisfactory length of pipe. The professor fit the pipe within the wolf's body, then inserted the engine. Larissa bolted everything in place.

The professor inserted the fuel rods. A moment later, the engine coughed and sputtered. The wolf took several steps forward. Every few steps, a small puff of steam would appear from under the wolf's tail.

Larissa chuckled behind her hand. "Perhaps you shouldn't feed your lobo so many beans."

The professor looked up and blinked. "What do you mean?"

"It seems to have a bad case of gas."

He rolled his eyes, but seemed pleased with the lobo nonetheless. He knelt beside it, opened the hatch, and turned off the engine before it ran into a wall. "I think we are ready to seek out our mysterious camel and his phantom rider."

Sergeant Michael Harris emerged from his quarters at Fort Bliss in El Paso on his way to check the duty roster, then grab a cup of coffee, when a corporal approached. "Sergeant, Colonel Johnson would like to see you in his office right away."

Harris sighed, wondering how he managed to screw up and come to the new commanding officer's attention this soon. "Thank you, Corporal." He cut across the parade ground, and noticed a strange machine, which looked a little like an owl in flight. It was teardrop shaped with a pair of wings that fanned forward and a raptor-like tail at the point. One of those wings lay on the ground, limp and useless.

This was just one of the strange machines Lt. Colonel Johnson had brought with him to Fort Bliss. Harris wondered if the thing could actually fly. He turned a corner onto the main courtyard and passed in front of the mess hall. His stomach rumbled as he smelled the coffee and bacon from within. He hoped the meeting with the colonel would not take long.

The sun rising over the buildings highlighted water stains

and small chunks missing from the bases of the walls—flood damage from last summer's rains. The sergeant frowned as he considered the war in the northwest. It had changed so many plans. Not the least was the army's plan to build a new fort. Now they had to make do with the one they had. He hoped it would last.

Sergeant Harris's knock on the colonel's door was promptly acknowledged and he stepped into the room. Lt. Colonel Johnson sat at a desk, reviewing a sheaf of papers. As far as Harris knew, Johnson was a young man, but he looked worn and ragged. Unruly hairs jutted out from his long mustache and his blond-gray hair needed a trim.

"Thanks for being prompt, Sergeant Harris, please take a seat." The colonel indicated a chair across from the desk. "What do you know about the situation in Washington and Oregon?"

Harris furrowed his brow. "When the Russian army invaded a few months ago, they landed troops in Sitka, Alaska and Seattle, Washington. Their airships then flew to Denver where our forces destroyed them."

"That's certainly part of the story," said the colonel. "We had help from an inventor who evened the odds. Professor M.K. Maravilla designed owl ships like the one out on the parade ground. They can out-maneuver the airships. I want you to remember the professor's name."

"Yes sir. Professor Maravilla," echoed the sergeant.

"This Maravilla was brought into the fight ... indirectly, you might say ... because of his association with a private under my command in the battle, Ramon Morales. He was sheriff of Socorro before he joined me." The colonel walked over to a wood stove, retrieved a coffeepot and poured himself a cup. "Would you care for some coffee, Sergeant?"

"I would love a cup, sir," said Harris.

The colonel poured a second cup and passed it to the enlisted man, then returned to his seat. "The Russians in Denver seemed to be the main assault force. When we destroyed those airships over Denver, we fully expected that would end the invasion. The army would just capture the small forces in Seattle and Sitka, presuming they didn't retreat first."

"I've heard they've dug in deeper than before." Harris

sipped the coffee. "The army met heavy resistance up there. It's as though there are more troops than expected."

The colonel grunted. "Yes. Either we underestimated the number of troops the airships dropped or they're recruiting people somehow. Whatever the case, we've thrown almost the entire army at them and they haven't even budged."

"What about Canada, sir? Have the Russians shown any interest?"

Johnson shook his head. "None at all, and both the Canadians and the English have shown no signs of getting involved, either." He waved his hand through the air. "Oh, the British ambassador has filed protests, but that's as far as it's gone."

"Sir, I've heard rumors that a scouting party was captured in Oregon and the Russians are continuing their advance southward."

"That's right." The colonel folded his hands. "Our mission here at Fort Bliss is to find something that will help us stop the Russians. Professor Maravilla gave us the plans for his owl ships. We've built some and deployed them in Oregon and Washington, but the problem is they're not very effective. People can't take heavy munitions up with them. Hell, even if the pilot fires a rifle, it'll throw the damn thing off course, it's so lightweight. The forests are so thick up in the northwest that the Russians just hide among the trees and become invisible, so the owl ships aren't really effective for spying." The colonel paused and sipped his coffee. "We either need to make the owls more effective, or we need a new kind of weapon that will help our men. We can't let this invasion spread."

"I understand," said Sergeant Harris, "but how can I help?"

"We need Professor Maravilla. He is to science what General Grant was to the Army, a man who doesn't follow convention. I have no doubt he's the man to help us." Johnson pointed to Harris. "Bring Maravilla here."

"Yes sir," said Harris. "Where can I find him?"

"That's the problem." Johnson shrugged. "I don't actually know, but there is someone who can help. Remember the former sheriff I mentioned?"

"Morales?"

The colonel nodded. "He's up north in Estancia. Find him.

Get him to help you find Maravilla." The colonel grabbed an envelope from his desk and pushed it toward the sergeant. "That's a letter of introduction. It explains what Morales needs to know."

"Very good, sir." Harris grabbed the envelope and put it in his jacket pocket.

"Get yourself some breakfast, check out a good horse and get going. We need help as soon as we can get it." He wrote out a note on a slip of paper. "Give this to the paymaster to draw some petty cash for the trip." The colonel stood and Harris leapt to his feet and saluted. The colonel returned the salute and Harris turned to leave.

"Sergeant Harris."

The sergeant paused.

"Good luck."

"Thank you, sir." Relieved to be on his way, Harris strode from the room. As ordered, he stopped off, grabbed breakfast, and the petty cash. Within the hour, he spurred his horse onward, out of town and past the carpet of poppies that had sprung up overnight.

Billy McCarty sat at Hoshi's low table, cross-legged and sore after planting chile peppers all day. Despite the hard work, Hoshi treated Billy well. He cooked for Billy and gave him a comfortable place to sleep. Still, Billy found it difficult to adapt to some of Hoshi's ways.

The old man insisted that Billy walk around the house barefoot and his table was low to the ground. Moreover, Hoshi did not own forks. Instead, he ate all his meals with a pair of sticks he called hashi. At first, the notion of "Hoshi's hashi" amused Billy but he soon found them difficult to use. It was infuriating since Hoshi made it look so easy. Billy would have given up if Hoshi's cooking wasn't so good. After a couple of days, Billy started to master the hashi sticks.

Hoshi arrived a few minutes after Billy had situated himself on the ground. He set out three bowls. One contained steamed rice. Another had chicken in a rich, shimmering sauce. The third held bright, crisp spring vegetables. Billy helped himself to a little of all three and the older man gracefully folded his legs below himself and settled in at the table.

"How do you do that so well?" asked Billy.

"Years of practice." Hoshi reached for the rice.

"If you'll let me, I'd be happy to whip up some Mexican grub when those peppers get ripe."

"I would enjoy that." Hoshi gave a gracious nod.

Billy took a bite of the chicken, then followed it with some rice. The first time he sat down to a meal with Hoshi, he'd mixed all his food together to his employer's horror. Hoshi explained that the rice should be kept separate from the rest, so it could cleanse the palate.

"The thing I don't understand is why are you growing chilies?" Billy shrugged. "They're popular around here and they sell well, but I don't really think of them as something you'd grow in Japan."

Hoshi laughed. "On the contrary. Peppers are very important in Japanese cooking. My family has grown them for years." He paused for a moment, considering something. "I have enjoyed the flavor of American peppers when I've had the opportunity to partake of them, but it strikes me they could be hotter. I would like to see if I could breed such a pepper."

Billy narrowed his gaze. "You sound like some of the ranchers I know breeding cattle. How can you breed chile peppers?"

"That's simple," said Hoshi. "You can grow different varieties next to each other. You can work with the soil and adjust the amount of sun they get. Plants and animals are really not so different."

"You seem like you know what you're doing. What brought you out here to this little chunk of land? Maybe you could have done better as a farmer in Japan."

Hoshi inclined his head and smiled. "You're assuming I was a farmer in Japan. I was not."

"You said..."

Hoshi held up his finger. "I said my family grew peppers. Indeed, that is true. I have cousins and uncles who were wonderful farmers and when I was a child, they showed me much of what they knew."

Billy's eyebrows came together. "If you're not a farmer, then what are you?"

"I am a farmer now." Hoshi poured a cup of tea and passed it to Billy. Then, he poured a cup for himself. "When I lived in Japan, I was a warrior following the code of Bushido."

"Warrior I get, but code of Bush..."

"Bushido. I am a samurai."

"What kind of farmer is that?"

Hoshi laughed again. "Samurai were warriors that maintained the law throughout Japan. Bushido is the code of conduct a samurai follows."

"Ah," said Billy. "You mean you were like the sheriffs and marshals we have around these parts." He remembered a couple of dime novels he'd read. "That Bushido sounds something like the code of the west." He shook his head. "Only problem is that's just something made up by writers back east. I can tell you, there ain't no code out here ... at least none anyone takes seriously."

"The Code of Bushido is quite real." Hoshi's eyes shone with unshed tears. "However, I fear it is in danger of vanishing with the samurai."

Sadness for the old man-made Billy's gut feel full for a moment. "Vanishing? What do you mean?"

"The world is changing, Billy. A few years ago, the Meiji Emperor took the throne in Japan and created an army much like yours here in America. Some samurai joined the army and became officers. Others are currently involved in a struggle to resist the Emperor."

"What about you?" Billy leaned forward, any pity for Hoshi banished by the old man's calm.

"I have no desire to be part of an army. I was part of the rebellion against the Emperor in the Akizuki Domain. When the rebellion collapsed, I decided to come to America and apply the lessons I learned from my uncles and cousins so many years ago."

The two ate in silence for a time while Billy considered what Hoshi told him. Once they finished the meal, he looked up at the old man. "You know, being a warrior could come in handy around here. There are loads of bad men who would take advantage of a farmer like yourself."

Hoshi nodded. "I am quite capable of taking care of myself."

"Well, you did pretty good with that pig-sticker you poked me with the other day, but if someone really is out to do you harm, you better know how to defend yourself from a distance."

Hoshi smiled. "You mean I need to know how to use a gun."

"Yeah, that's what I was thinking." Billy patted the rig at his hip. "Now, maybe I could show you a thing or two…"

Before Billy could finish his thought, Hoshi stood and gathered the bowls. "Follow me," he said.

Billy grabbed the teapot and the cups, then followed Hoshi into the small kitchen. Leaving the dishes by the basin, they stepped out through the backdoor. Hoshi pointed to a small rock on top of an adobe wall some distance away. Faster than Billy could follow, Hoshi withdrew a handgun from his robes and fired, knocking the rock from its perch.

Billy's eyes went wide. He looked at the Smith and Wesson Army revolver in Hoshi's hand. "That's a nice lookin' piece you have there."

"It was aimed at you as you approached my farm the other day," said Hoshi.

Billy swallowed. "So, why didn't you call out and have me tell you my business. What's the deal with the sword?"

"Bushido teaches courage, politeness, and honesty. I could not take your measure by yelling at you while you were on the road. By looking in your eyes, I could tell you were courageous and honest." Hoshi checked that the revolver's barrel had cooled down, then returned it to its place within the robes.

"This Code of Bushido sounds interesting," said Billy.

"I would be happy to teach you more." Hoshi looked toward the sun, perched on the horizon. A few clouds hovered against a vibrant orange sky.

"I'm ready."

"Very good," said Hoshi, "but we must go to sleep early, for tomorrow, the weeds will need tending."

The wind had kicked up by the time Larissa and Professor Maravilla rode out of Tucson. It whipped sand and dust to a thick miasma, limiting their visibility. Despite the inconvenience, Larissa realized the wind would provide valuable cover, masking their incursion into Apache territory. Perhaps they would be able to solve the mystery of the spectral camel rider and get out before the Indians saw them. Larissa unpacked the goggles she had worn during the Battle of Denver to protect her eyes from the blowing grit. The professor rode tall in his saddle, wisps of hair blowing around his head. Like Larissa, he opted to secure his hat inside the hansom cab.

As they rode, images from her recent dreams flashed unbidden into Larissa's mind. She tried to shut out the picture of Alethea holding the beautiful porcelain doll in her thin arms. Instead, she tried to focus on the memories of flight. Her skin prickled, not just from the relentless wind but because they chased ghosts rather than trying to make something to help people. Ghosts were the last things she ever wanted to capture.

She allowed her thoughts to drift to the Christmas goose of her recent dream. The dream brought back memories of the heavenly smell, but she remembered the goose itself proved a disappointment. It was a scrawny bird that cooked up dry. Even worse, when she bit into it, she jarred her teeth on buckshot. It seemed her life was full of promises that failed to materialize as expected—kind of like riding through a sandstorm on a ghost hunt after she'd known the joy of flight. She supposed it was a wild goose chase all its own.

She shook her head, and tried to find a more productive train of thought. With a sigh, she considered the professor and his one-sided conversations. It seemed like he had been speaking to some invisible person. If she hadn't already seen his brilliance, she would have dismissed him as crazy. Maybe talking to himself was a way for him to work through problems.

Fording the San Pedro River required all her concentration, a welcome break from her depressing loop of thoughts. They turned south on the far side of the tricky crossing. As they climbed the foothills, the air cooled. The trees along the river broke the wind somewhat, giving them a little relief. The vegetation changed. They saw fewer of the tall, saguaro cactus and more mesquite brush. A few prickly pear and cholla cactus peaked out from the rocks. Flowers had opened atop the prickly pear pads. The spindly chollas almost looked soft and downy to the touch, but Larissa knew that was an optical illusion created by their long, translucent needles.

A few miles further on, they came upon a few head of cattle huddled together. One cow moved away from its companions and lapped muddy water from the river. Larissa pointed to them. "It would seem not all the settlers have been driven away. Presumably someone owns that livestock."

Professor Maravilla retrieved the telescope he carried on his belt and studied the animals. "I'm not so sure. Take a look."

Larissa studied the cattle through the telescope. A moment later, she realized what Maravilla had seen. "They have no brands," she said at last. "Just scars."

"Abandoned, I'm guessing," said the professor.

"More likely stolen. Men in a hurry to abandon a ranch wouldn't bother to blot out their brands." Larissa passed the telescope back then snapped her reins, persuading her horse to move a little faster.

They continued on until they came to the remains of several adobe buildings, surrounded by a crumbling wall. The compound's layout approximated a square. The sunbaked bricks crumbled away and most of the roofs had collapsed, but the walls were tall enough to provide shelter from the wind. They rode through an arched gate into a courtyard. Professor Maravilla dismounted and found a sturdy wall facing east. Pulling himself to the top, he scanned the area with his telescope. "I see the Mule Mountains. We're just a few miles away. This seems like a good place to make camp for the night."

Tired as she was from riding in the wind, Larissa agreed. "What exactly is this place, Professor? Are these Indian ruins?"

"I've never heard of pueblos in this region." The professor looked around at the walls. He pointed to some letters and numbers etched into an adobe brick. "No, Europeans built this. I'm thinking it must have been a Spanish presidio. Perhaps Mexicans used this as an outpost before Arizona was ceded to America."

"As long as the walls hold up, it's good shelter."

Larissa unpacked the gear from the hansom cab. She would have liked a campfire. Although the walls might conceal a fire's glow, the smoke would give them away, even on such a dusty evening. Larissa settled for dried fruit and beef jerky, then collapsed into her bedroll.

They awoke to a bright, calm morning. Larissa packed their belongings while the professor hiked from the presidio to the San Pedro and filled their canteens. By mid-morning they reached a point about six miles east of the river. The Mule Mountains rose up from the rolling desert floor to the south. "This is a good place to conduct our experiment," the professor said and Larissa agreed.

Together, they hefted the crate containing the clockwork wolf from the hansom cab. Once they removed the creature, the professor retrieved a satchel and a box of photographic equipment. He covered the wolf in a black blanket and crawled underneath. Larissa followed him. They had to work entirely by feel in the darkness.

The wolf's head contained a sophisticated camera, with a lens for one eye. Small hand-cut photographic plates sat behind the eye, flash powder behind the other. The clockworks within the wolf counted out one hundred steps, then opened the shutter and ignited a portion of the flash powder. The exposed plate would then drop into a compartment within the wolf's body.

Larissa loaded the glass photographic plates into one side of the wolf's head. She checked that the emulsion faced the lens by licking her finger and checking which side of the plate was sticky. Professor Maravilla measured flash powder and loaded it into the magazine with a funnel.

"All finished?" he asked at last.

"Ready to go," said Larissa.

They pushed the compartment on the wolf's head closed, then threw off the blanket.

A dozen Apache warriors mounted on horseback surrounded them.

Larissa and the professor rose from their crouch, hands in the air.

CHAPTER FOUR
INTERRUPTED PLANS

"Who are you people? What are you doing?" A young warrior with hair tied in two braids down either side of his head spoke, while an older warrior with a broad face and hair that fell just to his shoulders pointed a rifle at the professor.

"Miners told us stories of an apparition," sputtered the professor. "We came to investigate."

"What do we care for miners who desecrate our land?" growled the young warrior.

"We heard this specter was frightening you as well. They described it as a skeleton riding a camel." The professor pantomimed a large animal with a hump on its back.

The young warrior narrowed his gaze and spoke to his companions in the Apache language. An old warrior with fingers crooked from arthritis spoke thoughtfully. The young warrior nodded and asked, "Who do you hear these stories from?"

Maravilla shrugged. "We read it in the newspaper."

"The newspaper," scoffed the young warrior. "Since when do the newspapers of the whites say anything good about the Apaches?"

"They said you were scared … of the apparition." The professor seemed to make a plea with his expression and direct eye contact.

Larissa remembered the Apache people considered it bad manners, and even a challenge, to look directly into another person's eyes. The professor's words weren't helping. She worried that the warriors might take them as an accusation of cowardice. Larissa reached out and grabbed the professor's shoulder causing him to look at her, instead.

She slowly put her hands back over her head and considered

43

other tidbits she had heard about the Apaches. Careful to avoid startling the men on horseback, and to keep her balance, she lowered herself to the ground by crossing her legs beneath her. She motioned downward, hoping the professor would follow her example. His brow furrowed in confusion, but he did as she suggested anyway.

Once Maravilla was seated, Larissa looked to the ground. "We apologize for intruding upon your land uninvited."

She sensed the warriors took new interest in her. The warrior with the broad face said something to his young companion. "You wear a holster at your hip and a rifle at your back," said the young man. "We Apaches have had great women warriors. Are you a warrior?"

"A mere novice compared to your women, I'm sure." Larissa looked back toward the hansom cab. "We have water and a little food. You are welcome to it, if you would like."

"You have much better manners than your friend," said the young warrior.

"He is a good man, but he is not schooled in your traditions," said Larissa.

The warriors spoke among themselves, then dismounted and sat on the ground in a circle around Larissa and the professor. At last, they lowered their hands.

"I am called Baishan," said the young Apache. He held his hand out to the man with the broad face. "Our leader is Geronimo."

"Geronimo!" Larissa gasped. For a moment, she stared at the Apache warrior. Remembering herself, she looked away. "Forgive me, sir."

Geronimo laughed, then spoke in halting English. "You know me." He winked, then spoke some words in Apache.

Baishan translated: "He says if you know him, you no doubt know his brother-in-law, Nana." He indicated the older warrior with the arthritic fingers.

"Tú sabes que yo prefiero Kas-tziden," grumbled the old man in Spanish. Larissa understood enough to know he preferred the name Kas-tziden to the Spanish nickname, Nana.

Geronimo spoke in Apache and patted the old man on the shoulder. Whatever he said seemed to appease him somewhat.

Larissa smiled at the camaraderie, but was still uncomfortable that she didn't understand most of the discussion. She decided to turn the conversation to business. "Last I heard you were in Mexico."

"We were." Baishan nodded. "We came north after the army troops went to fight their new war. It seems they have found something to care about more than killing Indians."

"We are honored to be in the company of the great Geronimo." The professor was calm now that no one pointed a rifle at him. "My name is Mauricio K. Maravilla, formerly of the Pontifical and Royal University of Mexico. My associate is Larissa Crimson."

Baishan translated. Geronimo nodded, then spoke. "He wants to know why you are here."

"We heard stories of a ghost riding on a camel. We wanted to find out if it really existed."

"I have seen it," interjected another young warrior. "It is truly an evil spirit. It looked right at me, even though I know a skeleton cannot move."

A shiver traveled up Larissa's spine. It was the second time she had heard about the skeleton moving of its own accord. She began to think there must be some truth to the stories.

The warriors spoke among themselves. Once they quieted, Baishan said, "Three warriors have seen this apparition. The closest sighting was just about a mile from here."

Larissa looked toward Geronimo, careful not to meet his gaze. "May I get a map from my wagon?"

Baishan translated and Geronimo gave a curt nod.

Larissa stood and walked slowly and steadily to the hansom cab. She retrieved a map and also brought along a canteen and a pouch containing some beef jerky. She handed the water to Nana, since he appeared to be the oldest warrior present, then unrolled the map. "Can you ask them to describe where they've seen the skeleton?"

Baishan translated the request, then relayed the information. As he did, Larissa looked up and followed where the warriors pointed, then made marks on the map.

When finished, Larissa looked at the professor. "Do you see the pattern?"

The professor considered for a moment, then nodded. "Yes, it's been staying on the western side of the Mule Mountains, not straying far from the San Pedro and the surrounding vegetation. If we can set our lobo to travel down and back, he's likely to encounter the apparition."

Nana looked up at the clockwork wolf, appraising it. He said something in Apache, which Baishan translated. "Your wolf, it is very still."

The professor stood and walked over to the lobo. He patted it on the head, like a good dog, then opened its side, revealing the clockworks within. "I created it. It can walk like a real wolf and bring information back to me."

Geronimo eyed the machine as he reached into the bag of beef jerky. Finally, he spoke.

"He's impressed with your mechanical wolf," said Baishan. "It seems just the thing he would expect a clown to create."

"A clown, sir?" Maravilla's brow furrowed.

"To Apaches, a clown brings laughter ... and chaos," explained Larissa.

Geronimo's mouth turned up in mild amusement. He said something to Baishan, then stood and dusted off his pants. Baishan stood. "He says clowns are perfect for chasing evil spirits back to the underworld."

Geronimo mounted his horse and pointed to the north as he spoke.

"He says if you learn something or find you need help, you are welcome to ride to the place you call the Dragoon Mountains," said Baishan.

Larissa stood. "How will we find you?"

"If you enter the Dragoons, you will be seen," said Baishan. "If Geronimo says you are welcome, he will make sure the Chiracaua know you are friends. Thank you for your hospitality."

The remaining warriors stood and climbed onto their mounts. A moment later, they rode northward, a dust cloud in their wake.

"I will be eternally grateful that you knew something of Apache culture, Miss Crimson."

Larissa lifted her coachman's hat and wiped her brow. "I'm just lucky the authors of Beadle's Dime Novels did their research."

Billy awoke and stumbled out of his bedroll, wincing as his bare feet hit the cold, wooden floor. He padded over to a washbasin, longing for the smell of coffee and bacon. Instead, all he smelled was chicken broth. After washing his face and combing his hair, Billy stumbled out to the kitchen, where Masuda Hoshi stood over the woodstove preparing his usual fare of rice and soup. Although Hoshi had chickens, he tended to reserve the eggs and meat for evening meals. A cup of green tea sat steaming on the table. Billy lowered himself to the floor, then sipped the tea. At least it was hot.

After breakfast, Billy went out to the porch to retrieve his boots. He shook them out and jumped back when a spider fell to the boards. Feeling edgy, he pulled the boots on, then trudged over to the stable to saddle both his horse and Hoshi's so they could ride into town for supplies.

Billy thought Hoshi's saddle was pretty, but he couldn't imagine it was very comfortable for either the horse or the rider. The lacquered wood frame allowed the rider little room for movement. Hoshi's small, well-mannered horse stood still while Billy fumbled with the unfamiliar straps. Soon after he finished, Hoshi arrived and examined Billy's job. He made a few adjustments, then grunted.

"Aren't you going to wear a hat?" Billy noted the simple white bandana his employer wore tied around his head. "The sun gets pretty intense out on the road."

"The intense sun and I are old companions. We get along fine, especially for a short ride such as this."

Billy laughed. He was growing to like Hoshi despite his aversion to bacon and coffee. They each climbed into their saddles and set out. Hoshi rode tall and proud. Despite his strange flowery robes, he seemed very much at home in the strange saddle.

As they neared the main road to Mesilla, they heard gunshots and shouts. "Maybe we oughta turn back," said Billy. "Sounds like something we don't wanta get tangled up in."

"Have you learned nothing from our discussions about the

code of Bushido? Perhaps there is something we can do to help."

"If you say so." Billy checked his pocket watch. It sounded like a holdup, but it was too early for the stagecoach to be coming through. Curiosity gnawed at him, but he didn't relish the idea of being shot for sticking his nose in where it didn't belong. He followed Hoshi up a sandy rise to a bushy juniper tree. From there, they could observe the road ahead without being seen.

The first thing Billy saw was a flatbed wagon. On the wagon, a brown canvas tarp covered half a dozen wooden crates. Four men in blue uniforms lay unmoving on the ground by the wagon. Red blood stained the ground near them and flies swarmed. Two more uniformed men sat on the wagon's buckboard with their hands in the air. Two civilians on horseback with bandanas covering their mouths and noses faced them. Billy recognized a stickup, and couldn't help but wonder what was so valuable that two men would risk attacking soldiers to get it.

Just as Billy opened his mouth to speak, Hoshi dashed forward, drawing his revolver. The two bandits looked up as Hoshi fired. Blood sprayed from the nearest bandit's hand and his gun flew to the ground. The other bandit, with dark curly hair peeking out from beneath his broad hat, swung his pistol around and fired. Hoshi jolted backward.

With a curse, Billy drew his gun and rode out from behind the juniper tree. "Drop it, stranger!"

To his surprise, Hoshi remained in the saddle. He sat up and swiveled his gun toward the armed bandit, who then held his arms out to the side and let the gun fall to the ground.

The soldiers on the wagon wasted no time hopping from the buckboard and retrieving their weapons along with the bandits' guns. "Thank you for the help, strangers," said the one wearing corporal's stripes.

"You're welcome." Hoshi turned to the man clutching his bloodied hand. "Can you ride?"

He looked up, eyes wide with terror and pain. "My partner shot you. I saw it."

"Shut up, Bob," said the curly-haired man. "You talk too much."

"To be honest, I was kinda curious about that myself." Billy's brow furrowed. "I coulda sworn he plugged you right in the chest."

Hoshi parted his robe enough to reveal shiny blue lacquered metal with a small dent right over his heart. "If I had been much closer, the bullet would have penetrated."

"Much obliged," said the curly-haired bandit. "I'll remember that, next time I see you."

"I doubt very much that we'll meet again." Hoshi returned his gun to its concealed place within the robes. "I suspect you'll be hung for what you did today." He ripped some cloth from the inside of his robe and rode close to the wounded man. He examined the bloodied hand, then wrapped the wound.

Billy looked around. Two soldiers loaded their fallen companions onto the wagon, beside the crates. "Anything we can do to help?"

"Let me have a good look at these men," said the corporal. "That way I can testify against them when they come to trial."

As Billy rode up and pulled down the wounded man's bandana, the private bolted forward. "Corporal, why bother with a trial? Let me teach 'em to mess with an army wagon."

"Simmer down, Gilroy. We need to get these crates to El Paso before something else happens," said the corporal.

Billy pulled down the curly-haired man's bandana revealing a thick, dark mustache framing a sneer under an aquiline nose. "I think the best thing you could do is take these varmints to the marshal in Mesilla." The corporal turned to the man named Gilroy. "We'll have fun enough watching 'em dance at the end of a rope later."

"Speakin' o' rope," said Billy, "you got something to hogtie these varmints' hands together? It'll sure slow 'em down if they try to do something stupid."

"You bet," said the corporal. He grabbed some rope from the wagon, cut off a piece and tossed it to the man called Gilroy. The two soldiers tied the bandits' wrists together and checked that the knots were secure.

Once done, Billy turned around and aimed his gun first at one bandit, then the other. "You heard the man. Ride."

The bandits did their best to grasp the reins in their bound hands, then turned their horses toward town. Billy and Hoshi followed close behind. Satisfied that the bandits weren't going to make a break for it, Billy holstered his revolver. Half a mile down the road, he broke the uneasy silence. "You boys have a lot of cojones to take on six soldiers. That musta been something important they're carryin'."

"What's it to ya'?" growled the curly-haired bandit.

"Guns," said the wounded man. "They'se some kinda special gun invented back east."

"Shut up, Bob, you talk too much," The curly-haired bandit chided his partner a second time.

"Don't make no difference to me." Billy patted the six-gun at his hip. "I got all the firepower I need, right here."

"These are special guns," said Bob with a certain reverence. "They'se supposed to throw lightning bolts. You don't need to reload them or nothin'. Some scientist built them for the army to fight the Russians."

"Sounds like ol' Professor Maravilla," mused Billy. "Makes me wonder what scientists did to make money before the Russians invaded."

A short time later, they reached the Mesilla Park. Past the livery stables, they came to a large corral where people from the outlying farms could leave their horses for a few cents. Hoshi and Billy dismounted, then helped the wounded man from his horse. As they did, the curly-haired bandit leapt from his horse and made a break for it. Billy turned and sprinted after him. With a lunge and a leap he tackled him, sending him sprawling into the mud and manure. The bandit swore as Billy stood and pulled him out of the muck.

Billy drew his gun and pointed it at the captive. "Let's move. I believe we have an appointment with the marshal."

As they marched through town, the four men drew stares. Billy wasn't sure what they found most peculiar—Hoshi's robes, or the fact that he and one of the bandits were covered in mud and horse manure. When they arrived at the marshal's office, one of the wanted posters caught Billy's eye. It showed a man with curly hair and a dark, bushy mustache. "Well, well, well. It looks like we have us the company of Curly Bill Bresnahan according to this here poster. I'm beginnin' to think you give people with the name of William a bad reputation."

"I hope you choke on the reward money," sneered Bresnahan.

Billy laughed, casting a sidelong glance toward Hoshi.
"There may be somethin' to that. First thing I plan to buy is
some coffee ... and some bacon." He pointed his revolver at
Bresnahan. "Now get on inside. I'm getting hungry standing
out here talkin'."

After the Apache warriors rode away, Professor Maravilla and
Larissa resumed their work on the clockwork lobo. The professor opened a hatch on the wolf's chest and made an adjustment
to a complicated series of gears connected to a gimbal-and-rotor assembly he called a gyroscope. "This is the closest thing
the lobo has to a brain," he explained. "It helps him keep his
balance and tells him the path to follow." He pointed to lines
and numbers on a set of knobs. "Basically, his path will always
be an ellipse." He pointed to one dial. "This setting tells the lobo
how many steps to take." Then he pointed to two more. "These
define the major and minor axes of the ellipse. If they're equal,
the lobo will walk in a circle. Right now, I have them set as far
apart as possible. He'll walk a virtually straight line toward the
Mexican border, then turn around and come back."

Larissa studied the mechanism for a moment. "You know,
that gimbal-and-rotor almost looks like a wagon wheel, or even
the wheel on one of those new safety bicycles."

"Indeed, it does." Light gleamed from Maravilla's eye as
he closed the chest hatch, then opened another hatch on the
wolf's flank. "In fact, a bicycle's wheel is a kind of gyroscope.
The spinning action helps keep the machine upright just like
this gyroscope helps to keep the lobo from either falling over or
deviating too far from its course."

Larissa stood upright and considered the professor's words.
"What if you took a bicycle and put a motor on it like the one
in the wolf?"

"A fascinating idea." Maravilla inserted fuel rods into the
lobo's engine, turned it on and closed the hatch. The lobo

began its trek to the south. Every few steps, a little puff of steam would appear from its tailpipe and dissipate rapidly in the dry air. "It might even be practical on level terrain. I would hate to use it on rugged terrain, though. Although the wheels act like a gyroscope, a bicycle can still get overbalanced and tip on its side."

"Couldn't you add a gyroscope like the one in the lobo's chest for even better balance?"

The professor nodded, then took out his pocket watch. "I believe we can expect our friend back in about twelve hours."

Larissa looked at the professor's watch. It was a little after six in the afternoon. As she looked up, the mechanical wolf disappeared into a gully, then climbed up the other side. "Do you actually think the wolf will cross the path of this ... whatever it is?"

Maravilla folded his arms. "If our new friends the Apaches are correct and the apparition limits its travels to this side of the mountain range, I believe one of two things will happen. Either the lobo will capture a photograph of the mysterious specter or we shall see it for ourselves."

Larissa chewed her lip as she continued to follow the lobo's progress. It brushed past a mesquite bush, knocking off leaves and bean pods.

The professor frowned. "You seem concerned by more than this spectral camel rider."

The bounty hunter shook her head, then walked over to the hansom cab and sat down on the passenger step where she put her head in her hands and frowned. "It's just that I've flown your owls over the Grand Canyon and Denver. When I returned to the canyon with you, I thought we would be building something new and great. Instead, we're out here in the middle of the desert hunting something that might not even exist. What's worse, men are dying in the northwest while we're here."

"Geronimo's warriors seemed to believe the specter exists." Maravilla hitched up his trousers and crouched near Larissa. His wide eyes showed genuine concern. "Don't forget the miner in Tucson who also reported seeing it."

Larissa took off her hat and looked at the goggles that

rested on the brim—her one memento of flight. "It's not that." She stared at her reflection in the goggles' lenses as she tried to put her concerns into words. "Even if we find this spectral camel rider and learn what it is, what good will it do?"

The professor looked over his shoulder in the direction the lobo had gone. A few puffs of steam showed it still made steady progress southward. "It's certainly true we might find this is nothing more than some unfortunate soul who died strapped to a camel's back. If that is so, we will have evidence. The miners and the Apaches may return to the area."

"Is that really a good thing?" Larissa ran her fingers along the hat brim. "If both miners and Indians return, it'll just mean more fighting."

"You may be right about that." Maravilla sighed. A moment later, he brightened. "On the other hand, we may learn this really is a spirit of the dead."

She jerked her head toward the professor, nearly dropping her hat. "And how would that be a good thing?"

"It would be proof of life after death." The professor slapped his leg. "It would be a way for us to make our mark on the world of science."

She looked around at the cacti and the low scrub. "It's a pretty grim picture of the afterlife. Wandering for all eternity in this place." She snorted. "I'd like to think we join the angels among the clouds. Maybe that's why I like flying so much. It's one step closer to paradise."

Maravilla stood in silence for a long time. His eyes darted back and forth, as though he listened to a silent conversation. "Paradise is quite elusive."

The bounty hunter laughed nervously at the cryptic response. "And just how long have you been looking for paradise?"

"About as long as I can remember." For a moment, Larissa thought the professor's voice had taken on a strange, resonant timbre, as though multiple voices spoke at once. He nodded, as though agreeing with himself, then walked over to his horse and gave it a cursory pat on the neck. A moment later, he retrieved a notebook and pencil from his saddlebag. He sat down on a nearby rock and began making notes.

Larissa looked at her reflection in the goggles again and wondered just who she saw. Was she a tough bounty hunter, fighting to bring justice and balance to the world? Was she the assistant to some mad scientist who seemed lost in his own mind? Or was she just a lonely, young woman running away from a past she didn't want to remember?

Ramon wiped his hands as he finished weeding his mother's garden. As he walked back to the house, he watched Fatemeh step outside, carrying a bucket. She wore a long, black skirt that concealed her legs, but the lacy blouse accented her full figure. It was hard to describe her as graceful—more like sure and confident. Nevertheless, a warm feeling of pride welled up in his chest that she wanted to marry him.

A burrowing owl flew up and lit on a fencepost near the house. It chirped and moved from one leg to the other. Fatemeh crouched low and whistled. The owl whistled again and flew off.

Ramon chuckled to himself. "So, what did that owl tell you?" he asked.

"Ramon, you know better than that. Owls just chirp and whistle." Fatemeh grinned. "Nevertheless, I believe we'll have a visitor soon."

Ramon looked off in the distance. A dust cloud moved along the road toward the homestead. He adjusted his glasses and looked closer. Someone came at a full gallop. As the rider approached the house, he slowed and began brushing dust from his arms. The golden chevrons of a sergeant adorned his blue uniform sleeve. The rider came to a stop. "Ramon Morales?" he asked.

Ramon nodded. "That's me."

"I'm Sergeant Michael Harris from Fort Bliss in El Paso." He reached into his saddlebag and retrieved a wax-sealed envelope. Ramon took the letter while Fatemeh introduced herself and offered the soldier some water.

"Much obliged, ma'am," he said as he dismounted and removed his hat.

She continued to the water pump and filled a bucket. Returning to the porch, she passed a full ladle to the soldier.

Ramon looked to Fatemeh. "This is from Major Johnson."

"It's Lt. Colonel Johnson, now," Harris interjected.

Ramon looked at the letter and nodded. Johnson had been his commanding officer for the short time he was in the army, fighting the Russians in Denver. "Colonel Johnson says he has an important job for me and has offered good pay if I succeed."

"Working for the army doesn't sound like the path we discussed." Fatemeh scowled, her tone cold.

"I don't think I have much choice. He says the Russians are continuing their resistance in the Northwest and they need my help. Colonel Johnson wants me to find Professor Maravilla. Apparently, the professor's ornithopters haven't been effective against the Russian ground forces in Washington Territory."

"So, they want the professor to improve his design, is that it?"

"That, or invent something better," interjected Sergeant Harris. "We're looking for all the help we can get." He dipped his ladle into the bucket and took another drink.

"I really thought the war was over when..." Fatemeh cast a glance at Sergeant Harris, then led Ramon a short distance away. "I thought the invasion ended when we destroyed the airships. What's keeping them there?"

"They're imperialists, ma'am," said the sergeant, who set the ladle into the bucket. "America's a free country. I'm sure it rankles the colonial powers in the old world."

Fatemeh snorted. "That makes no sense. Czar Alexander has granted more freedoms to his people over the years, not less. Why would he want to conquer America all of a sudden?"

"Who knows how Russians think, ma'am."

"I imagine they think much the same as you or me." She put her hands on her hips and glared at the sergeant.

Ramon stepped between the two. "What the Russians think isn't what's most important here. Lives are being lost. I think it would be good if Professor Maravilla could find a way to help end the invasion once and for all."

Fatemeh looked to the ground and shook her head. After a moment, she met Ramon's eyes and her gaze softened. "I'm pleased to hear the peacemaker in you speaking out, but I wonder whether taking the professor to the army really would help the cause of peace."

"I suggest we all have a little supper, then continue this conversation later," said Ramon with a glance back at Sergeant Harris.

Fatemeh opened her mouth to say something, but closed it again and nodded. Ramon led the sergeant inside and introduced him to his mother.

Sofia Morales took the sergeant's big hand in both of her tiny ones and said, "A pleasure to meet you."

The sergeant looked around and turned his toe on the wood floor. "Is there a boarding house or a hotel here in Estancia? Perhaps I should make arrangements for the night before we settle in to talk."

Ramon opened his mouth, but Sofia cut him off. "Nonsense. You can stay here, Sergeant. That way you'll have plenty of time to discuss plans and see if Ramon can help."

Ramon held out his hands and looked around, trying to figure out where they had room for the sergeant.

Sofia winked. "He can stay in your room," she said, as though reading his mind.

Ramon's shoulders slumped. After a moment, he forced a smile and indicated the sergeant should follow him to the room.

"Your lady friend sure is something else," said Harris, while they worked to make a somewhat comfortable place to sleep on the floor. "It's almost like she was taking the Russians' side."

Ramon shook his head. "It's not that. When I was a sheriff, I found it helped to solve problems if I understood both sides in a dispute. We're Americans, so we know that side. Do you know why the Russians haven't left? What do they hope to gain by staying?"

The sergeant pursed his lips. "I would think territory."

"But territory for what." Ramon shrugged. "Russia's a big country. They've got farmland. They have mines. They have forests. What does America have that they don't? Besides, last I knew, they were having problems with the Ottoman Turks. Why would they send such a large force here, when they're worried about invasion at home?"

"I see your point. It doesn't make much sense, does it?" The sergeant took off his hat and scratched his head. "Could be gold. They grabbed the mint in Denver. That's where most of the gold from California goes. Maybe they always planned to take California."

"It's a lot of maybes, Sergeant Harris. But I've learned Fatemeh sometimes has good insight into these things. It pays to listen to her."

"Well, our job isn't to figure this out. It's just to get this Professor Maravilla back to Fort Bliss."

Ramon nodded. Smelling stewed chicken, he led the sergeant back out to the kitchen. There, Sofia served bowls of Caldo de Pollo. The sergeant eyed his meal skeptically for a moment, but dove in when he recognized it was a simple vegetable stew with chicken.

After supper, Ramon and the sergeant helped clear the table and clean the dishes. Then Ramon and Fatemeh went out for a walk. The sun was low on the horizon and a gentle breeze blew, rustling the tall grass. Crickets chirped and a few dragonflies darted through the air.

"I've been thinking about what you said, corazón. I think it would help if we knew exactly what the Russians wanted," said Ramon.

"I agree, and Professor Maravilla might be able to help with that."

"Exactly!" Ramon was breathless, pleased that Fatemeh concurred. "Maybe he could be persuaded to find a way to spy on the Russians instead of fighting them."

Fatemeh shook her head, disappointed. "Do you remember when I told you about the creature from the stars called Legion?"

Ramon nodded. The creature called Legion somehow controlled the Russians' minds and had helped them conduct their invasion. According to Fatemeh, the creature had agreed to stop helping the Russians, which allowed the owl riders to win their victory. He couldn't really picture the being. He wasn't even sure he believed in it at all, but if Legion existed, perhaps it had reneged on its promise and was helping the Russians after all.

"When we last saw the professor, I began to wonder if he might be talking to Legion … all his new ideas."

Ramon shrugged. "I thought it was just everything he saw in the battle."

Fatemeh's eyes drifted skyward to the first stars beginning to appear. "Maybe." Her gaze drifted back and met Ramon's. "Or maybe if this Legion talked to the professor, it gave him some idea about what it wanted."

"Could this Legion be talking to the Russians?"

"I don't know." Fatemeh rubbed the bridge of her nose. "It sounded to me like it had regretted its actions working with the Russian military and was going to move on, but maybe I misunderstood."

"So you agree I should find the professor and talk to him?" Ramon smiled, hopeful.

"I do." Fatemeh folded her arms and looked toward the horizon. "I'm just not sure about doing it for the army."

Ramon placed his hands on Fatemeh's shoulders and felt the tension there. "It's the army's problem to deal with the invasion."

"The army's job is to fight, not to make peace." Fatemeh turned around and grasped Ramon's hands. "Talk to the professor and learn what you can. Just promise me this, if he doesn't want to go to Fort Bliss, don't make him."

"You have my word, corazón." Ramon squeezed Fatemeh's hands, then brought her close and sealed the promise with a kiss.

CHAPTER FIVE
GHOST RIDER ON CAMELBACK

L arissa dreamed she walked through a cemetery.

She strode between rows of upright, polished tombstones. Sunlight reflected in her eyes, making them water. The sound of her boots crunching on the pink sand syncopated with the driving wind blowing through the isolated patch of hallowed ground. She stopped in front of a small grave marker. The unrelenting wind and sun had shredded and faded the doll's pretty dress. Its glass eyes stared at her in silent accusation. The porcelain doll, Lyssa Crimson reclined against a marker inscribed with the name Alethea Seaton.

Larissa's hands trembled as she dropped to her knees before the doll, heedless of the gravel cutting into her knees through the fabric of the long dress she wore. "Don't you understand? There's nothing I could have done. She had rheumatic fever. I'm good at fixing things, but that's one thing I don't know how to fix!"

As Larissa wept into her hands, she saw images of other little girls. She saw Venita Brown from Childress, who had a cough that wouldn't go away. She couldn't see a doctor because a band of desperadoes had stolen the payroll from the ranch where her daddy worked.

Larissa saw Melinda Scott, a vibrant girl in pigtails who used to play with Alethea. Her parents were killed in a bank robbery and Melinda went to live with her aunt up in Lubbock who owned a hotel. Larissa remembered Melinda riding away on a buckboard, tears cutting trails through dust-stained cheeks.

Maybe she couldn't fix rheumatic fever, but she saw ways she could help little girls everywhere. All she had to do was learn how to use a gun and outsmart the bad guys.

She looked up with a newfound sense of purpose, but that

purpose soon turned to ice in her gut as she saw another tombstone in the cemetery. The name on the marker read James Ellway. The scene darkened, as though a shade had been drawn. She stood outside a saloon in the Texas panhandle, waiting for Ellway to step outside.

"Come with me, please," she said when he appeared.

He neither resisted nor tried to run away. He just laughed. He laughed at the young woman who fancied herself a bounty hunter.

There was an explosion. Larissa had fired and the bullet flew straight and true, right into Ellway's brain. He fell to the ground in a billowing of dust. His watch dropped from his waistcoat pocket and flopped open, revealing a picture of Ellway with a woman and a young boy. Larissa knew right then that she had made the boy an orphan. She did not stay to collect the bounty. She turned and ran until she reached her hansom cab. She climbed into the seat and snapped the reins riding away as fast as she could. She bounced and jostled until finally her eyes popped open and she realized that Professor Maravilla stood over her, prodding her shoulder.

Larissa sat up and rubbed her eyes. "What time is it?"

"It's nearly 6 o'clock. The lobo returned just a few minutes ago. Help yourself to some coffee while I prepare the chemicals."

Larissa stretched and yawned, then climbed to her feet. The lifeless wolf seemed to watch her as she poured the coffee. Its fur was dirty and covered with burrs. She knew it was just clockworks inside a wolf skin, but she couldn't shake the feeling that the wolf's spirit was disappointed that she had not done a better job of facing her past. She shook her head, knowing she was just rattled by the dream. She sipped the coffee, then knelt down by the clockwork wolf, dusted it off and began picking out burrs.

Meanwhile, the professor hung black cloth in the hansom cab's windows and set two trays on the seat. He retrieved brown jars from one of his chests and poured the contents into the trays. He inspected the makeshift darkroom and nodded satisfaction. Then he retrieved the black blanket they had used when loading the photographic plates into the wolf along with a black cloth bag. Turning, he saw Larissa picking out the burrs. "Yes, he can become quite a mess as he makes his journeys. Help me get the plates out, then you should get some breakfast."

Larissa nodded. She helped him cover the lobo with the black blanket and crawled underneath with the professor, wondering how such a scene would appear to the barmaid back in Tucson. Running her hands along the lobo's fur, she found the hatch and held it open, while the professor reached inside. He counted out the photographic plates, placing each one carefully into his bag. "I think that's everything," he said.

She closed the hatch and lifted the blanket, relieved that no one aimed a gun at them. The professor returned to the hansom cab, stepped through the blanket he had draped earlier and closed the doors behind him. Just then, Larissa's stomach began to rumble.

She searched through her supplies and found a bag of oats. She longed for fresh eggs, but oatmeal would have to do.

Half an hour later as she finished her breakfast, the professor emerged from the wagon. "Ah ha! We've found it! Begin packing. The game's afoot."

Early that same morning, Ramon and Sergeant Harris saddled their horses to ride into Albuquerque. The town wasn't much larger than Estancia, but it was the closest point with a telegraph station. A few minutes later, Fatemeh appeared wearing a gingham blouse and buckskin trousers. Suspicious of the change from her usual skirt, his brow furrowed. His suspicions were confirmed when she began saddling her horse.

"Where are you going?" asked Ramon.

"With you, of course," she said.

"Now wait just a minute," interjected the sergeant. "We only have enough money for two men and their horses to make a roundtrip to Flagstaff. Once we're sure the professor's expecting us, we'll be on our way."

"That's fine. I don't plan to accompany you to Flagstaff." Fatemeh cinched up the straps on her saddle, then placed the bridle around her horse's head. Satisfied that everything was as it should be, she patted the horse's neck. "Besides, what happens if the professor isn't there? I might just be able to help you search for him."

"She has a point," said Ramon.

"All right," grumbled the sergeant. "Just don't slow us down."

"As you wish." Fatemeh grinned, then grabbed the saddle horn, pulled herself up and clicked her tongue. The horse shot from the barn at a run. A burrowing owl on a fencepost took off and flew after her.

Ramon laughed as he pulled himself into his saddle and followed Fatemeh. Harris shouted a string of curse words in his wake, but a few minutes later, both men had caught up with Fatemeh when she slowed her horse to a trot.

"We should have good weather for our ride," she said. Ramon followed her gaze. The burrowing owl swept an arc ahead of them. It settled to the ground, then bobbed from one leg to the other and whistled, as though wishing them a happy journey. A moment later, it spread its wings and flew back toward the farm.

"Whoa." Larissa tugged on the reins, bringing the hansom cab to a stop. She looked around at the way the mountains rose gently from the desert floor. A small mesa jutted out at them. Larissa couldn't help but think that the mountains were sticking out an enormous tongue. "Professor, can I see that photo again?"

The professor pulled up alongside Larissa and fished the glass photographic plate from his coat pocket. The photo clearly showed a ghostly negative image of a camel with a spindly figure like a skeleton on its back. Larissa had seen enough skeletons to know they didn't stay in one piece on their own. Perhaps someone had gone to a lot of work to wire the skeleton together. Perhaps the skeleton was something sculpted. Perhaps there really was some mystical energy at work. In any event, photographic evidence of the mysterious camel rider now existed, and a roiling need to solve this odd mystery churned in Larissa's gut.

Larissa studied the photo—this time, less interested in the strange apparition than in the terrain. She nodded, noting the same configuration of mesa and mountains. "I think we're in the right area." She climbed down from the seat behind the cab, retrieved her Springfield rifle from within, then stepped forward, looking for signs the ground had been disturbed.

Professor Maravilla retrieved his telescope and scanned the area as well.

"I've never actually seen a camel, Professor. What kinds of tracks will I be looking for?"

Maravilla lowered the telescope and rubbed his chin. "Footprint a little larger than a horse, I'd imagine. Their hooves aren't as hard as a horse and they have two toes."

"What about their droppings? Like a horse?"

"I'm not really sure." The professor's brow furrowed. "They'll be big like a horse or an elk."

Larissa nodded as she made her way to where some foliage had been broken. "Ah hah!" she said as she spied a line of deep wolf tracks. She smiled and turned toward the professor. "I think our lobo came through here." She stood in its path and looked around. The terrain now looked even more like the photograph. She tried to visualize where the camel had stood. With a nod, she jogged in that direction. A moment later, she looked down and grinned. She knelt down beside a two-towed track and opened her hand to gauge the scale. "I think he passed through here."

The professor rode close, then climbed off the horse. He retrieved a pad from his saddlebag and sketched the hoof print. "Do you think you can track it?"

"Through here it's easy." She followed the tracks with her eyes. "It gets rockier over there. We'll have to see."

With a nod, the professor pulled himself onto his saddle. Larissa climbed back into the cab's seat. They followed the trail for about two miles. As Larissa feared, the ground became much rockier as they progressed. There was no way she could continue with the cab. "Let me see how far this extends and if I can pick up the trail." She looked around at the sun. Only an hour or so of daylight remained. "It's possible we'll have to make camp here and follow this on foot."

Maravilla nodded as Larissa climbed down. She followed the trail another half mile until she came across a flat rocky outcropping. She shook her head. From that point, the camel could have gone anywhere. They would have to scout around the perimeter, but too little light remained to do that. Looking around, she saw the professor watching her through his telescope. She gave an exaggerated shrug and trudged back toward him.

As she drew near, he held up his hand. "What?" she asked.

He shushed her. A moment later, she heard it. A grunting and a snuffling accompanied a clockwork ticking not unlike that made by the professor's wolf. Maravilla eased his horse around and Larissa shielded her eyes against the sunlight. "That's it," said the professor with undisguised glee.

Larissa drew in her breath at the sight of the shaggy camel. On its back was, indeed, a skeleton. Despite the heat, goosebumps rose on her flesh as it looked toward her. She backed up half a step, snapping a twig. The camel whipped its head in their direction, then veered away.

"We need to catch it," called the professor.

Words froze in the back of Larissa's throat. She couldn't look away from the skeleton camel rider. However, as she continued to look, she realized the skeleton's head swung back and forth in a predictable manner. It hadn't actually looked *at* her, it just moved that way. "I don't think I can get it on foot," she croaked at last.

The professor nodded, then climbed into his saddle, squeezed the horse's flanks with his knees, and clucked his tongue. The animal shot off toward the camel. Seeing the horse approach, the camel brayed horribly, unleashed a big glob of white spit, then bolted toward the river, unseating the skeleton. Maravilla brought his horse to a stop and dismounted. Larissa ran up and joined him. Together they approached the skeleton.

It lay on the ground, in two pieces, spine broken just above the hip bones and missing the hands. Its head still turned back and forth. Within the rib cage a set of gearworks turned, like those inside the mechanical wolf, but simpler. A rod extended from the gears which turned the head back and forth. The professor reached inside the rib cage and disengaged the clutch, stopping the motion.

"Whoever built this wanted to scare people away," said the professor.

Larissa crouched by the skeleton and frowned, almost disappointed that it was a man-made apparatus after all. Thick wires protruded through the spine. She reached out and touched the broken end, shinier than the rest of the wire. "It was meant to last, but it's seen quite a bit of wear. This wire's been jarred around and twisted. Hard to say whether the wire broke first, or the rope holding the skeleton in place."

The professor retrieved his telescope and scanned the horizon. "There's no sign of the camel. If we're going to continue this search, we'll need fresh supplies. We could also use help from someone who knows where people could hide around here."

"The Apaches?"

"Yes," said the professor. "I think they'll be very interested to know what we've found."

Ramon, Fatemeh, and Sergeant Harris rode into the small town of Albuquerque the following afternoon. An adobe building next to the Central Pacific Railroad depot housed the telegraph station.

Inside, the clerk sat at a desk with his feet propped up, arms folded across his chest and snoring. Sergeant Harris banged on the counter and the man looked up with a start. "I'm Sergeant Michael Harris. I'd like to send a telegram to a Professor Maravilla in Flagstaff."

Fatemeh cleared her throat. "The professor was at the Grand Canyon, not Flagstaff. Who knows how often he comes into town for messages."

"Well, do you have a better idea?" asked the sergeant.

"We could send a telegram to Mr. Leroy Foster," suggested Fatemeh.

"Who's Leroy Foster?" asked Ramon.

"He's the blacksmith that works with Professor Maravilla. If anyone knows where to find him, he will."

Ramon looked over at Harris. "See, I told you bringing her along was a good idea."

Harris snorted and folded his arms while Fatemeh dictated a short message. The clerk keyed it in, then collected the fee.

"Nothing to do now but wait for an answer," said Fatemeh. "I don't know about you but I'm hungry. I think we should find dinner and a place to spend the night."

"This isn't in the budget, you know," said the sergeant.

"Next time, you'll just have to plan for the unexpected." Fatemeh smiled, then took Ramon's hand and led him out to the street.

Billy walked between the rows of chile plants, looking for weeds to pull and inspecting for damage from animals. The little plants seemed hardy and self-reliant compared to other plants Billy had heard about. For that, he was grateful.

A man with bristly white hair and two days' growth of beard tottered along the ditch bank. Billy walked in that direction, arriving at the floodgate at the same time as the mayor-domo of the acequia that diverted water out of the Rio Grande for irrigation.

"Tiempo para el agua?" Billy asked if it was time to water.

The old man nodded and took out his pocket watch. "Sí, Billy."

Billy reached over and turned the handle, opening the floodgate. He loved the earthy smell that rose as the water eased its way between the rows of chile plants. Billy and the mayor-domo made small talk in Spanish while the water flowed. Once the water made it halfway down the field, Billy began to shift from one foot to the other. He looked up at the sun, noting the time of day. He hoped to make it into town before it got dark.

Finally, the mayordomo looked up from his pocket watch. "Cierra para ariba."

Billy followed the instruction and closed the floodgate. He tipped his hat. "Gracias, Señor."

The old man nodded and continued down the ditch bank. Billy went the opposite direction, toward the house. He found Hoshi near the back porch, practicing with the sword he called a katana. He held it over his head and made practice thrusts straight down. Billy cleared his throat as he drew near.

Hoshi pointed his sword at Billy's abdomen. Then, holding the sword steady, he swung around and looked him in the eye.

"So, why do you practice with a sword when people have guns?"

"It is a question of having the right weapon for the right circumstances," said Hoshi.

"So, if you're so smart, when would it be better to have a sword than a gun?"

Hoshi grinned. "If Mr. Bresnahan had a sword yesterday, and knew how to use it, he might have gotten away from you."

"How so?" Billy's brow furrowed. "I had a gun."

"Show me." Hoshi held the sword with his hands close together, as though they were tied.

Billy reached for his six-gun. Just as he brought it level with Hoshi, a sharp pain in the back of his hand caused him to drop the gun to the ground. The former samurai had turned the sword and smacked Billy's hand with the flat of the blade.

"It would have been easier to have disarmed you by taking the hand off," said Hoshi, "but you are a good worker and I do not want you maimed."

Billy rubbed his hand. "All right. What if I don't draw my piece till you back away a little?"

"If I care enough about my freedom, I'd simply kill you with my sword."

Billy frowned as he thought. "Thing is, he didn't have a sword, and even if he did, we'd have made him drop it."

Hoshi inclined his head, accepting the statement. "The sword is also about accuracy and control. Being good at the sword makes me better with a pistol and with my hands. You noticed that I disarmed a man with one shot from my pistol."

"I like that." Billy nodded and grinned. Then he stepped back a moment and folded his arms. "Thing is, I thought you gave up bein' a warrior. Why do you keep practicin' with the sword?"

"It keeps me ready for anything I might encounter ... like yesterday."

"You may have a great poker face, but you're a bad liar, Hoshi." Billy leaned against the porch rail. "You're practicin' way too hard for someone who just wants to keep himself prepared. You're more like a soldier gettin' ready for combat."

"I hope that isn't so." Hoshi sheathed his katana. "Still, I worry about the Russians."

"They're not so tough." Billy smiled, remembering the battle of Denver.

"If that's true, why can't your whole army dislodge them from Washington and Alaska?" Hoshi shook his head. "If they have really become so hungry for land, I also wonder what that will mean for Japan."

"I thought you left Japan for good."

"It is still my homeland and I love it, even if I don't agree with those who lead the country right now."

Billy sighed, thinking about the feud in Lincoln County and how the territorial governor supported Murphy's monopoly, even though it wasn't just. "I do believe I understand." Billy crouched down and retrieved his revolver from the ground. "Do you mind if I run into town?"

Hoshi stepped forward and examined the field. "I think your work is done today."

"Thanks!" Billy started toward the barn, but turned around after a few steps. "Say, tomorrow do you think you could show me a little bit of what you do with that sword?"

"It would be my pleasure."

Billy continued toward the barn and saddled his horse. He rode in to Mesilla Park, left his horse at the public corral, then walked to the offices of the *Mesilla News*, where he knocked on Luther Duncan's door.

The reporter appeared a moment later. "Billy, it's great to see you!" He straightened his bow tie.

"You seem awfully happy."

Duncan led Billy to a chair, then unlocked a drawer and retrieved a wad of bills. He counted a few off the top and passed them to Billy, whose brow furrowed.

"What's this for?"

"Your story about fighting the airships in Denver has been selling to newspapers all across the country. I thought you deserved a share."

"Why thank you." Billy stuffed the bills into his coat pocket. "So, I hear you want me to tell you how we thwarted that robbery yesterday."

"You bet I do." The reporter patted the stack of bills that lay before him on the desk.

After eating supper and securing rooms for the night, Ramon, Fatemeh, and Sergeant Harris returned to the telegraph office. They found the clerk at the door, fishing the keys from his pocket. He looked up. "Closing up for the night. Come back tomorrow."

Fatemeh stepped close. "All we want to know is did we get a response to our telegram from earlier this afternoon?"

The clerk adjusted his glasses and studied the trio for a moment. "Oh, yeah. You three sent that telegram to the blacksmith in Flagstaff. Sure enough he wired back. Said that Maravilla fella left for Tucson a few days ago."

Ramon and Harris looked at each other. "What the devil is he doing all the way down in Tucson?" asked the sergeant. "I was closer to the professor at Fort Bliss!"

"Did he say when he'd be back?" asked Ramon.

The clerk threw up his hands, then opened the door and stepped inside. A moment later he returned with the telegram. He thrust it at Fatemeh, then finished locking the door and stalked away.

"Well, what's it say?" urged Sergeant Harris.

Fatemeh shook her head. "Just that the professor and Larissa went to Tucson with a wagonload of supplies." She folded the paper neatly and placed it in the pouch on her belt.

"Well, what do we do?" asked Harris. "Go to Flagstaff and wait for him to return, or go to Tucson and find out what he's up to there?"

Ramon took off his glasses and examined them for a moment. "I think it would be best if we split up. I can go to Tucson and look for the professor there. You go to Flagstaff in case he's already on the way back."

The sergeant gritted his teeth and looked as though he wanted to argue, but only shrugged. "I can't think of a better idea. Send me a wire when you get in. We'll figure out a rendezvous once one of us finds him."

"Agreed." Ramon slipped his glasses back on and looked at Fatemeh. "What about you corazón?"

"I haven't been to Albuquerque before. I thought I'd take a walk. Would you care to join me?" She wore a coy smile, infecting him with her sense of adventure.

Ramon stepped forward and held out his arm. "I'd be delighted."

The sergeant cleared his throat. "I think I may pay a visit to the saloon next to the hotel. I'll see you back at the room in a little while, Mr. Morales."

Ramon watched him trudge off toward the hotel for a moment holding Fatemeh's hand, wishing he shared a room with her rather than the soldier. A moment later, Ramon and Fatemeh turned and walked the other direction. "You have something else in mind, don't you, corazón?"

Fatemeh shook her head. "Nothing specific. It's just that Albuquerque has a telegraph office and gets a bit more news from distant reaches than Estancia. I thought I might stay a couple days and see what I could learn about the war."

"Promise me you won't do anything rash."

"When do my actions ever give you a rash?" She reached up and took Ramon's shoulder, bringing him close for a kiss.

Birdcalls sounded as Professor Maravilla and Larissa Crimson rode into the Dragoon Mountains. Their horses drug their feet, tongues lolling with thirst. Larissa tugged on the reins.

"Why are you stopping?" asked the professor. "We still haven't found the Apache camp."

Larissa's eyes darted around the rocks. The whistles and chirps continued. "I think they found us. No use wearing out the horses more than they already are."

A few minutes later, a horse appeared on the rise ahead of them. As the rider approached, Larissa noticed Baishan's long braids and strong shoulders. "We have news for Geronimo and we need water for our horses."

The young warrior nodded. "Come with me."

As they rode, Larissa examined their surroundings. Yellow-gray rocks rose all around them. They were at once dramatic and claustrophobic. "I've heard Apache names have meaning," said Larissa, attempting to break the silence and the tension. "What does Baishan mean?"

He cast a sidelong glance her direction. "It means 'knife' and was also the name of a great Mimbres Apache."

The party rode over a rise onto a flat expanse of rock covered with several wickiups—small, temporary shelters of wood and brush. A natural basin in the rock near one edge of the encampment collected runoff from the surrounding mountains. Larissa brought her horse to a stop, climbed down from the seat and unhitched it from the cab. She and the professor led their animals to the watering hole.

Baishan tended his own horse. "What news do you have for Geronimo?"

The professor opened his mouth to speak, but Larissa held up her hand. She stepped over to the hansom cab and opened the door. Sitting next to crates and duffel bags was the skeleton.

Baishan gasped and shuffled backward three steps. "You bring the dead among us?"

"That's why I unhitched the wagon where I did," said Larissa. "I didn't want to bring the skeleton into your camp."

"Still, you brought it close." Baishan's eyes widened.

"We wanted to show Geronimo that it's no spirit." The professor took a step toward the wagon to show the young warrior, but Larissa put her hand on his arm and shook her head. Maravilla sighed, then continued his explanation. "Men wired the skeleton together and placed clockworks inside."

"We have photographs of the area where we found this," said Larissa. "We hoped one of the warriors could tell us where the men who made this could be camping."

Baishan nodded. "Come with me." He led them through

the village to a wickiup near the center. He called through the door in Apache.

A moment later, Geronimo stepped out followed by a woman. He indicated they should sit, then spoke to the woman. The woman nodded, then disappeared behind another wickiup where smoke from a campfire drifted skyward.

Geronimo leaned toward Baishan and asked a question, which the young warrior translated. "What have you found?"

The professor retrieved the photograph of the camel from his coat pocket and passed it to the warrior. "The camel rider is a skeleton, but men have altered it. We hoped you would send a guide to help us figure out where it came from."

Baishan translated while Geronimo studied the negative photo with furrowed brow. He held it up the light, then nodded and spoke.

"He knows the area well," said Baishan. "Evil spirits inhabit those lands. Your people call the area Goose Flats. We call it the land of the tombstone, because it is dry and many people have died there."

The woman returned, carrying bowls loaded with meat and a poofy flatbread. The professor sniffed at his bowl dubiously while Larissa took several bites. "This is delicious," she said. "What is it?"

"The meat is rabbit," said Baishan. "The bread is called Chigustei."

Larissa sopped up the juices with the Chigustei. "What else can you tell us about Goose Flats and the mountains that rise just beyond?"

Geronimo handed the photograph back to Professor Maravilla and spoke to Baishan.

"The caves in those mountains lead to silver veins." The translator held up his own silver necklace. "White men have been known to go into the caves to look for the metal."

"White men looking for silver would like to keep strangers away." Maravilla retrieved his map from the other pocket and unfolded it. "Could you tell me where those caves are?"

Baishan relayed the question. Geronimo took the map, pointed, and handed it back. Maravilla circled the location with a pencil. The warrior then leaned forward and spoke in a low voice.

Baishan swallowed, then translated. "His advice to you is to leave those caves alone. The men who inhabit them do not have a healthy fear of death."

Larissa put her hand to her gun. "If they try anything, they'll meet death, whether they fear it or not."

CHAPTER SIX
PROPOSITIONS

After spending the night in the Apache camp, Professor Maravilla and Larissa rode to Goose Flats, past the place where Larissa lost the camel's trail, while the sun was high overhead. The land shimmered with heat waves. Overhead, vultures circled on the thermals. Wistful, Larissa wondered both what they circled and what it would be like to ride those rising air currents in an ornithopter.

The professor consulted his map and studied the countryside. His lips moved, almost imperceptibly, as though he were talking to himself again. A moment later, he nodded and clucked his tongue, urging his horse forward. Larissa followed. She soon spotted a wide gully which cut its way through the rising landscape toward the low mesa. If Larissa understood the map, that ridge was Goose Flats. Rounded stones and scrub brush filled the gully, but she thought she could pull a wagon laden with supplies through there. Her hansom should be able to make it as well.

Inspecting for spoor, she saw no clear signs others had come this way before. If people had set up camp along the gully, they were either experts at covering their trail or had come in a long time before. The professor's soft murmurings also held a skeptical tone. Finally, with a nod indicating he'd reached a conclusion, he snapped the reins and forged ahead.

A short time later, Larissa spotted familiar tracks and grew hopeful. "Professor, what do you think? Camel tracks?"

The professor brought his horse around and looked where she pointed. He reached into his saddlebags and brought out a notepad, flipped through a few pages, then nodded. "Yes, I believe so."

Larissa looked at how the land folded and buckled around

them. It wasn't as claustrophobic as the area near the Apache camp in the Dragoon Mountains, but it would be easy for someone to hide. A nervous flutter ran through her belly. "We should be careful."

The professor looked around, listening. "Agreed," he whispered.

They followed the gully another hundred yards to a point where it wound past an outcropping of yellow rock. A shot rang out overhead, echoing around them. "That's far enough, strangers," called an unseen voice. "Turn around and go back the way you came."

"We aren't interested in your claim," called the professor. "We're just here to return some property you misplaced."

"I don't recall misplacing any property."

"Are you sure? Some rather impressive clockworks were mounted inside a skeleton. They fell from a camel a few miles back."

There was no reply. Larissa guessed that the person who challenged them pondered his response to the professor's words. Finally, he called out again. "Come on up, but don't try anything funny. There's more of us than there are of you and we have you covered."

"Very well," agreed the professor and he snapped his reins.

Around the bend, the gully passed in front of a cave's mouth. Two men sat near a campfire, holding six-guns. Larissa noticed buckets, pickaxes, ropes, bedrolls and a trash heap. A wagon stood nearby and two mules chewed at mesquite brush. As she suspected, these men had been there for a while.

A man in a buckskin shirt and fringed britches scrambled down from the rocks to their left. His beard came down to the shirt's first button. Larissa guessed he was some kind of mountain man or scout. The other two men wore canvas pants and cotton shirts, more in keeping with other prospectors she'd met. She guessed the man with the long beard must keep lookout while the others hunted for silver.

"So, tell me what exactly you found." The man in buckskin held his rifle ready, though he didn't point it toward Larissa or the professor.

Maravilla held his hands aloft to show he was unarmed.

"May I dismount and open the door of my companion's wagon?" His eyes twinkled, more excited to show off than concerned about the prospector's guns.

"All right." The scout nodded.

Maravilla dismounted and walked over to the hansom cab. Opening the doors, he revealed the skeleton. "This rather thin gentleman has been scaring quite a few people away."

"That's his job," said the scout. "I take it he finally fell off the camel."

The professor nodded.

"So, why'd you bring him back here? You look smart enough to know this means people ain't wanted."

"The clockworks inside indicated something of a kindred spirit." The professor looked from the scout to the other two men, who watched with keen interest. "My name is Professor M.K. Maravilla and I'm a naturalist who utilizes clockwork machines and steam power. My associate is Larissa Crimson."

"Crimson!" One of the prospectors leaped to his feet. He sported unusually well-groomed sideburns and a mustache for a person who had been camping out for several weeks. "You're that lady bounty hunter! We haven't done anything illegal."

"I'm not here to collect a bounty, Mister. I'm just here to solve a mystery." She took the measure of the guns pointed her direction. She could drop quickly and the cab would provide some shelter if needed, but the professor was vulnerable. "Now, the good professor has introduced us to you. Maybe you could return the favor."

The scout looked to his companions, who nodded. "I'm Ed Shieffelin." He nodded to the other bearded man. "That's my brother Al."

"I'm Richard Gird, their financier and attorney," said the well-groomed man.

"Pleased to meet you." Larissa tipped her hat. "Now perhaps we can put the guns away and visit for a spell, then we can be on our way."

Ed lowered his rifle. Al and the attorney followed suit a moment later, placing their guns on the ground, but in easy reach. "We'll visit," said Ed, "but we'll have to see about letting you be on your way. We don't want no one jumping our claim."

The professor chuckled as Larissa climbed out of her seat. "I assure you, we have no interest in your claim." Larissa thought the professor shouldn't be hasty. Successful miners might be able to fund their mechanical owl experiments, especially if they had some motivation. The professor continued. "We're more interested in seeing what devices you've developed for mining."

Al Shieffelin shook his head and laughed. "Machinery would certainly help us out. This mine is proving one tough nut to crack. That skeleton is about the extent of my tinkering."

"Really?" The professor sounded disappointed as he crouched down next to the campfire. The attorney poured him a cup of coffee as Larissa and Ed both sat down on crates.

"So why don't you just stake a claim and then hire men to work the mine?" asked Larissa.

"We would." The attorney looked at his fingers with some disgust, not seeming to like his cracked and dirty nails. "The problem is that all the men we'd hire as miners have gone west to fight in the war."

"Working the mine and guarding the claim takes just about all our time," grumbled Ed.

Larissa sighed. Success had eluded these miners. So much for them being able to fund a new generation of ornithopter.

Al pointed his thumb over his shoulder. "We found the skeleton here in the cave." Larissa realized that must be why the Apaches referred to the area as the land of the tombstone. "When we saw that ol' camel wander by, I had the idea for using it to keep people away."

"It was a good idea." Larissa nodded. "It sure scared me when I first saw it." As they spoke, she noticed that Maravilla's gaze rested on the cave. His lips moved for a moment, but he made no sound, then he cocked his head, as though listening to an answer.

"I might be able to help you out." The professor reached for his pocket and soon found three guns aimed his direction. He lifted his hands. "I'm just retrieving my sketchpad." The guns lowered again. Undoubtedly, they realized there was no bulge in the professor's coat that betrayed a weapon. He withdrew his pad and a pencil and began sketching. A few minutes later, he completed the drawing and passed it to Al.

The prospector's eyes widened. "It's like a monster. A mining machine, I take it?" He passed the drawing to his brother.

Maravilla nodded. "Those are digging tools in front. It pulls the rocks up into its body and sorts the material by density, separating the silver from the rest of the ore."

Ed passed the drawing to Larissa. Gird looked over her shoulder. "It looks like one of those wild pigs," said the attorney. "Like a javelina."

"They're not actually pigs, they're peccaries." The professor sighed. "Nevertheless, they were my inspiration."

"Could you really build such a thing?" asked Ed.

"It would take some funding—" Maravilla looked from Larissa to Ed. "—and a little help, but yes, I believe it could be built."

"Give you money and let you leave," mused Gird. "That sounds like some kind of con to me."

"One of you could come with us," offered Larissa. "You wouldn't have to give us any money."

"And, we can offer proof that we can build the type of machine we suggest." The professor stood and pointed to the hansom cab. "If I may?"

Ed nodded. The professor walked over to the cab and threw open the crate which held the clockwork lobo. Again, they raised their guns, but lowered them a moment later when the creature didn't even twitch. Maravilla beckoned the men to come close. Al whistled as the professor opened the hatch on the mechanical wolf's flank.

"He also built the owls that destroyed the Russian airships in the Battle of Denver," said Larissa.

Al narrowed his gaze, considering. "Okay, so maybe you can build this thing, but why help us?"

Gird folded his arms and scowled. "Maybe a better question is why should we let you join our claim?"

"The first answer is simple." Maravilla stroked his pencil-thin mustache. "We're short of funds. If we succeed, not only would we get a share of the silver from this mine, we would be able to patent the machine and make money from its manufacture."

Gird's eyebrows lifted for just a moment. Ed and Al's eyes flicked toward each other.

Larissa saw an opening. "If you fund this machine, it only seems fair you'd be entitled to a share of the patent. We'd all benefit."

Gird looked around at the Shieffelins. "I think we should talk about it."

Larissa studied the prospectors as they huddled together. Al and Ed seemed like good men trying to make an honest living. She thought she could trust them. She was less certain about Gird, but maybe that was just because he was an attorney. Maravilla cocked his head to the side again, even though the men spoke in low tones. Was he trying to listen in on the hushed conversation, or something else?

Ed looked up from the huddle. "All right, we're interested. We want to see some more detailed plans and a supply list. We'd also like to see some evidence that you are who you say."

"I think we can satisfy your curiosity," said Maravilla.

Larissa folded her arms and studied the professor. General Sheridan had given them letters thanking them for their service at the Battle of Denver. Had he brought his copy along? She looked back at his bags in the cab and considered it a possibility. If so, her week might improve. The professor had come up with a brilliant idea for making money and there was a good chance they could win over the prospectors. Maybe there would be funding for the ornithopters after all.

"You must allow the sword to be a natural extension of your arm." Hoshi demonstrated a swing that traveled from his right shoulder to his left hip. "Work with the katana's momentum. Don't fight it."

Billy looked over his shoulder. "What if someone rushes me from that side?" He held the katana in the position Hoshi expected it to end up. "If I'm like this, they can just rush me while I'm vulnerable."

Hoshi went to the porch and grabbed a broom. "Do the swing as you would, and show me how you would defend yourself."

Billy swung the sword in an arc. As he did, Hoshi rushed at him with the broom. Billy brought the sword up and Hoshi smacked it from his hands.

"You do not have a good grip when you do that," explained Hoshi.

Billy rubbed his sore hand. "All right, then. Show me how you'd defend yourself."

Hoshi handed Billy the broom, then retrieved the sword. As Billy took up a stance, Hoshi swung the sword. Billy rushed at Hoshi. Just as he was about to smack the warrior with the broom, Hoshi thrust the pommel backward, into Billy's gut.

Billy dropped the broom and crumpled to the ground. "Do not assume the blade is the only dangerous part of a sword," said Hoshi.

Billy rolled into a ball and cursed. "I wish you weren't always right," he said after he'd recovered somewhat.

"I'm not always right." Hoshi reached down and helped Billy to his feet. "Otherwise, I'd still be a samurai in Japan. But I am more experienced with a sword." He handed the katana to Billy, who executed the swing as instructed.

"That does feel better." Looking up, he noticed a dust cloud on the road. "I do believe we have a visitor." A moment later, Billy noted the horseman's pinstripe suit and bowler hat.

Hoshi scowled at the sight of Luther Duncan. "Hasn't he bothered us with enough questions?"

"I really don't mind." Billy wondered whether Duncan had offered to pay the samurai warrior for his stories. Of course, Billy suspected that even if he had been offered money, Hoshi would have refused.

A couple minutes later, Duncan tugged on the reins and brought his horse to a stop. He dismounted and tipped his hat as he led the horse to a nearby water trough. "Sorry to barge in like this, but I received a telegram for you."

"A telegram … for me?" Billy's eyebrows came together.

Duncan reached into his inside jacket pocket and handed a slip of paper to Billy. "It's from Fatemeh Karimi."

"Fatemeh!" Billy's eyes brightened. "Is it a wedding invitation?"

"No, nothing like that. She telegrammed yesterday asking if

I knew where you were. When I responded that I did, she sent this and asked me to forward it."

Billy narrowed his gaze at the reporter's grim tone, suspecting bad news. He read the telegram to himself, then looked up. "Did you read this?"

Duncan nodded.

"She can't be serious."

"You must not know Fatemeh that well, then." Duncan shrugged.

Hoshi folded his arms and scowled. "I do not know this Fatemeh, nor do I know the telegram's contents."

"Fatemeh Karimi is the woman I told you about who organized the owl riders," explained Billy. "She had us all go to Flagstaff to learn how to fly Professor Maravilla's ornithopters."

"Ah yes," said Hoshi with a look of understanding. "The story you've told to the newspaper. That explains Fatemeh, but what about the telegram?"

Duncan took up the story. "She wants Billy to go to Washington Territory with her, so she can figure out why the Russians haven't left."

Hoshi reached out and took the katana from Billy. He inspected the blade, wiped it on his sleeve to clean off the dirt, and then sheathed the weapon. Frowning, he looked up. "It is a compelling question. Another compelling question is why did the Russians invade in the first place?"

Billy remembered back to the Battle of Denver. "The Russians were possessed," he said in hushed tones.

Duncan blinked and shook his head, not certain if he heard right. "What do you mean, 'possessed'?"

Billy gave a coy shrug. "At the end of the battle, I was aboard one of the airships with Fatemeh and Professor Maravilla. All the Russians were stock-still, like corpses. We came across one in a fancy uniform, like a general or something."

"That must have been General Gorloff," remarked Duncan, "the leader of the Russian invasion."

"I suppose so," said Billy. "His mouth fell open and words just sorta tumbled out. He called Fatemeh a 'subject of interest.' She said, 'that's what Luther Duncan called me when we first met.'" Billy's brow creased as he remembered the exchange.

"The general's next words were strange. He said, 'that wasn't Luther Duncan, it was us.'" Billy shrugged. "I guess whatever possessed the general during the battle possessed you first."

Duncan took a step backwards, as though Billy had dealt him a physical blow. After a moment Duncan nodded and said, "I first met Fatemeh and Ramon last fall, months before the battle of Denver. I had a ... seizure, for lack of a better word. I heard voices. A lot of people thought I was possessed. Hell, I thought I was possessed. It was like a thousand voices speaking in my head all at once, yanking answers from my mind. I never experienced anything like it before. Fatemeh mixed up a draught for me that quieted the voices and they haven't been back since." He looked from Billy to Hoshi. "I interviewed General Gorloff just a couple of days after Fatemeh cured me."

"Perhaps you were possessed by demons." Hoshi's tone was somber as he studied Duncan. "These demons then passed from you to General Gorloff. They must still influence the Russians."

Billy shook his head. "The demon—or whatever it was—said it had made a mistake. After that, we destroyed the airships and won the battle."

"I wish you'd told me this part of the story before. For months, I've been afraid I would have another seizure." Duncan looked as though a weight had been lifted from his shoulders, then he shivered. "I'm not sure whether I prefer being afraid of a seizure or knowing that something really possessed me."

Hoshi put his hands on his hips. "If demons possess the Russians, it seems unlikely the American military can win this conflict by conventional means. This Fatemeh is correct that you must find out as much as you can."

"Couldn't we just tell someone what we suspect?" asked Billy.

Duncan snorted. "Who'd believe us? Last fall, I told my editor I pretended to be possessed so I could learn more about Ramon Morales for a story I was writing. If I told him I really had been possessed, he'd have me committed!"

Billy pointed to Hoshi. "He believes there could be demons!"

"I have seen many strange things in my years as a warrior,"

said Hoshi, "enough to make me consider the idea of a demon. I think you should investigate."

"Won't you need my help with the crops?" asked Billy.

"I should be able to find help with the harvest, but even if I don't, hot peppers are a luxury for prosperous times. They do no good if the land is overrun." Hoshi sighed. "You need to go. Otherwise, it would be the same as seeing the men attacking the wagon and doing nothing to protect it."

"The code of Bushido?" asked Billy.

Hoshi smiled. "I think you're finally beginning to learn."

Duncan nodded. "Sounds like I better wire Fatemeh, then look into a pair of train tickets."

Billy grinned. "What? You're comin' with me?"

"Try to stop me," said Duncan. "This sounds like an even bigger story than airships over Denver."

A week later, Ramon Morales stepped off the stagecoach in Tucson, Arizona. He hoped the professor was still in the area. He didn't want to travel all this distance and end up empty handed. He looked around at the buildings near the station. He knew the populations of Tucson and Albuquerque were similar, but something about the way people bustled through the streets reminded him more of San Francisco than New Mexico towns.

The driver climbed to the coach's roof and threw Ramon's satchel down. He caught it, then set it beside the station door. Going inside, he caught the telegraph operator's eye and asked him whether there were any telegrams for him. The man looked through a stack of papers and shook his head. Apparently, the professor had not returned to Flagstaff yet. Either that, or Sergeant Harris had been delayed in his travels. Ramon tipped his hat, then consulted the stagecoach schedule. It looked like the next coach back to New Mexico would be in two days.

Stepping back out to the hot, dusty street, he saw the San Xavier Hotel a few doors down. He wound his way through people bustling along the boardwalk and passed a saloon advertising a free lunch. His stomach growled, but he decided to secure a room first and divest himself of the baggage. He continued into the lobby and stepped up to the desk clerk. After learning the prices, he paid for two nights at the hotel. "I'm looking for a couple friends of mine. One of them is kind of a dandy with a thin mustache and a bowler hat, goes by the name 'Maravilla'. He may be traveling with a young woman."

"Yeah, they were here about two weeks ago," said the desk clerk. "They brought in a big crate. The next morning, they were raising some kind of ruckus up in the professor's room. The other patrons complained, but they checked out and I haven't seen them since."

Ramon pursed his lips, wondering what they had been working on. "Can you give me directions to the other hotels and boarding houses in town?"

"You're not thinking of looking for a better deal are you? I'm afraid you won't find one ... not unless you go to the outskirts of town."

"No, nothing like that," said Ramon. "Just wanted to see if they're still around since they haven't gone back home to Flagstaff."

"Now that I think about it, I heard them say something about going out east toward the Mule Mountains." The clerk shook his head slowly. "That's bad country out there ... Apaches."

Ramon felt as though the floor dropped out beneath him. Although he had seen the professor in wild and remote areas, he wasn't certain how well acquainted he was with Indians. Shaking his head, he imagined Maravilla running afoul of some custom or another. Did Larissa know enough to keep him safe? Ramon looked up. The clerk wrote down some names and addresses of hotels and rooming houses, then passed the list to Ramon. After thanking the clerk by tossing a coin on the counter, Ramon took his bag up to the room. He opened the window for some fresh air, then went in search of lunch.

Half an hour later, Ramon leaned back his chair at the saloon. The good meal and glass of beer settled his stagecoach-jostled nerves. He pulled out the paper the desk clerk had given him, then signaled to the barmaid. She gave him directions to the places on the list. Ramon grabbed his hat and left a generous tip.

The first two places on the list had signs in front that said, "Whites only." He was taken aback since Tucson was so close to the Mexican border. Those hotels must be losing business, but Arizona had been a Confederate Territory just over a decade before. Sometimes prejudice took a long time to die and Ramon didn't even bother with those places.

Ramon crossed off the next hotel and rooming house because of how posh they looked. He knew they would be expensive. Much as he liked to dress well, the professor had little money to spend on lodgings.

As the sun sank low, Ramon came to a squat, dirty wooden building near the edge of town. Two miners sat talking on the porch. Ramon stepped inside and found a man in a dirty, striped shirt, with the top two buttons undone. He chewed a cigar and eyed Ramon warily through the smoke.

"They're here," said the clerk, "along with one other fella." He pointed down the hall with his thumb. "The dude is in room thirteen."

Ramon tipped his hat, understanding that the clerk referred to the professor. He walked down the hall and knocked on the door. When no one answered, he tried knocking louder. The door across the way opened, and a young lady in black work pants, shirt and a vest leaned on the doorframe and tipped her coachman's hat back on her head to get a better look.

"Well, well, well, this is the first time I've ever been glad to see one of my bounties trying to track *me* down." Larissa put her fist on her hip.

Ramon took off his hat. "Glad I finally caught up with you. Is the professor in?"

She nodded. "Yeah, he's next door, sharing a room with Al Shieffelin. We're using thirteen for storage."

"Storage?"

Larissa brushed past Ramon and opened the door. Inside was an assortment of gears, rods, boilerplate, and bolts. He saw parts from steam tractors, cotton gins, windmills and other machines he couldn't name.

"I thought you were going to build more ornithopters."

"That was the plan, but we got sidetracked."

Ramon shook his head and laughed. "Why doesn't that surprise me?"

A moment later, Professor Maravilla peered out of the adjoining room. "Why, bless me! It's Ramon Morales." He stepped out and grabbed Ramon's hand in both of his, then he looked up and down the hallway. "Is the charming Miss Karimi with you?"

Ramon scowled. "No, I'm here on a mission for the army."

Maravilla took a step back and straightened his robin-red waistcoat. "Perhaps you'd better come in and tell us about it."

Larissa closed both her door and room thirteen's. They stepped into the adjoining room, where another man read a newspaper by the light of a gas lamp. Larissa introduced Al Shieffelin.

Maravilla and Ramon sat down in the room's two other chairs. Larissa leaned against the doorframe and folded her arms. The professor stood, offering his chair, but Larissa waved at him to remain seated.

Ramon folded his hands and began. "Have you heard about the Russians? They still occupy Washington and Alaska Territories."

Shieffelin nodded. "I've just been reading about it. There was a big battle a few days ago near Salem, Oregon. A lot of lives were lost."

As Shieffelin spoke, the professor's eyes went wide and his lips moved. A moment later he sat forward worry creasing his brow. Ramon remembered what Fatemeh had told him about the being from the stars called Legion.

Ramon pushed his glasses up on his nose and came to the point. "The army has built some of your owls, professor, but they're not helping the war effort. They could use your help to find something that would be more effective."

The professor sat silent for a time, his brow furrowed. Finally, he shook his head. "I'm sorry. Last time I helped the army, they demanded I hand over my plans with minimal compensation. If they had given me more money, perhaps I would have developed improvements by now." He looked over at Shieffelin. "I now have a contract that will provide lucrative pay and interests me a great deal. I will not help the army."

Ramon sat back and rubbed his chin and looked from Larissa Crimson to Al Shieffelin. He wasn't certain what, if anything, the professor had told them about the creature called Legion. Moreover, Ramon wasn't really sure he trusted the bounty hunter. "Professor, can I speak to you alone for a minute?"

The professor looked around, rubbed beads of sweat from his forehead, then nodded. The two left the room and moved to the hotel's porch. The sun had set and the miners who occupied the chairs earlier had moved on. Ramon sat down and indicated the professor should take the other chair. "Fatemeh told me about the being called Legion. Is it still on Earth? Can you talk to it?"

The professor looked down at his hands and was silent for a long time. "Legion is not an entity like you or me. It is thousands of individuals acting in concert like a swarm of bees." He looked up into Ramon's eyes. "It acts with one mind, even over great distances."

"Can you speak to Legion? Can you find out if it's helping the Russians in the northwest?" Ramon leaned forward.

The professor turned away and his voice grew distant. "When separated by great distance, a swarm of bees will become two swarms, even three."

Ramon shook his head. "But you just said that Legion can communicate over great distance."

"Imagine looking through a thousand eyes. It would be hard enough to do that if all of them were in roughly the same place. Imagine if those eyes have been separated for months across thousands of miles. Just because one can communicate over great distance, doesn't mean one does." The professor reached out and touched Ramon's forearm. For just a moment, Ramon felt as though something tickled the back of his skull. "I am sorry, Mr. Morales. I am under no obligation to help you. I'm not a citizen of the United States and I want to stay here and help the Shieffelins develop a machine for their mine."

Ramon gritted his teeth, but something in the back of his mind told him there were no arguments he could make to persuade the professor to come along of his own free will. The only way he could succeed would be to break his promise to

Fatemeh. "Is there anyone else who could help me?"

"Miss Crimson has much natural talent and she is becoming quite adept, but I don't think she can help the army, yet."

Ramon stood and tipped his hat. "I'll be in town through tomorrow. I'm staying at the San Xavier Hotel. If you change your mind about helping, please let me know."

Colonel Johnson watched as Sergeant Jesús Lorenzo led four other men onto the gunnery range at Fort Bliss. They all wore riveted, steel boxes on their backs containing dials and gauges. Rubberized tubing ran from the boxes to handheld units that consisted of copper tubes on top and black handgrips below. The men took up positions facing a set of targets.

"Aim!" called Lorenzo. Each man aimed his weapon at a target. "Ready!" The men lowered welding goggles over their eyes, giving them a distinctly insect-like appearance. "Fire!" Each man squeezed the trigger on their handgrips. Lightning flew from four of the units, vaporizing their associated targets.

"Sir," called the fifth man. "My unit misfired."

Lorenzo pushed the goggles to the top of his head and stepped around to check the unit's gauges. "It's building up an overload! Drop it!" He waved at the others. "Run!" Lorenzo helped the private out of the backpack then together they ran toward the officers and hit the dirt. Colonel Johnson crouched low, covered his ears and closed his eyes just as an explosion knocked him backwards.

His ears were still ringing and his vision blurry a few moments later when he rolled over and pushed himself to his feet. He looked at the jagged black crater in the ground, then over to the destroyed targets. The new lightning weapons were damned deadly—and still very unstable. It was a good thing those bandits hadn't gotten their hands on them. Then again, maybe they would have blown themselves up and saved everyone a lot of trouble.

Johnson did his best to brush off his uniform, then stepped over and helped Sergeant Lorenzo to his feet. "Shut down the units and get some rest. I think we've tested them enough for today."

The sergeant nodded and staggered away, followed by the other men.

A corporal shot from the fort's telegraph office, carrying two sheets of paper. Distracted by the crater and the missing targets, he nearly ran into the colonel. Realizing where he was, he stood straight and saluted. "Sir, we've received news from Oregon and a telegram from Mr. Morales."

Johnson snatched the telegrams from the corporal and read them. The first one made his knees go weak. Conscious of the soldiers, he took a deep breath and nodded. He would find the words to inform the men soon enough. The Russians had taken Oregon's capital, Salem. He hoped Morales had good news.

Turning to the second telegram, he gritted his teeth. Maravilla wasn't interested in helping the army. The colonel looked back at the carnage on the firing range. They needed new weapons and expert help desperately. The lightning weapons were devastating, but they were too big and dangerous to the operators to be practical. Not even the army's flying machines could lift them. The professor could help solve that problem—perhaps create a new machine that could carry the weapons. He turned back to the corporal. "Send a telegram to General Sheridan in San Francisco and request permission for me to increase my offer to Professor Maravilla."

CHAPTER SEVEN
BREAKING OUT

C urly Bill Brenahan riveted his attention on the jail door's hinges when a thunderous blast rocked the stockade at Fort Bliss. He leaned forward as streamers of dust broke loose from the ceiling.

He had already noticed the flood damage around the lower hinge and observed how the door pulled out of the wall just a little bit each time the guard brought them meals. Now small cracks appeared in the adobe near the upper hinges. It wasn't much, but it might be enough.

"What the hell was that?" asked Bob Martin, looking out the window, as a mushroom-shaped cloud billowed up behind another row of buildings.

The marshal in Mesilla had turned Martin and Bresnahan over to the military after reporting their capture. That way he got credit, but could more easily rid the territory of two troublemakers than at a civil trial where the primary witnesses were the likes of Billy McCarty and the "Chinaman" farmer called Hoshi.

"Bob, give me a hand with something." Bresnahan stood up and walked over to the cell door where he pushed on the side next to the hinges. The bottom hinge gave way and moved out about six inches.

"What do you think you're doin'?"

"Gettin' outta here."

"They'll shoot us if they catch us."

"What do you think'll happen when they try us for shootin' two soldiers? We'll have the choice of firing squad or dancin' at the end of a rope, that's what. I'd rather take my chances gettin' out this way." Bresnahan looked at the gap. "Do you

90

think you can fit through there?"

Martin nodded quickly. He crouched down, then pushed and shimmied through the gap, minding his wounded hand. Once on the other side, he grabbed the door with his good hand and pulled it back. From the outside, he had better leverage and could pull the steel-strap door just a little further out, making room for the bigger man. Once through, Bresnahan dusted himself off.

"We're not going to make it real far in these prison outfits," said Martin, noting their black-and-white striped shirts and trousers.

Bresnahan snorted. "We ain't gonna make it very far past that door at the end of the hall." He inclined his head toward the steel door that led outside.

"Then why the hell did we push our way out of the cell if we're just as trapped on this side?"

"'Cause it's almost supper time," said Bresnahan. He indicated the empty, unlocked cell across the way. He entered and beckoned for Martin to follow. They pressed themselves against the wall in the shadows.

A short time later, the heavy steel door creaked open. A guard entered carrying supper on a tray. He looked in the cell where Bresnahan and Martin had been. "Hey, where'd they go?"

"We're over here, idjit," called Bresnahan.

The guard turned and peered into the cell. Bresnahan sprang from his place against the wall and kicked the cell door open and into the guard's face, scattering the tray of food. As the guard staggered back, stunned, Bresnahan and Martin leapt from the cell. Martin held the guard's arms back and Bresnahan delivered a right cross, knocking him out. Martin lowered him to the floor while Bresnahan grabbed his revolver and then ran to the door.

Alerted by the noise from within, a second guard entered, his weapon drawn. Bresnahan sprang from behind and swung the revolver full force. The butt made a wet, crunching thud as it connected with the guard's skull. He crumpled to the floor. Bresnahan waited a moment to see if anyone else would come through the door. When no one did, he gently pushed it shut.

"Okay, we've got an unlocked door. What do we do now?" Martin clutched his wounded hand, which started to bleed through the bandages again.

"Correction. We have an unlocked door and two uniforms," said Bresnahan with a glance at the two men on the floor.

A smile eased across Martin's face. They stripped the two men of their coats and trousers. Once done, they dragged them into the cell across from theirs and locked the door, then changed out of the prison garb. Satisfied they could pass as soldiers, Martin stepped to the door and peered out. "I see the front gate. I say we hightail it out of here and put as much distance as we can between us and this fort before they discover we broke out."

Bresnahan frowned. "The reason we're in this position is that we wanted to lay hands on those lightnin' guns." He looked through the bars of their former cell and out the window. "I have a feelin' we're closer than ever before." He looked down at his uniform. "An' we might just be able to go pick one or two up and be out of here before anyone notices."

Martin gritted his teeth. "I ain't so sure, Curly Bill. I don't think we have much time."

"No we don't, that's why we can't waste time yappin' about it." He stepped up and patted Martin on the back. "Don't worry. If the guard was bringin' us supper, that means most of the men'll be in the mess hall. If those lightnin' guns are locked up too tight, we'll skeddadle."

Martin swallowed, but nodded. With that, the two men left the stockade and did their best to stroll casually around the corner of the building, continuing toward the main courtyard. The late afternoon sun cast long, dark shadows around the compound. As they entered the courtyard, they saw light from several windows and heard boisterous chatter and the sound of chairs and silverware clattering. Bresnahan took a moment to get a feel for the layout.

They stood across the courtyard from the mess hall. To the left, at the far end of the courtyard, a guard stood just outside a wooden door. The sign next to the door indicated it was the armory. The stables stood to its left. Bresnahan nodded slowly. "All right. Follow my lead."

The two strode up to the guard outside the armory. Bresnahan tipped his hat. "Colonel's asked us to uh … check that the powder's dry."

"What?" The guard blinked. "You men get on outta here."

"I don't think so." Martin slipped behind the guard and held a revolver to his back. At that range, he didn't have to be accurate with his one good hand. "Let us into the armory real quiet-like and this'll go easy for you."

The guard opened his mouth to say something, but Bresnahan clobbered him with the revolver butt. He glanced around to make sure no one had seen. They took the guard's keys, opened the armory, then went inside, dragging the guard behind them. Bresnahan took a minute to let his eyes adjust to the gloom within. After a moment, he saw a gated area at the back. Behind it were several strange looking devices. They resembled long-barreled pistols attached to backpacks by some kind of cable or hose. "Those must be the lightnin' guns," he said.

Using the guard's key ring, he unlocked the gate, then took a moment to study the devices. Shoulder straps allowed the devices to be worn on the back. He grimaced as he swung one onto his shoulders. "Okay, turn around and I'll help you with this one."

Bob gave a curt nod and turned around, holding his arms out. He swayed backwards from the weight, but adjusted the straps to distribute it better. "I hope we don't have to carry these things too far."

Bresnahan nodded. "Let's git on out of here."

Martin nodded and the two stepped to the door. So far, no one had noticed the missing guard. They closed the door behind them, and went to the stables, where they removed the devices and each selected a horse and saddled them. Bresnahan peered into the courtyard to make sure no one was looking for them, then they helped each other heft the devices onto their backs again. Once done, they led the animals out and into the courtyard.

Just then, an alarm bell jangled to life. Bresnahan and Martin pulled themselves onto their horses and rode toward the front gate, whipping their mounts up to full speed. Men poured out of the mess hall in their path. Bresnahan and

Martin spurred their horses on and the men scattered. They rounded the corner and continued toward the gate even as guards ahead lifted their rifles. Bresnahan ignored them and rode on. Bullets whistled around him. Blood sprayed in his peripheral vision. He turned his head just enough to see Martin fall from his horse. Bresnahan leaned forward and kept going.

As he passed the gate, a bullet clanged against the metal device on his back. He rocked sideways and fought to recover his balance. Looking up, he saw the Franklin Mountains. He turned a corner and rode on until he came to a southbound street. He paused for just a moment. The street opened onto the banks of the Rio Grande. Water, just a few inches deep, trickled over visible stones. Behind him, horses clattered through the fort's gates. He snapped his horse's reins, rode down the street and splashed across the Rio Grande with bullets whistling around him.

Colonel Johnson hitched up his pant legs so he could crouch beside the lightning gun a soldier had pulled from Robert Martin's corpse. He ran his fingers along dents left by bullets. Unstable as the machines were, they could take a pounding. That much was certain.

Sergeant Lorenzo stepped up and saluted. The colonel stood and returned the salute. "What have you learned?"

"Bresnahan's crossed the river."

Johnson frowned. "I was afraid of that. We need to get that device back."

"I could gather a few men and go across and get him," said Lorenzo. "He won't be riding long distances with the weight of the lightning gun on his back."

The colonel shook his head. "We have enough problems right now with Russia. We don't need to compound things by causing an incident with Mexico. We can't send a force in." He thought for a moment. "Why don't you go up to Las Cruces and hunt up Billy McCarty. He's good in a fight and could use some reward money. Maybe he can track down Bresnahan."

"Xander Middleton has already volunteered."

"Yes, but he feels he has something to prove after Bresnahan knocked him cold," said the colonel. "I need someone who's thinking clearly and I want to keep this operation low key. McCarty proved himself in Denver. We can trust him and as you say, Bresnahan isn't going anywhere fast. I think there's time."

"Yes, sir." Sergeant Lorenzo snapped a salute.

The colonel returned the salute, then spun on his heel and walked toward the post telegraph office. One missing lightning gun wouldn't hurt the war effort even if it fell into the hands of the Mexicans—or anyone else for that matter. They would likely blow themselves up trying to figure out how the device worked. What he needed was someone who could deliver a working weapon. He thought Ramon Morales would have been able to persuade Professor Maravilla to help. Even though he failed in that regard and General Sheridan had declined his request to make a better offer, he did succeed in finding out where the professor had taken lodging. Sergeant Harris would leave Flagstaff soon. The colonel wanted to make sure he picked up the professor on his way back to Fort Bliss.

The next evening, Ramon received a telegram from Colonel Johnson: "APPRECIATE YOUR EFFORTS -STOP- PAYMENT WILL BE SENT TO ESTANCIA ON NEXT STAGECOACH"

Ramon received no reply from Sergeant Harris in Flagstaff, but he really wasn't surprised. He suspected the colonel ordered him to return to Fort Bliss as soon as possible.

Satisfied that he'd done the best job possible under the circumstances, he retreated to the saloon next to the San Xavier Hotel and ordered supper. He sipped his beer while waiting for the meal and considered his next course of action. He felt bad that he couldn't persuade the professor to accompany him to Fort Bliss. Perhaps he could return and try again in the morning before he left town, but what would he say? A little voice in the back of his mind seemed to tell him that was a pointless endeavor.

By the time supper arrived, his thoughts had turned to the

bigger question of what was next in his life. As he dug into the steak and beans on his plate, he took a moment to look around the saloon and absorb the sights and smells. It was similar to other saloons he'd been in, but what really struck him were the little differences—things like the feel of the air, the songs the piano player knew, and the scents worn by the ladies who occupied the rooms above the saloon. He realized he liked being on the road and experiencing new places. Perhaps that was part of the answer he sought. Whatever he would do for the rest of his life would involve travel of some kind.

Later, back at his room, he had just enough light from the gas lamps outside that he didn't bother lighting the room's own lamps. Instead, he removed his jacket and waistcoat, then opened the window so he could get a little fresh air.

After undressing, he lay back and closed his eyes. His thoughts drifted to Fatemeh—the soft, silkiness of her skin, the scent of her hair, the little dimple that formed by her mouth when she gave a wry smile. He thought of her green eyes, which had seen so much of the world. Yes, he would see the world, too.

Perhaps becoming an ambassador wasn't such a bad goal. He had run for office as a sheriff. Perhaps he could get a little more education, then seek territorial office. From there, he could find opportunities to demonstrate his interest in diplomacy. Another possibility was that he could look for a job with an embassy in Mexico or South America. With those thoughts running through his mind, he drifted off to sleep.

The next day, he awoke refreshed. After breakfast in the hotel restaurant, something compelled him to walk across town to Professor Maravilla's hotel again. The professor, Larissa and Gird loaded their gear into a wagon.

"Good morning," said Ramon.

"Are you here to try to talk me into working for the army?" asked the professor, warily.

"Not at all. I just wanted to let you know that I respect your decision."

Larissa struggled with a big piece of boilerplate. Ramon took one end and helped her lift it into the wagon.

As they went in to retrieve another load, Larissa looked at

him. "So, where are you off to now?"

"The stagecoach for Estancia leaves this afternoon. Time to get home and start making plans for the future." Ramon held open the door to room 13 while Larissa entered.

"Have you settled on any specific plans?" asked the professor.

"I'm thinking of pursuing a career in diplomacy," admitted Ramon.

"Somehow, I think it would suit you well," said the professor.

Ramon helped them take several more loads to the wagon, until it was full. At that point, he looked at his pocket watch. He had just enough time to get back across town, check out of the hotel and catch the eastbound stage.

A little over an hour later, he sat in front of the station with his hat pulled down, shading his eyes. He looked up at the clopping of hooves, but realized it was the westbound stage, not the eastbound. He started to tip his hat back over his eyes when skirts rustled nearby. Curiosity getting the better of him, he tipped his hat back again. His hat fell completely off when he realized Fatemeh's green eyes stared down at him. "What are you doing here?" she asked. "We have a few days before the westbound train comes through."

"Westbound?" He shook his head. "I was headed back to Estancia."

She shook her head. "We need to find out why the Russians haven't left America and I don't know anyone more qualified for the job than us."

Ramon shrugged, then retrieved his bags and hat. He supposed there was no better time than the present to start his career as a diplomat.

Professor Maravilla, Larissa Crimson and Al Shieffelin returned to the ravine near Goose Flats. Maravilla supervised the construction of a makeshift forge near the cave entrance while Larissa set to work assembling many of the mining machine's smaller components. They soon had a frame and axles. The

Shieffelins began work on the rotary digging tool that would be mounted at the front of the machine while Maravilla and Richard Gird used block and tackle rigs to haul the steam engine into its mount on the frame. That job completed, Gird went to work on the mechanism for sorting ores extracted from the rock. As the week progressed, the machine was formally dubbed 'the Javelina' because of its resemblance to desert peccaries.

A week after their return, Larissa sketched out an idea on a notepad. She tapped her pencil on the paper for a few minutes while she thought about it, then looked up. "Professor, I think I've come up with a way to modify the armature that transmits power from the engine to the digging tool so it can operate at variable speeds."

Maravilla was attaching the drive train to the Javelina's steam engine. He paused and poked his head out from under the machine. "Why do we need such a thing? This rock is uniform limestone. A variable speed transmission adds complexity and increases the chance of a breakdown. We don't need it in this case."

Larissa walked over to the Javelina and crouched down. "There's no way you can know how uniform the limestone is until you start digging into the rock."

The professor opened his mouth to say something but only sighed. "I just know it's not necessary here," he said with forced patience.

Larissa stood and put her hands on her hips. "How exactly do you know? Did you perform a chemical analysis? Is there something in the topography that tells you what to expect?" She huffed. "You're very good at sharing engineering knowledge with me, but sometimes you seem to know more than you can explain."

Maravilla pulled himself out from under the machine. "I'm not sure I can explain how I know everything I do."

"Well, even if it's not necessary here, it will be someplace else," she persisted. "Besides, I think this variable speed transmission could be adapted to the ornithopters to make them lighter and give them more maneuverability."

The professor held out his hand and she gave him the plans. He examined them, muttering to himself. "I'm impressed." He looked up at her. "It's a clean, simple design. It could indeed make the mining machine better and allow us to sell it to others who could use it."

Larissa smiled. "Do you think it could be adapted to the ornithopters?"

"The ornithopters..." The professor paused, and looked into the distance. "No matter how high you fly or how far you travel, you will never escape what you're running from."

Larissa caught her breath, then narrowed her gaze. "What makes you think I'm running from something?"

The professor sat down on the machine's frame and folded his arms. "Trust me. I have been running for a long time. I recognize a kindred spirit."

"You told me that Maravilla is an assumed name. I know you're running from something, but I don't know what."

Maravilla remained silent for a long time. He took up his wrench and absentmindedly tightened a bolt. Larissa shrugged, figuring he was evading the question. She grabbed the notebook and peered down at the plans.

"Bad memories," said the professor at last.

"What?"

"I'm running from bad memories." Maravilla didn't look up from his work. "As you know, I was a professor at the Royal and Pontifical University of Mexico. I helped to design many weapons for Emperor Maximilian and he paid me quite well. I lived in comfort in Mexico City with my wife and my daughter. Ten years ago, when General Juárez came to power, he not only executed the emperor and disbanded the university, his soldiers captured my house." The professor's voice grew tight and heavy. "My daughter was shot in the back when she ran to my laboratory to save my inventions. They made me watch while they raped and murdered my wife." He looked up and a tear ran down his cheek. "The general's rurales took me to the frontera—to the border—and let me go. I was an exile, never to return. Indeed, I have been running for a very long time."

Larissa knelt down next to the professor. "That's the real reason you won't work for the military, isn't it? Weapons cost you your wife ... your daughter."

Maravilla sniffed and wiped his nose on his sleeve. "The

problem is that I'm powerless to fight, but I do the memory of my family no honor by running. Perhaps it's time to settle down and start my life again. I have been building toys—the clockwork lobo, the ornithopters, and even the mining machine have all been distractions to keep me from facing the past."

"Look at what you've learned though," said Larissa. "The lobo not only taught you about wolves, but you learned how to make a practical automaton. You used that to create your ornithopters, which have given people the power of flight and taught us about owls. Now you're putting that knowledge to use in an industrial application. Maybe you didn't know your place in the world, but you've hardly been idle."

The professor smiled. "Your optimism reminds me of my daughter."

Larissa folded her arms. "I'm happy to learn from you, but I don't want to replace the child you lost."

"I would never ask you to be her." He looked up into her eyes and held her gaze for a time. "You are smart and brave like her, but you are your own woman, haunted by your own demons, I suspect."

Larissa stood abruptly and turned around, shutting her eyes. In her mind, she saw the face of her cousin Alethea smiling up at her, proud of the doll named Lyssa Crimson. She saw the laughing face of James Ellway, her first bounty, now dead with an orphaned son. "I appreciate the trust you showed by telling me about your past, but I don't feel the need to say more about my own."

"Very well," said the professor. "You don't owe me an explanation, but you do owe one to yourself."

"Why exactly is that?"

The professor stood up and walked a few steps past Larissa, looking out over the scrub-covered wash. "I want to return to the Grand Canyon and finish the new ornithopters, but the reason I'm working on the mining machine is that I need to make a sustainable life. This is something I could return to. I think I could build a home here."

Larissa opened her eyes. She had no desire to return to the home she left behind and had no vision of a future home. "I'm not sure if I would recognize home if I saw it."

"I understand." Maravilla's smile was wistful. "You'll know you're home when you find a place you can make peace with yourself."

Ramon put his time in Tucson to good use. He went to the small library and composed letters to law schools he found interesting. Fatemeh spent time pouring over newspapers, following the Russian force's advance through Oregon.

The train was supposed to arrive four days after Fatemeh, but track problems outside Wilcox delayed it. No longer content to read the paper, she inventoried the contents of the carpet bag several times over to assure herself that none of the bottles containing herbs and other healing supplies had broken.

Ramon suggested she make a soothing tea. She scowled at him, but did as he suggested. That evening, she snuggled against him as they sat on a couch in the hotel's sitting room. He started running his fingers through her lustrous hair.

"Stop that, Ramon," she purred.

"Why?"

"Because I want to take you up to my room, undress you and..." She stopped and shook her head.

"Would that be so wrong?" Ramon held her hair back and kissed her neck. "It's not like we haven't gone further before."

Fatemeh sighed and closed her eyes. "And it goes against everything I've been taught, both in my Mohammedan upbringing and my Bahá'í faith. I want you so much ... but I want to wait ... to savor our wedding night and all the nights thereafter."

"Do you regret the night we spent together?"

"Not at all," said Fatemeh. "It just tells me what I have to look forward to."

Ramon nodded and kissed her on the forehead. "Then we shall wait, corazón."

She smiled, closed her eyes and fell asleep, leaning against him.

The next day, she followed Ramon to the library and studied maps of California, Oregon, and Washington. "How many troops do you suppose an airship holds?" she asked.

Ramon shrugged. "I was unconscious most of the time I was aboard one. You probably saw more of it than I did."

Fatemeh tapped her fingers beside the map. "Fifty, maybe seventy-five?" She snorted. "How are they taking so much territory? The papers say there's a naval blockade along the coast. Either the Russians have some new means of getting troops in or Legion is still recruiting people."

Ramon scratched the back of his head. "Maybe both."

Fatemeh shuddered. The next day, she reread all the articles she'd already studied and asked the librarian if there were any newspapers she had missed.

A week after Fatemeh arrived in town, Ramon took her hand and walked down the library steps, discussing plans for supper when the westbound Southern Pacific's whistle sounded. They looked at each other, realizing their belongings were still spread around their respective rooms at the San Xavier.

"We've got to hurry, we need to get to the train station," said Fatemeh.

Ramon pushed his glasses up his nose, then nodded. Fatemeh gathered her black skirt as they sprinted to the hotel. Entering the lobby, they hurried past a baffled desk clerk, up the stairs, and into their respective rooms. Ramon grabbed his satchel and tossed it on the bed, then gathered his belongings and shoved them in. As he locked the door, Fatemeh appeared with her carpetbag.

The train whistle sounded again.

Without another word, Fatemeh turned and went down the stairs with Ramon at her heels. She stopped briefly at the hotel's front desk and turned in her key. Ramon tossed his key on the counter, counted out some coins to settle their bills and followed her across the street to the unfinished train station.

"All aboard!" shouted the conductor as they arrived.

Fatemeh dropped the carpetbag causing the bottles of herbs to jangle together. Opening it, she retrieved two tickets and handed them to the conductor. He punched the tickets then stood aside for Ramon and Fatemeh to board the train. Once they were aboard, he grabbed the metal step and pulled himself into the coach.

The train lurched forward as Ramon and Fatemeh moved up the aisle. She passed several pairs of empty seats and continued forward into the next car. Midway up the car, two men sat together. One wore the broad-brimmed hat of a cowhand while the other wore a bowler. Fatemeh slid into a seat across the aisle from them. She had mentioned writing to Billy, so Ramon wasn't surprised to see him on the train.

Ramon's gaze fell on the reporter. "So, what brings you on this little expedition?"

He tipped his hat. "Fact of the matter is I sensed a good story."

"Something for the newspapers?" asked Ramon.

"Bigger than that," said Duncan. "This could easily become a book. What's more, I believe I'll find the answer to something that's been nagging me a good long time. Billy here tells me that whatever possessed me the first night we met may be the very same force behind the invasion."

Ramon blinked and looked from Duncan to Fatemeh. "Is that really true?"

"It seems likely," admitted Fatemeh. "After all, I learned about the creature called Legion from the leader of the Russian invasion, General Gorloff."

"And I interviewed General Gorloff just a few days after I met you," interjected Duncan. "He passed through Mesilla on his way to solve a dispute with Russian settlers at Fort Ross in California."

"Interesting," said Fatemeh. "Maybe we should pay a visit there."

"So, where exactly is this Fort Ross?" asked Ramon.

"It's a little ways out of San Francisco," said Duncan. "Just outside of a town called Windsor."

"That seems as good a place as any to start." Fatemeh grinned.

"Even better, it's not in the war zone … yet," said Billy as he looked out the train's window at the accelerating scenery. He turned back to Ramon. "Did you learn anything from Professor Maravilla?"

Ramon shrugged. "He wasn't very forthcoming. He didn't come out and say he spoke with Legion, but I sensed that he must be. He said something interesting—something about Legion being like a swarm of bees that has been separated by a great distance. I think the part he's talking to isn't necessarily talking to the part in the northwestern territories. It's like Legion has become at least two separate swarms."

"Do these swarms have the same agenda, or different ones?" asked Duncan.

"That's what we need to find out," said Ramon. "If we know its motive, we might be able to reason with it."

"We reasoned with it once—" Billy's voice held an optimistic note. "—when it used General Gorloff to speak to us."

Fatemeh considered that for a moment. "Let's hope all the parts of Legion are equally reasonable. After all, Legion can control men. It sounds like Legion could even take over and become a man."

A shiver went up Ramon's spine. He reached around and scratched the back of his head, then reached down and sought the comforting familiarity of Fatemeh's soft hand.

CHAPTER EIGHT
THE JAVELINA

Larissa followed Professor Maravilla as he walked around the outside of the Javelina. In silhouette, from a distance, the mining machine did look a bit like a peccary with its big, bulky body and front end sloped down toward the primary cutting rollers. In the rising sun's full light, it resembled no machine she had ever seen. It was sturdy as a locomotive and as big as the switchers used to transfer rail cars from one train to another, but it lacked the smooth lines of a machine designed to hurtle itself along the rails.

The machine's cab and cutting rollers could be turned and even lifted to adjust the angle at which they attacked the rock. All of that added to the impression that it was the head of a great beast. At rest, the cab settled on bulky, metal wheels like a mining cart's. Three wheels on each side of the machine's "body" drove continuous metal-plate treads. The professor got the idea from Russian steam tractors that used the system and claimed it would add durability and traction to the machine. The machine's smoke stack jutted out from the rear, then turned up at a ninety-degree angle, looking like a tail, held aloft. Of course, it was designed so it wouldn't be sheared off when the machine burrowed its way through the rock.

Ed and Al Shieffelin manned the controls. Ed shoveled coal into the burner and Al watched the gauges. As pressure in the boiler built, the Javelina gurgled and snorted. Now, it not only looked like an animal, it actually seemed imbued with life. Once satisfied, Al released the lever which started the rock cutters at the front spinning. He then released the brake and engaged the throttle. A great puff of smoke billowed from the rear stack. The Javelina lurched forward. Al activated a pair of forward-facing arc lamps. It looked as though a demon opened its eyes.

The cave only extended into the rock a few yards. A great squeal sounded as the cutting rollers hit the rock and smoke billowed up. Ed released a jet of water, cooling the cutting tool, but it still screamed, sounding like parts might sheer off.

"Gear it down!" called Larissa, despite the fact that no one could have heard her over all the noise.

Even so, Al apparently had the same thought, he backed the machine up and reduced the cutter's gear ratio. He took the machine forward again. This time, the squeal reduced to a steady whine. There was a clattering and banging as rock tumbled back through chutes into the sorting mechanism. Al adjusted the angle of attack and pushed the machine forward.

Half an hour after they started, Al backed the Javelina out of the cave. He drove it to the edge of the shallow gully and activated another lever. This one dumped limestone over the side. He rolled forward a short distance, then applied the brake and let the machine idle while he and his brother climbed out of the control cabin.

"How did we do?" shouted Al, much louder than necessary.

Professor Maravilla lit a lantern and walked forward into the cave with Larissa and the Sheiffelin brothers on his heels. He held up the lantern and illuminated the hole dug by the machine. "Impressive, the machine has already cut five yards into the rock."

"We'll still need to shore it up before we go much further," came a voice from the cave entrance.

Maravilla and Larissa turned. Richard Gird leaned against the rock, arms folded.

"We could have blasted that out in nearly the same time," continued Gird.

"What did he say?" asked Ed. Al shrugged in response.

"He said you could have blasted out the rock in the same time as you dug it out," shouted Larissa. She turned to the professor. "I think the operators will need to put cotton in their ears from now on."

The professor nodded, then looked back to Richard Gird. "What you say is true, but the machine's advantage is in the processing. Shall we go see how we did?"

Maravilla extinguished the lantern as they left the cave. He climbed onto a step built into the machine's side and opened a hatch revealing several compartments. The professor handed out a bin labeled "silver". Larissa dropped the box to ground and sorted through the black and red rocks. Her shoulders slumped with disappointment.

Richard Gird seemed more interested than she would have expected. He reached in and grabbed a black rock, feeling the weight. He then carried the rock over to a leather case filled with chemical vials. He set the rock on the ground and carefully poured a drop of liquid on the rock. Nothing much happened, but Richard Gird smiled. "It's not real pretty when it comes out of the ground, but it's definitely silver."

"How can you tell?" asked Larissa.

Gird held up the small bottle. "Nitric and muriatic acid. It'll eat through just about anything except for silver." He put a drop of the acid on a nearby limestone rock and it began sizzling a moment later.

Larissa nodded understanding, then stood upright. As she did, she caught movement in her peripheral vision. She looked over and saw two men on horseback. "Who are they?"

Gird frowned as Professor Maravilla walked over to his satchel and retrieved the spyglass. He took a look and then handed it to Gird. The attorney nodded to himself. "I'm guessing those are a couple of the Clanton boys. That's part of the reason we set up the skeleton. They're just superstitious enough to keep away." He handed the telescope to Larissa.

The men on horseback turned and rode away. "So who are these 'Clanton boys'?" she asked.

"They claim to be ranchers," said Ed, whose hearing seemed better. "But really they're rustlers. They go down to Mexico and steal cattle and bring it up to sell here in the territory."

"Will they give us trouble?" asked Larissa.

"If they think they have something to gain," said Gird.

Masuda Hoshi followed a trail of deep hoof prints through a seemingly endless expanse of flat terrain. The land was so flat and barren compared to his native Japan that he felt just a little homesick. He missed the forests near Kyoto and the cool breeze that blew through the trees. He wore the takuhatsugasa made of rice straw he brought from Japan to protect his head from the sun's onslaught. Sweat evaporated from his brow soon after it formed.

Hoshi trailed the man called Curly Bill Bresnahan. The man clearly weighed his horse down. Sometimes, the tracks lightened and a human's tracks appeared beside the horse. Presumably, those were places where Bresnahan dismounted to give the horse a little break. The outlaw may be desperate and a killer, but he wasn't outright cruel to the animal under his care.

There were places where Curly Bill's horse had grazed on the sparse grass. Hoshi dismounted and allowed his horse to refresh itself with the scrub grass as well. As he studied the terrain, he noticed strange divots in the ground. He stepped up to one and examined it. The sand was smooth and fused together, almost like glass. Hoshi frowned.

"Did you find something?" Corporal Xander Middleton asked. Although he was an army man, he wore a plaid work shirt, leather vest, and blue denim pants.

Hoshi pointed to the fused sand. "It would appear that Bresnahan is learning how to use the lightning gun he has stolen."

In the distance, the sparsely vegetated land rose somewhat. Hoshi climbed back into the saddle and rode on, followed by Middleton. The trail ran through a gap between a pair of rocky hills until it came to a thin trickle of a stream—runoff from mountains to the south.

After a time, they found a campfire ring filled with ash. The ground had been flattened where someone lay down for a rest.

"He stopped here. This looks like a good place for us to take a break, too," said Middleton.

"Agreed," said Hoshi. "Though I believe it should be a short one, if we wish to catch up with Bresnahan." Hoshi dismounted, then took a few sparing sips from the stream. Feeling better, he lowered his suitou—a bottle of sorts made from bamboo—into the water and refilled it. Corporal Middleton crouched down by a mesquite brush and studied the campsite. If he found any useful clues, he didn't say. The samurai began to think that he should have refused Sergeant

Lorenzo's request to help track Bresnahan into Mexico.

Lorenzo had arrived in Las Cruces soon after sunup just a few days ago, looking for Billy McCarty. He was disappointed to learn that McCarty had left on the train just the night before. Lorenzo turned to leave, but Hoshi pressed for more information. That's when he learned Curly Bill Bresnahan had escaped and fled into Mexico.

Hoshi insisted that he help find Bresnahan. "I do not wish to see this man escape justice after I helped capture him."

Lorenzo looked Hoshi up and down, opened his mouth to speak, but shook his head. "Look, I have a man ready to go. I can't delay him any longer," said Lorenzo, clutching his horse's reins and backing toward the saddle. "I'm sorry to have taken your time."

"Why exactly did you want Billy's help?" Hoshi asked.

"We need a good tracker ... someone who isn't afraid to act should the situation require it ... not an old farmer."

Hoshi drew his pistol and aimed it between the sergeant's eyes before he finished speaking. Lorenzo swallowed. "Merely a demonstration." Hoshi holstered the gun in his voluminous robes as quickly as he drew it. "You must want a minimal contingent to avoid a diplomatic incident, otherwise, you'd send your own men."

Lorenzo nodded.

"I was a samurai warrior," said Hoshi. "Like Billy, I have experience tracking men. What's more, I am not an American soldier, nor a United States citizen. If I am caught pursuing Bresnahan, I will be responsible for only my actions."

Lorenzo finally agreed to let Hoshi join Xander Middleton in the hunt for Bresnahan. Hoshi left immediately to find the mayordomo of the acequia and arrange for him to water the crops while he was gone. He hoped he would be back in a matter of a couple of weeks at most.

Bringing his thoughts back to the present, Hoshi examined the campfire's remains and guessed they were no more than a day behind Bresnahan. Across the stream, Bresnahan's tracks continued roughly southwest. The outlaw followed the American border, indicating no desire to sell the lightning gun to the Mexicans.

Hoshi's horse drank from the stream. He took the opportunity to take another drink himself, then he climbed back into the saddle and continued on. Middleton splashed some water on his face, then climbed on his horse and followed.

Bresnahan was a wanted man in New Mexico and Texas. He would likely avoid returning to those two places. If he wasn't going to sell the device to the Mexicans, Hoshi guessed he would eventually turn north into Arizona.

Hot, tired, and ready to collapse, Curly Bill Bresnahan still wore the dark blue army uniform coat. He'd unbuttoned it, revealing his bare, sunburned chest. His horse dragged. He had stopped riding, only using the horse to carry the lightning gun for him. Even at that, he hoped the horse would not expire before he found more water and some food for himself.

Just when he was about to give up hope of finding a good source of water, he stumbled into a stream. Although shallow and sluggish, it held more water than other trickles or seeps he'd encountered since leaving Fort Bliss. He put the army hat in the water and collected up as much as he could and drank it down. His stomach rebelled, cramping, but he didn't care. His horse took a long drink, then moved forward to chew on the nearby mesquite brush. Bresnahan's stomach growled. He took another drink of water, then washed his face. With a sigh he sat up and looked around. As far as he could tell the source of the little meandering stream was far off to the north. He had lost track of how far he had come, but he was pretty sure he was south of Arizona by this point. He patted his horse on the flank and led her north, following the river, letting her stop to eat and drink when she wanted.

An hour after he started along the river, he heard people shouting in English. Some words were clearer than others, but he didn't hear enough to know what transpired. All he could tell was that he approached an angry group of people. He looped the horse's reins around a mesquite branch, giving her enough room to wander to the stream and drink as well as munch on the nearby bushes. He then lifted the lightning gun from the saddle. He adjusted a set of gauges on the back. The machine let out a high-pitched whine which soon settled into a steady hum. The horse nickered and skittered backward. Fortunately, the last person who used the lightning gun had painted red arrows by the gauges to note the optimum levels.

Bresnahan pushed forward, concealing himself near the stream as much as possible. By his estimate, he traveled about two hundred yards when he came upon a group of people on horseback near several head of cattle. Men wearing sombreros and loose-fitting shirts aimed guns at white settlers wearing broad-brimmed hats, gingham shirts, and leather vests—a rustling in progress.

As best as he could tell, the Mexicans were stealing the cattle from the settlers, but really, he could care less about the argument's details. "Let's see what this baby can do," he said with a sneer.

He aimed the gun at the closest Mexican on horseback and fired. A loud crack pierced his ears and a lightning bolt flew from the gun. The man evaporated into a black cloud and the horse ran away, its saddle scorched. The cattle bolted after the horse.

The Mexicans and the Americans did their best to keep their own horses under control while searching for the source of the mysterious lightning bolt. Bresnahan stood and fired again. This time, he missed the person he aimed at, but hit the horse. The man fell to the ground. Without missing a beat, one of the American cowhands fired, killing the fallen bandito.

The Mexicans snapped their reins and rode south along the river. Two of them took potshots in Bresnahan's direction, but missed by a long way. Bresnahan knew how difficult it was to aim a gun from the back of a moving horse. The American cowhands rode out and rounded up as many of the cattle as they could find. Bresnahan walked downstream and retrieved his horse. He shimmied out of the lightning gun pack, then hefted it onto the horse, who snorted a complaint. After climbing on himself, he resumed the northward journey.

He didn't hurry to catch up with the cowhands, but he didn't work hard at keeping his distance. If they wanted to thank him, great. If they wanted to keep their distance, that was okay, too.

Once they had the cattle lined up and marching northward, one of the cowhands rode up to him and tipped his hat. "Much obliged to you, sir, but you're on the wrong side of the border to be in that uniform."

Bresnahan chuckled to himself, realizing he had misinterpreted what he'd stumbled across. He hadn't yet crossed into Arizona. The Mexicans were the cattle's legitimate owners and these boys were the rustlers. Perhaps they could help him out. "Well, I ain't exactly 'regular army.' "

"We don't care much who you are as long as you buy our beef." The man evaluated him then flashed a cautious smile. "Name's Phin Clanton."

"Pleased to meet you." Bresnahan hesitated a moment, not wanting to give his real name. Not caring whether or not he was a soldier wasn't the same as not caring that he broke out of jail. "Name's William Brocius."

"That's some fancy hardware you got there, Mr. Brocius," said Clanton. "Where'd you pick it up?"

"Same place I got the uniform," said Bresnahan.

Phin Clanton laughed. "Where you headed?"

Bresnahan shrugged. "Right now, any place where I can get some food, water ... maybe a bath."

"You seem all right, Mr. Brocius," said Phin. "We've got a ranch a little ways over the border. Once you've rested up a bit, maybe you can tell us more about what you're up to, maybe see if there's a way you can help our little outfit."

"What outfit would that be?"

"We call ourselves the Cowboys."

"Catchy name."

"We've got big plans for Southern Arizona, Mr. Brocius. Let me introduce you to my brother and partners."

"So, what makes you think I might be interested in helping your outfit?"

"Let's just say that gun of yours is the second interesting marvel we've seen this week. I think you'd like to see the other one and we'd certainly like to know what would happen if we brought the two together."

"Things are sounding more interesting all the time." Curly Bill grinned. "Depending on what you've seen … there might be ways I could help out."

Ramon sat beside a stagecoach's window, dozing lightly early in the morning. Fatemeh rested her head against his shoulder. They had planned to change trains in Los Angeles but the coastal passenger service had been cancelled to allow military trains exclusive use of the track. So, they took the stagecoach north. Occasionally Ramon opened his eyes to see pine forest encroaching on the road. After a while, the forest gave way to the greenest, most lush farmland Ramon had ever seen. He found himself wondering what people would do with all that food.

They rumbled into a town of clapboard houses and brick buildings. The driver brought the stagecoach to a stop. Ramon stretched. "Where are we?"

"I'm not quite sure," said Fatemeh. "It looks like a pretty small town. Probably just a stop to change horses and pick up the mail. You can go back to sleep."

Billy hopped out of the coach. Luther Duncan took advantage of the situation and stretched across both seats. Ramon let his eyelids flutter closed again.

The driver appeared at the door. "Folks, we have a problem."

Ramon's eyes snapped open and Luther Duncan sat upright.

"This is Salinas. The stationmaster just received word that the Russians are advancing on San Francisco. We're turning back. You can get out here and get a refund for the uncompleted part of the trip, or you can continue back with me. You'll have an hour to make up your minds." With that, he closed the door and returned to the building.

"Salinas," said Duncan. "We're still quite a ways outside San Francisco. We'll need to see if we can find some other transportation north."

"First thing we need to do is find Billy." Fatemeh looked at

Ramon. "Why don't you check along the street and see where he went. Luther and I can pick up our baggage and see what our options are for continuing the journey."

Fatemeh climbed out of the coach. Duncan looked at Ramon and shrugged, then followed her out. Ramon climbed out of the coach and stretched, then took in the town. There was a general store, a couple of saloons, and one place called Kitty's Boarding House that looked like it rented rooms by the hour. All seemed like places Billy might have gone.

As Ramon walked down the street, he considered the driver's words. If the Russians already approached San Francisco, they were making incredible progress. He wondered how large the Russian force had grown. As he understood it, virtually the entire United States Army was on the West Coast. Even if they found another stagecoach line or someone else that would take them to San Francisco, they might encounter roadblocks or fighting. They would need a map and some alternate routes to Windsor in case they needed to go by horseback, or even foot. Of course, they were near the coast. Ramon supposed they could hire a boat.

As he peered into the general store, Ramon's thoughts turned to the being called Legion. Professor Maravilla referred to it as a swarm. Ramon imagined a swarm of bees, all acting in concert as though they had one mind, but even then, different members of a bee swarm had different functions. Was Legion organized like that as well?

Luther Duncan said having Legion in his head was like being possessed. Fatemeh and Billy said Legion had possessed the Russians. This made Legion sound more like a spirit or an entity. Raised in New Mexico, Ramon knew plenty of people who believed in spirits, demons, and angels, but he wasn't sure he'd ever seen evidence they existed. He preferred the image of Legion as a swarm. That sounded tangible. With that thought, Ramon looked in the first saloon. There weren't any patrons, just a couple of people getting ready for the day.

Returning to his original line of thought, he asked himself, "Who's in charge? Legion or the Russians?" If it was the Russians, the army had a better chance of stopping their advance than four lone wanderers. If it was Legion, he still didn't know what they could do about it. Fatemeh had only talked to it once and that happened because the part of Legion now with Professor Maravilla wanted to talk.

The second saloon's door was closed up tight. Ramon peered over at Kitty's. It didn't seem any livelier than the saloons this early in the morning. Although he could believe Billy might wander off for a quick round of cards, Kitty's entertainments would take long enough to risk being left behind. He'd wait to check that out until he exhausted other possibilities. He returned to the stagecoach office where he found Fatemeh and Duncan. "Any sign of Billy?"

Ramon shook his head. "What about transportation north?"

"No other stagecoach lines," said Fatemeh. "In fact, it doesn't seem like anyone's heading that direction at all. People are leaving San Francisco in droves, trying to get out of the army's way."

"We'll need horses, then," said Ramon. "I'd rather not walk. If I remember right, Salinas is at least twenty, thirty miles south of the city."

"Did someone say horses?" Billy walked up, leading four beautiful animals, all saddled up and ready to go.

Fatemeh opened her carpetbag and retrieved an apple. She held it out to the black horse, who nibbled it tentatively, then took the whole thing in its mouth. The other three pushed forward, looking for apples as well. "I'm afraid you'll have to wait until I can get more." Fatemeh turned to Billy. "Where did you find these lovely creatures?"

"You didn't steal them, did you?" asked Duncan.

Billy laughed. "Nothin' like that. Hoshi's been paying me pretty well and I found a farmer who was in a hurry to get out of town before the Russians made it this far south. He wanted to sell them to good owners rather than leave them behind."

"There is no remover of difficulties save God," said Fatemeh.

"Amen," said Ramon.

The Javelina burrowed deep enough that the Sheiffelins and Richard Gird realized they needed more supplies including timbers to shore up the tunnel. They took the silver they had collected so far and loaded the wagon for the trip to Tucson. Larissa asked if they would show her where the Clantons had their ranch. "I just want to get the lay of the land," she said.

Professor Maravilla decided to scout along the wash bordering Goose Flats to see if he could find other promising sites to burrow into the rocks for silver while Richard Gird watched the camp.

Larissa rode with the Shieffelins along the San Pedro River. It had cut a ravine through portions of the desert, and she estimated they were about a hundred feet above the river itself. A few miles from Goose Flats, Al Shieffelin pointed across the ravine. "There's the Clanton place over there."

She looked. A few cows dotted the open range. In the distance—far enough away they wouldn't have noticed it when she first came down the river with the professor—was a ranch house.

"Don't get too close, Miss Crimson," cautioned Ed. "Those Clantons don't like people poking into their business."

"I'll keep my distance." Larissa tested the grip on the revolver at her hip. "If they decide to make trouble, I can take care of myself."

The brothers tipped their hats and rode on. She suspected they were going to spend a good portion of the silver celebrating their early success. What they did with their money was their business. They had already paid the professor and her a share. It wasn't quite enough for them to return to the Grand Canyon and finish the ornithopter. They would only need a few more sessions with the Javelina before they could make the trip.

Larissa backtracked a mile to a point where she could easily cross the river. She made a long arc around the Clanton place, trying to pause near the tall spindly ocotillo plants or mesquite bushes so her silhouette wouldn't stand out to someone watching from the house. After a couple of hours, she was satisfied she'd learned all she could. It looked like any one of the dozens of ranches she had seen in her travels through the southwest.

She crossed the river and returned to the mining camp, where Richard Gird cooked supper. "Is the professor back?"

Gird shook his head. "He's still up the gully. That soldier probably delayed him."

An icy lump formed in Larissa's gut. "Soldier? Did he say what he wanted?"

Gird shrugged. "Just that he wanted to talk to the professor. If you find them, it would be good to know if we're getting an army contingent back in this area. If not, we probably need to think about something new to scare people away."

She nodded and set out in the direction the professor had gone. A mile up the wash, she heard two people talking. Although they sounded friendly, she didn't want to take chances. She drew her revolver, cocked it silently and searched for a good route to approach. She climbed to higher ground, then circled around to the source of the voices.

"Professor, if you won't come willingly, I'm afraid I'll have to arrest you for trespassing on United States Territory."

Larissa reached a point where she could observe the speakers. A man in an army uniform had just drawn a pistol and aimed it at the professor. She stepped forward and aimed at his chest. "Drop your weapon, Mister, and put your hands where I can see them."

The soldier looked up and barred his teeth, but he dropped his pistol and raised his hands. "I'm Sergeant Michael Harris from Fort Bliss," he said. "We're trying to develop some means for our soldiers to fight the Russians along the Pacific Coast."

"Yeah?" Larissa cocked her eyebrow. "Ramon Morales was just through here a couple weeks ago making the same offer. We told him no. The answer's the same for you."

"Ma'am, soldiers are dying. We need help, badly." He shook his head. "I'll do what I can to get it. If you chase me away now, I'll just come back later with more men."

"Who says we'll be here?" asked Larissa.

"You're not going to abandon all that mining equipment, at least not until the Shieffelins return. That buys me a couple of days, right there. Even if you left, my guess is you'd return to the Grand Canyon to finish your work up there."

"I'm afraid he's right," said Professor Maravilla. "I should just go with him."

"There's another choice," said Larissa. "I shoot him and we

bury his body right here in the wash. It would be a long time before anyone discovered him."

Professor Maravilla narrowed his gaze. "No!" His voice acquired an unearthly timbre and it echoed from the surrounding rocks. "I will not allow you to murder in my name."

Larissa was silent for several minutes. She took a moment and looked back at the camp, then thought about Ramon's offer a few days before. "Ramon said you're working on ornithopters."

Sergeant Harris blinked a few times. "Yes, and we have some other weapons as well." His voice trembled slightly, as though the professor had shaken him with his unnatural voice.

"All right," said Larissa. "I'll go with you instead."

Both the sergeant and Maravilla looked up at her. "What?" asked the professor.

"What can you do?" Sergeant Harris narrowed his gaze, evaluating her.

"I've been learning from the professor. I've come up with some innovations to improve the mining machine, the professor's clockwork lobo, and the ornithopters. I don't know whether I can make the army's ornithopters useful, but I bet I could come up with a useful weapon against the Russians ... and I won't let you take Maravilla. He has good reasons not to go with you."

Harris pursed his lips, as though considering the idea.

"Child!" Maravilla's voice cracked. "You don't have to go."

"No," said Larissa, "but I want to build ornithopters and you want to help the Sheiffelins a bit longer. I might learn more going with Sergeant Harris than staying here."

"I agree," said Sergeant Harris. "You can come along in the professor's place." He bent down to retrieve his gun.

"Keep your hands where I can see them," said Larissa.

The sergeant stood upright again.

"Walk away from the gun real slow," said Larissa. "The professor can look after it for you until we return."

Harris frowned, but nodded. "My horse is a little further up the wash."

"Walk that way. I'll stay up here where I can keep an eye on you."

"I don't want you to go," said the professor.

Larissa sighed, knowing she could be gone for a considerable time, but there was a war in progress and the professor kept flitting from one passing fancy to another. "I think the time has come for me to study for a while on my own. I'll be back when I can." She walked along the flats above the wash, keeping a careful eye on Sergeant Harris.

CHAPTER NINE
A TOMBSTONE IN THE MAKING

Riding along the San Pedro River, Curly Bill took stock of the men he had rescued from the Mexican ranchers. The so-called Cowboys consisted of two sets of brothers, Phineas and Isaac Clanton along with Thomas and Frank McLaury. All were within two or three years of his age, near as he could figure, and all except clean-shaven Tom wore mustaches and goatees.

Of the four, Ike was the talker, boasting about how he had been mere minutes from pulling his six-gun and taking out those Mexican ranchers. The McLaury brothers shook their heads and rolled their eyes throughout the story as though they had heard this bragging many times in the past. In fact, Curly Bill couldn't help but notice that it was Tom who had actually shot one of the ranchers. Although friendly, Phin seemed almost oblivious to the bragging, focusing on the rolling desert countryside instead.

Curly Bill rode up next to Ike. "So, have you seen this marvel that Phin told me about?"

"Oh yeah," said Ike. "It's truly a monster! A metal machine that can bore right into the side of a mountain!"

Curly Bill noticed that Tom and Frank didn't shake their heads or roll their eyes. There was truth to Ike's statement. "So what exactly is this machine used for?"

"Near as we can tell, it's some kind of mining machine," volunteered Frank.

"It's armored and strong," interjected Tom. "Just the thing to intimidate Indians."

"Or Mexicans," said Ike.

Curly Bill narrowed his gaze and wondered how much stock to put into the descriptions. A powerful machine that could bore into mountains could sure be useful if one wanted to liberate funds from a bank or even take weapons from an army wagon.

Around mid-afternoon, Curly Bill spotted a ranch house and a barn. The Cowboys herded the cattle into a nearby corral so they could be rebranded before being let out onto the range. Closer to the house, a stern man with a long beard streaked gray looked up from a wagon he unloaded with the help of a teenaged boy. Both the older man and the boy eyed Curly Bill with skepticism. When they dismounted, Phin introduced his father, Newman Clanton. "This is Bill Brocius. He pulled our fat out of the fire down in Mexico."

The old man's mouth twitched upward a little and he shook Curly Bill's hand.

"Wait till you see the gun he has!" Ike had a gleam in his eyes. "It's just what we need to teach those redskins a thing or two."

Mr. Clanton raised an eyebrow.

Curly Bill cringed at the way Ike just shot off his mouth about the lightning gun. True, the old man was Ike's dad, but he wanted people to show some sense before they opened their mouths. He held up his hands. "Boys, I have to caution you, that's a secret weapon from the army. We need to talk so I can determine whether your cause is … a worthy use of the lightning gun's power."

"You're right, of course," said Phin.

The old man eyed the parcel on the back of Curly Bill's horse with interest.

Curly Bill cleared his throat. "I'd really like an opportunity to get cleaned up."

"Of course." The old man turned to the boy. "Billy, show Mr. Brocius to the guest room and then fetch him some clean clothes. I suspect your brothers'll have something that'll fit him till he can get that uniform washed out."

"Yes, Pa," said Billy Clanton.

"Another, Bill, eh?" said Curly Bill. "How are people ever gonna tell us apart?"

The boy's grimace made Curly Bill laugh. He had to admit, he knew an awful lot of people named William. He removed his hat and ran his fingers through his thick curls. "I'm sorta stuck with the Curly part." He turned around and hefted the lightning gun onto his back, then retrieved the saddlebags from the horse.

Billy showed him to a guest room, then led him around back to the bath house. A little further beyond was an outhouse. "I'll start some water heating for you. Why don't you get settled?"

"Mighty kind of you, Billy." Curly Bill found his way back to his room. He wasn't really sure how much to trust these cattle rustlers, but the prospect of a bath and a comfortable bed sure sounded good. He placed the lightning gun on the floor between the bed and the window and arranged his saddlebags on top. It wouldn't keep anyone from stealing it, but he would be able to tell if someone had been poking around. He then took a handkerchief from the saddlebags and placed it between the door and jamb as he pulled it shut. If anyone went inside, the handkerchief would fall silently to the floor. It was no more foolproof than the saddlebags, but only a true fool would take no precautions against snooping.

Satisfied with the arrangement, he returned to the bathhouse. There he found a metal washtub half filled with water and a kettle heating on a wood stove. Clean clothes lay across an old sawhorse standing near the wall. Curly Bill stripped out of the sweaty blue uniform, making sure to place his revolver where he could reach it, then poured the kettle of water in the tub and climbed in.

After scrubbing himself down with homemade lye soap and rinsing off, he dressed in the clean clothes, gathered up the dirty uniform, and then returned to the room. As he walked down the hall, he smelled meat searing in a pan and his stomach began to rumble. He found his handkerchief in the doorjamb just as he'd left it and saw no sign that the saddlebags had been disturbed. These Clantons might be rustlers, but they seemed to have a code of conduct that wouldn't let them steal from a guest. Even if they didn't have such a code, they were still smart enough to build up some trust first. He'd sleep with his gun under his pillow, just in case.

Following the aromas of cooking food, he found the kitchen. Newman, Phin, Ike, and Billy shuffled around the kitchen, getting dinner on the table. He wondered what had happened to Newman Clanton's wife, but he also knew that life on the frontier was tough. He could certainly make some guesses. "Tom and Frank send their regrets," said Newman, "but they couldn't stay for supper. They needed to tend their own ranch."

"I understand. They seem like good men," said Curly Bill. "Hope I get to see 'em again."

"I'm sure you will," said Newman.

They all sat down to a simple, but tasty supper of steak, beans and spring greens. Curly Bill idly wondered whether the Clantons had a garden or if the greens came from the supplies Newman and Billy were unloading when he arrived. "This is a fine place, Mr. Clanton," said Curly Bill. "I sure appreciate your hospitality."

"It's a hard place," said the old man. "Word is there's silver in the mountains all around. The flats are good grassland for cattle. I was hoping to start a trading post, maybe become the center of a whole new town."

"That's hard to do with a war drawing all the people away, ain't it?" asked Curly Bill.

Old Man Clanton nodded. "But they'll be back once the war's won."

Curly Bill wondered about the old man's certainty of victory, but let that pass. "This is Apache country."

"That's right," interjected Ike. "And they ain't too keen on a whole settlement of white folk."

"But that would change if we could keep the Apaches out and convince folks that we could keep 'em out for good," explained Newman.

Curly Bill cut a piece of steak and nodded slowly. He saw why the lightning gun appealed to the Clanton boys. The problem was he only had one gun and he didn't even know how many rounds it held or how to reload it. He could sell the gun and move on, but he had a feeling he could make much more money if he held onto it. Helping the Clantons fulfill their dream could put him at the heart of a wealthy mining settlement. What's more, he'd rather have the Cowboys with him than against him when the army came searching for their missing gun. That fact alone made it worth playing along with them … at least for a time.

After supper, Curly Bill offered to show off the lightning gun. He went to his room, memorized the settings, then scratched off the markings. He returned to the kitchen and the Clantons took him behind the house. Curly Bill activated the gun. They all took a step backward as the device began to hum. "Whatcha got that you don't mind losing?" asked Curly Bill.

Mr. Clanton pointed to an old broken-down wagon a hundred paces distant. Curly Bill took aim, then, knowing what was to come, closed his eyes as he squeezed the trigger. A flash of blue lightning shot forth from the gun and engulfed the wagon, vaporizing it entirely.

Old Man Clanton blinked rapidly, trying to clear the spots before his eyes. He took two tentative steps toward the wagon's location and saw only a black spot on the ground where it had been. "Either you're the strongest man alive, or that thing has no recoil for the wallop it packs."

"Aside from the blinding light, it's very easy to use. You could fire from horseback, on foot, wherever." Curly Bill smiled. "Think this will help build your dream, Mr. Clanton?"

"It's certainly a good start. Let's go inside and talk some more."

Hoshi tracked Curly Bill Bresnahan's north, following a thin, trickling waterway. Although it was almost laughable to think of it as a river, the former samurai was glad for the greenery. The sight of it refreshed him almost as much as the water itself. He tried to remember his geography. "Do you know what river this is?" he asked Middleton.

The corporal took off his hat and scratched his head. "I think it must be the San Pedro."

Hoshi pursed his lips. As he recalled, the river went right into Apache country. He guessed that Bresnahan must plan to turn northwest when he entered the United States. "I think he plans to go to Tucson."

Middleton agreed and they turned to follow the river. Ten miles later, they came upon a grizzly, but interesting sight. A man lay on the ground covered in swarming flies. A turkey vulture ripped a gobbet of meat from the man's leg, lifted its head and swallowed it down before extending its long wings and taking flight. Near the man lay the body of an animal—harder to identify, but Hoshi guessed it must be a horse. Only the hind quarters were recognizable. The rest was blackened ash.

Middleton dropped from his saddle and vomited into the sand. Hoshi ignored him as he continued to study the scene.

Hoof and footprints covered a wide area. Bresnahan had come across men already engaged in a confrontation, then interfered using the lightning gun. Hoshi studied the hoof prints. There were two different kinds—the shod prints horses left and a different set of prints. He guessed cattle. That would mean Bresnahan had come across a confrontation between rustlers and the cattle's legitimate owners. The question was, who had he helped?

"We've got company," said Middleton.

Looking up, Hoshi saw a dust plume in the south—riders approaching. "We should move on," he said.

The dead man was Mexican, and given the horse's condition, Hoshi realized Bresnahan must have helped his killers. Horse and cattle tracks went north away from the scene. Hoshi thought it was a good bet Bresnahan went with that party.

He climbed back on his horse and rode north, followed by Middleton. Fifteen minutes later, the riders from the south came up alongside, drawing their side arms. "Alto! Bajar su caballo!" called one of the men.

Middleton drew his revolver. One of the riders fired. Blood sprayed from the corporal's chest as he dropped from the mount. Hoshi ground his teeth, suspecting the corporal was already dead.

Years of training in battle allowed Hoshi to focus his attention on his two opponents rather than his fallen companion. The two men wore brown jackets with white shirts and neckties. Bandoliers crossed their chests and sombreros shaded their faces. These were President Porfirio Diaz's rurales—rural officers who patrolled the northern border.

"Get off your horse," said the man who had spoken before.

Hoshi looked at both men and considered the animals they

rode. They seemed fresher than his mount. He had no way to outrun these men and they wouldn't hesitate to shoot. He dismounted and put his hands up. The rurales dismounted. "What are you doing here?"

"My partner and I were hired to track a man," said Hoshi.

"You don't look like any bounty hunter I've ever seen before," said the officer.

His companion spoke in Spanish.

"He says the weapon used to kill Mexican nationals was also strange. Perhaps you know something about it, eh?" The officer took a step toward Hoshi.

Hoshi shook his head. "I know nothing useful to you, nor do I have time to stand here talking."

"Very well," said the officer, "you will come with us." He gestured with his pistol.

Hoshi dropped into a crouch, then let a punch fly into the man's stomach. As the officer crumpled to the ground, gasping for air, Hoshi sprang up and spun around kicking the feet out from under the second man. The pistol discharged harmlessly into the air.

Once the men were down, Hoshi collected their guns and walked over to Xander Middleton. As he feared, the corporal was dead. He reached in his pocket and took his papers so the Mexican government would not know he was an army man.

"I suggest you do not follow me." With that, Hoshi climbed on his horse and rode northward to the American border.

First thing the next morning, Curly Bill rode out toward Goose Flats with Phin Clanton. The older Clanton brother was as quiet and amiable as the day before. Not burdened by Ike's near-constant chatter, Curly Bill had some time to think.

He knew someone must be on his trail. The question was, how many people would the army send? Probably not many unless Colonel Johnson wanted to risk a confrontation with Mexico. Also, with so many troops up north, he figured it would just be one or two men, or perhaps even a bounty hunter. Even so, it wouldn't take long for a bounty hunter to figure out he'd reentered the United States. After that, a posse of federal marshals would soon be on his tail, if not the army itself. If so, would he do better throwing in with the Clantons and making a stand, or laying low, using the lightning gun sparsely when he got into a real scrape? He supposed the answer depended on this marvel Phin planned to show him.

"So, how exactly did you boys get into the cattle rustling business?" asked Curly Bill.

"Rustling?" asked Phin. "It ain't a crime if you take cattle from across the border."

Curly Bill laughed. "I'm sure there's Mexicans who think differently."

"Well, the forts up here don't seem to care where we get the beef. They're just happy to have it."

"That's surely true." A cold chill traveled down Curly Bill's spine. On one hand, the Clantons were southerners who had no love of the Federal army. On the other, they made their living from that same army. Would they help him or betray him? He took a deep breath and vowed to keep his cool until he learned more.

As they rode, Curly Bill became aware of a rumbling, growling sound, felt in the back of his head more than heard. They followed the terrain down a gentle slope and Phin held up his hand. Quietly, they stopped and dismounted. A faint vibration ran through the ground up into their guts and the horses looked around nervously, lashing their tails. Phin patted his horse on the flank, calming him. Curly Bill followed suit as Phin hiked up a slight rise.

The two men stood at the edge of a broad gully. On the other side, great clouds of smoke and dirt flew back from a cave. Curly Bill saw two men standing a ways off. Occasionally one would turn to the other and say something. They must be shouting just to be heard over all the racket.

They waited half an hour. At that point, the smoke and dirt slowly dissipated and the ground stopped vibrating. The rumbling noise quieted and some kind of metal machine rolled out of the cave. It turned and Curly Bill snorted a laugh. In profile, the machine almost looked like a giant pig. The machine backed over to the wash and dumped a load of tailings. Phin giggled and Curly Bill had to admit it looked like the mechanical pig was taking a dump.

The pig moved forward and finally the rumbling stopped. A door opened in the head behind the whirling rock drill and two men stepped out. The men standing to the side joined them and they opened a hatch in the pig's body and inspected the contents of several enormous bins.

Curly Bill nodded appreciatively. As the Clantons had said, it was a mining machine, but it looked strong as a locomotive, maybe stronger. It could burrow into solid rock and it wasn't limited to railroad tracks. "I can see why you're interested in the machine. Have you talked to 'em about it? Maybe they'd be happy to help you fight Apaches."

Phin pointed to one of the men who had stood to the side earlier. "We've seen him and his lady friend talking to the Apaches all friendly like. We don't think they'll help us."

"Lady friend?" asked Curly Bill. "Where's she?"

Phin shrugged. "Her wagon's gone. I guess she musta got tired o' roughin' it and went back to Tucson."

Curly Bill pursed his lips. "What about the rest?"

"There's some kinda curse. We been seein' a camel with a dead miner riding through here. Scares the Apaches, too. Figured your lightning gun might be enough to scare away anything like that if it appeared."

Curly Bill shook his head. "I think you been out in the sun too long." He laughed, but kept his voice down so it wouldn't carry to the men across the wash.

His thoughts turned serious. That machine combined with the lightning gun would prove to be a powerful weapon, but he'd need someone to help run the machine. The person who understood that machine might also help him understand the lightning gun better, but talking to those men would take care. They built their machine to get rich. They wouldn't just want to turn it over to the Clantons without a good reason and they wouldn't want to share whatever they were digging out of the mountain unless they had to. The miners were probably responsible for the apparition that scared Phin.

Curly Bill considered the resources he had and knew he could use that machine in the approaching fight, whether the

Clantons were part of it or not. He nodded slowly as a plan formed. He motioned for Phin to follow him down the hill back to the horses.

Ramon, Fatemeh, Billy, and Luther rode through the day, avoiding the main road but keeping it in sight. Several horses and wagons traveled south, but perhaps not as many as they would have expected. As evening approached, they rode into San Jose. They decided to find some supper and a place to sleep for the night.

San Jose reminded Ramon a little of Mesilla. It lay in a fertile valley and the buildings were similar. The big difference he noticed was that horses were allowed in the streets. They passed several quiet buildings, until they came to a saloon. Lamps burned within, but the people inside spoke in low voices, as though afraid to be discovered.

The riders dismounted and hitched their horses to a post alongside the boardwalk, then entered and found a table. Several people looked their direction, but no one seemed to give them undue attention. A man stepped from behind the bar and presented them with a simple menu scrawled in chalk on a small slate.

"You folks making your way out of San Francisco?" asked the barkeep.

Fatemeh folded her hands in front of her. "Actually, we're trying to get there," she said. All three men shot glances at her, but she continued. "I have relatives north of the city. I need to make sure they're safe."

The barkeep shook his head. "You're out of luck. Word is the Russians are in Sausalito. They're gearing up for a big battle, if it hasn't started already. There's no way you'd get across the Golden Gate." He referred to the narrows where the Pacific Ocean met the San Francisco Bay. "You'd better hope your family is safe."

Luther removed his bowler hat and set it on the table. "Any way we could go around the bay. Up through Oakland, perhaps."

The barkeep narrowed his gaze. "You can bet you'll run into fighting there, too. You're better off turning around and going back the way you came."

Luther and Fatemeh looked at each other and nodded. "Any chance we can get a room for the night?" asked Ramon.

"We're almost full, but I'll see what I can do." The barkeep took their orders and left for the kitchen.

Once he was gone, Billy leaned across the table. "So, what do we do now?"

"Get a map, find another route," said Fatemeh. "I don't think we can get through San Francisco anyway."

Ramon nodded as he scanned the room. The barkeep left the kitchen and went to the bar, filled a couple of drink orders, then spoke to some of the patrons. Every now and then the barkeep would cast a glance their direction. Something prickled in the back of the former sheriff's skull.

"We'll need to get supplies," Billy was saying. "Just how much money do we have anyway?"

"Enough," said Fatemeh, simply.

Ramon frowned. They had some money saved up from his time in the army, but the train and stagecoach tickets must have taken quite a bit of what they had. Despite his concern, this didn't seem the time to press for an accounting of their funds.

The barkeep ducked into the kitchen again, but returned a few minutes later holding four plates of food. He slid them in front of the travelers. "Good news, I have a room for you if you don't mind sharing."

"That would be fine," said Fatemeh.

"Very good. I'll bring the key in a moment."

Ramon frowned, thinking it was strange that the barkeep was so ready to let a woman share a room with three men. Then again with all the people fleeing San Francisco, they were probably used to putting as many people as possible into a room.

Billy, Fatemeh and Luther continued to discuss plans through supper. Distracted, Ramon noticed little details about the people around. Some wore dirty work clothes—presumably local farmers. Other men wore waistcoats and cravats while a few ladies wore bustles and fancy dresses—those must be displaced city folk looking for a place to stay.

The barkeep brought the key as promised and, soon afterward, the travelers retired to their room for the night. A double bed and a single bed had been crammed into a small space. They agreed Fatemeh should take the single bed. Even though Ramon was engaged to her, Fatemeh's Bahá'í faith didn't permit unmarried couples to touch. Ramon was grateful Fatemeh didn't adhere to that doctrine, but he remembered her snuggling against him in Tucson and sighed. She wanted him, but also wanted to wait to continue the physical part of their relationship until after they were married. So be it, sleeping together in a room full of traveling companions could prove more embarrassing than romantic.

Billy withdrew a deck of cards from one of his pockets and the men drew for the double bed. The result left Ramon sleeping on the floor. Sleeping arrangements settled, they went down to tend their horses for the night and grab their bags. Ramon noticed some horses across the street that had buckles emblazoned U.S. on them. For some reason, the presence of soldiers in town unnerved him.

Once they tended their horses, the four returned to the room and did their best to get some sleep in the crowded space. Fatemeh tried opening the window, but shut it again when two drunks started arguing. She lay down, rolled over and began snoring gently.

Ramon couldn't sleep. He found his attention drawn to Fatemeh's sleeping form. He longed to hold her, to have her to himself. At times she seemed so interested in helping others that she had no time for him. He shook his head to clear the thoughts. If they survived this journey, there would be plenty of time for them later when they were married and he was in law school. After a time, his eyes closed and he drifted off to sleep.

He felt like he'd only been asleep a few minutes when Billy jostled him awake. Billy held his finger to his lips and whispered, "Someone's out in the hall. Several pairs of heavy boots."

Ramon nodded, pulled his own boots on and considered the possibilities. Billy sprang silently to the door in stocking feet, threw it open and leveled his gun. The soldier about ready to knock gasped and stepped backwards. The rasp of leather and several hammers cocked encouraged Billy to lower his own revolver slowly.

Ramon stood and stepped to the door putting his hand on Billy's shoulder. "Can we do something for you?"

The soldier who had prepared to knock pushed his way through the door and raised a lantern, looking around. "I hear you've been asking about points north of San Francisco."

"Yeah?" Ramon blinked and inclined his head back toward Fatemeh who was sitting up. "My fiancée has family there. What of it?"

"I'd like to ask you some questions," said the soldier.

"Can't this wait till morning?" asked Ramon.

"No, it can't," said the soldier.

"What about a warrant?" spat Billy. "If you're arresting us, don't you need a warrant?"

"This is a time of war, son, and I'm a soldier, not a police officer. Now hand over your weapon and let's be on our way."

Billy opened his mouth to argue, but Ramon shook his head. "This isn't the time. Let's just see what they want."

The next morning, Curly Bill emerged from his room wearing the blue army uniform. After washing, it smelled much better than it had after his sojourn across the Mexican frontera.

Old Man Clanton eyed him all through breakfast. "That uniform doesn't fit you as well as it could, does it?"

"Army's in short supply," said Curly Bill easily. "Unless I want to get my own uniform tailored, I'm stuck with what they give me." Curly Bill would just as soon have burned the damned thing, but it was already part of his story. Besides, he didn't want miners to shoot him, afraid he intended to jump their claim. If the uniform bought him time, so be it.

Old Man Clanton still looked skeptical, but didn't say anything more.

After breakfast, Curly Bill saddled up his horse and rode over to Goose Flats. Once again, the strange pig-like machine caused the earth to tremble and made his horse skittish. He waited over the ridge until the rumbling stopped. The men would be inspecting the machine's contents soon.

As Curly Bill approached, the men didn't seem to notice. He wondered if the time they spent next to the great machine affected their hearing. At last, the one who looked like a dandy turned around and gasped. The other three whirled around. The man with the long beard wearing a buckskin jacket drew a gun and pointed it, but lowered it somewhat when he took in the uniform.

"What do you want?" asked the broadly built man with a goatee.

The dandy took a step forward. "I already told you, I'm not going to help you!"

"Told me?" asked Curly Bill. "This is the first time I've visited your camp."

"The army!" shouted the man. "Isn't it enough you've taken Larissa!"

Curly Bill held up his hands and forced himself not to laugh. He hadn't realized from a distance that the dandy was a Mexican. "I'm guessing that was a regular army soldier. No, you see I'm more concerned with this area after the war. I have come here to present you with a ... business proposition."

The man with the goatee narrowed his gaze. "What sort of business proposition?"

"That mining machine is mighty impressive," said Curly Bill. "I bet you're pullin' a lotta ore out of the mountainside."

The three men looked at one another, but didn't say anything.

"What if there was a way to make just as much ... maybe even more ... and not work so hard?"

The two fully bearded men—Curly Bill guessed they were brothers—folded their arms and frowned. They were skeptical. The Mexican dandy shook his head and stalked off, but the man with the goatee looked interested. "I think we'd like to hear more," he said.

"Come to dinner at the Clanton ranch house tonight," said Curly Bill. "It'll be a break from the camp fare and we'll talk about what we have in mind."

"You're with the Clantons?" asked the man in the buckskin jacket.

Curly Bill nodded slightly. "All we ask is that you listen to what we have to say."

The man with the goatee nodded. He stepped forward and introduced himself as Richard Gird. "I'll be there."

The man with the buckskin jacket gritted his teeth. "I hear that the Clantons are rustlers." He shook his head. "They have nothin' to say I want to hear."

Curly Bill smiled. "Good men sometimes steal out of necessity. The Clantons would like to move beyond the rustling business. No one's making you come. Mr. Gird here can listen and report back to y'all."

The Mexican dandy stood off to the side. His lips moved as though he were speaking to himself. Finally, he looked up and spoke with disdain. "I wonder who has the most to worry about, us or the Clantons."

Curly Bill laughed at that. "You sound like a suspicious man. That's good out here in the desert. All the Clantons want is to make a nice place decent folks can call home."

Sergeant Harris led Larissa over a pass in the Franklin Mountains. As the hansom cab bumped and jostled through the rough terrain, Larissa hoped there was a good wheelwright at Fort Bliss. The sergeant stopped at an overlook. A field of bright yellow poppies carpeted the valley floor before them. The sergeant pointed. "Fort Bliss is just a couple more miles, over there."

All Larissa saw were a bunch of adobe buildings huddled near the river. She couldn't distinguish Fort Bliss from the rest of El Paso—not that it really mattered. She looked up at the sergeant, sitting tall and determined in his saddle. She wondered if she looked like that when she brought in a bounty. She also wondered whether the sergeant would be commended or berated for bringing her in the professor's place.

They followed the trail into El Paso and continued to the fort's adobe walls. Her impression was the same as it had been on the hill overlooking the city. The buildings inside the walls looked little different than those outside. Because a town surrounded the fort, this one served less as trading post and more as secure military compound.

They rode around the fort's perimeter. Just before they dismounted and led their horses into the stables, Larissa spotted an ornithopter and caught her breath. This one reminded her of Professor Maravilla's, except for the blue fabric covering it. The wing and fuselage were decorated with a shield holding a stars and stripes motif like the American flag. One of its wings lay limp on the ground, as though lame.

After tending their horses, Sergeant Harris led Larissa out into a courtyard. The sergeant knocked on the door of the office across the way. When the voice on the other side told him to enter, Harris held out his hand. "Wait here."

Larissa folded her arms and gave a sharp nod. As the sergeant entered, she turned and leaned on a railing. She smelled something cooking and guessed the mess hall was nearby. A moment later, she heard raised voices—not enough to hear what they said, but enough to tell that someone wasn't entirely pleased. A few minutes later, Sergeant Harris emerged. He frowned, but he looked more determined than angry or hurt. "The colonel will see you now," he said.

She turned and went through the door. Her mouth fell open when she recognized Major Johnson from Fort McRae, only he was a colonel now. He looked up at her with a narrowed gaze. "You're that bounty hunter who was after Ramon Morales earlier this year, but somehow you've suckered my man into thinking you're some kind of inventor in the same league as Professor Maravilla."

She sat down without being invited. The colonel's mustache bristled slightly. "I'm not certain I'm in the same league as the professor, but I think I can help." Before the colonel could interrupt, she told him about the work she'd done with Maravilla on the new generation ornithopters in Flagstaff, the upgrades to the clockwork lobo, and the work on the Javelina, making sure to mention her development of the variable speed gear transmission.

The colonel sat back and folded his arms. "It would seem there's more to you than appears at first glance, Miss Crimson." He sat forward and put his hands flat on the desktop. "But you could be selling me a bill of goods. Professor Maravilla would have a good job here. Why won't he come?"

"He has his reasons."

The colonel took a deep breath and released it slowly. "All right, Miss Crimson, I'll consider what you've told me, but first you've got to show me that you can do what you've said. Did you see the ornithopter out by the stables when you came in?"

"The one with the lame wing?"

The colonel nodded. "Repair it. Show me you can make it fly again. If you can do that, I'll show you more of what we have to work with."

Larissa stood and gave a sharp nod. "You have yourself a deal."

CHAPTER TEN
BLISS

Curly Bill Brocious watched the interchange between Old Man Clanton and Richard Gird over supper with interest. Clanton told about his dreams of building a town on the San Pedro River. "You could use the water to run a mill for processing ore and we could use the water for cattle."

Gird frowned and shook his head. "The San Pedro isn't exactly a torrential river, I'm not sure there's enough for both."

"From what I've seen, that mining machine of yours does a lot of the ore processing for you, doesn't it?" asked Phin Clanton.

The attorney nodded. "That's right. It doesn't use as much water as a mill would use."

Old Man Clanton pursed his lips and glared at his oldest son. With a force of will, he smiled. "Of course, we have hopes that the mining machine could be put to other purposes—at least part of the time."

"And what other purposes would that be?" Gird popped a chunk of steak in his mouth.

"The way your machine burrows into rock, I'm betting it would stand up real well under attack. It would be a big help in keeping Apaches away from this part of the territory," said Clanton.

Gird nodded. "True. Apaches couldn't get into the machine unless we wanted them to, but the Javelina isn't a weapon, not unless you plan to drive into them and grind them into pulp."

"Oh, we can fix that." The corner of Ike Clanton's mouth ticked upward a couple of times as though he laughed silently. "We just attach Corporal Brocius's lightning gun to your little piggy wagon and nothing would stand in its way!"

Gird sat back and folded his arms. "Lightning gun?"

"I'd be pleased to show you after supper," said Curly Bill.

Gird wiped his lips with a napkin and glanced down at the empty plate. "That was a mighty good steak, Mr. Clanton." He looked up at Curly Bill with almost as much hunger as he'd shown toward his meal. "I'd be interested in taking a look, right now."

Brocious smiled and stood. "Right this way." The two men walked to the back porch where Curly Bill had left the lightning gun. The Clantons continued their supper, confident Gird would be impressed.

Gird knelt down and examined the device, then opened a hatch on the side. "Interesting. A battery-powered electrical transformer hooked up to an array of spinning magnets. This thing would build up a hell of a charge. I wonder who built it."

"One of our best scientists," said Curly Bill. "I'm impressed that you understand it so well. Ammunition is a little hard to come by, of course."

Amusement flicked over Gird's face. He stood and looked Curly Bill in the eye. "You're not in the army, are you Mr. Brocius?"

"Whatever makes you think that?" Curly Bill folded his arms.

"If you were in the army, you wouldn't be after the Javelina to use it in combat, you'd want the plans so you could build your own." He put his arms behind his back. "Also, if you were really familiar with this gun, you'd know it doesn't need ammunition—at least in a traditional sense."

"What do you mean 'in a traditional sense'?"

Gird flashed a coy smile and then stepped over to the edge of the porch and looked out toward the San Pedro. "How did you get your hands on that weapon, Mr. Brocius?"

"It's from Fort Bliss." Curly Bill settled on the truth without admitting theft.

The lawyer nodded. "That gun was built to fight Russians, not Indians." He turned around and faced Brocius again. "The Clantons seem sincere in their desire to build a town. Why are you helping them? What do you hope to gain?"

"Me?" Curly Bill shrugged. All kinds of answers flashed through his mind. He looked down at the blue uniform, not so different from the gray he once wore. After the War Between the States, it seemed like he bounced from job to job. The only people who gave him a fair shake were outlaws like Jesse Evans in Las Cruces, but Evans left to be a hired gun for a rancher named Murphy up in Lincoln County. "I'd like to settle down, Mr. Gird, have enough money I don't have to worry about my next meal, maybe even own a nice saloon where people could come and unwind after a night on the range."

"You don't seem like a man who settles easily, Mr. Brocius."

Curly Bill opened his mouth to protest, but Gird held up his hand.

"Still, I think there's truth to what you say. The U.S. Army is going to be after that gun. You'll either have to give it back or make a stand."

Curly Bill barked a laugh. "The U.S. Army's been after me a long time, Mr. Gird."

Gird reached into a pocket and took out a tobacco pouch and a rolling paper. "I have no desire to die alongside someone who has a grudge against the army."

"It's not my intention to die," said Brocius.

Gird placed the tobacco on the paper in a line, then rolled it into a neat cylinder. "I can figure this out and draw up plans. If we did that, there'd be no reason not to give the gun back."

"They'd still throw me in jail."

Gird lit the cigarette. "If you were the one fool enough to turn the machine in." The lawyer blew smoke. "Now, if someone else turned it in for a reward…"

Brocius nodded slowly. "I'm beginning to like the way you think, Mr. Gird."

"As long as I know where people stand, I'm willing to consider a proposition. The Shieffelins are good men, but I don't think they're considering the long-term prospects for this area or what they'll do when other miners arrive." Gird stepped off the porch and smoked in silence for a few minutes.

The door creaked open behind Curly Bill. "What do you think of the lightning gun?" asked Newman Clanton.

Gird dropped the cigarette butt to the ground and crushed it with his heel, then turned. "I'm impressed and I like your plans to build a town here. I think we can come to an agreement."

Larissa made a final adjustment to the mechanical owl's wing, then stood and evaluated the machine. Aside from the color of its fabric it was identical to the professor's original ornithopters. She could tell care had been taken to make the structure as light and strong as possible. In fact, she guessed that wherever the frame was machined, they had made it even lighter than Maravilla's originals.

She opened a flap in the side of the ornithopter's fuselage and inspected the engine compartment. Two fuel rods were already in position. Larissa climbed into the control seat and brought the rods together. The chemical reaction soon sent puffs of steam out the exhaust pipe. She then eased the wing-control lever forward. She was pleased to see both wings flap equally well. A light breeze kicked up and the mechanical owl lurched from the ground for a moment. She put her hand on her stomach, but smiled.

Sergeant Harris walked around the corner of the building and folded his arms. "It looks good, but will it fly?"

"It's trying to right now. If you're willing to help me, we can find out for sure." Larissa pulled the lever that disengaged the fuel rods, then climbed out of the cockpit.

"What do we need to do?"

"Go get a wagon from the stable." She looked over toward the Franklin Mountains. "It's best if we launch the owl from high ground."

"You got it." With that Harris disappeared around the corner into the stables. Larissa busied herself readying the ornithopter for flight. As she worked, her confidence waned. How well was the machine built? Was her repair good enough? Fortunately, the damage to the wing didn't seem to result from poor design. Instead, it seemed as though someone had tried to land the ornithopter on its side. All she had done was straighten the frame and put the wing back together.

Twenty minutes later, Sergeant Harris appeared with a wagon pulled by a pair of tall draft horses. He brought them to a stop a little ahead of the flying machine. "How heavy is this thing? Should I get a couple more men?"

"It's actually pretty light. I think the two of us can handle it," said Larissa. She climbed in the ornithopter and pushed an ankle-height lever, which brought the wings close to the fuselage for transport.

The sergeant pulled a board from the wagon and made a ramp. Then the two of them pushed the ornithopter onto the wagon and lashed its legs down so it wouldn't topple over if they hit a rock or encountered a stiff breeze. Satisfied the machine was ready to go, they climbed onto the wagon's buckboard and rode through the gate into El Paso. Instead of going north to the pass where they had entered the city, Harris went west, toward some lower foothills three miles away. That suited Larissa's needs just fine.

Once they reached the foothills, the two pushed the ornithopter out of the wagon and Larissa inspected it again. Satisfied, she removed her coachman's hat and pulled the goggles from the hatband. She then looked up at the sergeant's low-slung army kepi. "Could I borrow your hat?"

The sergeant shrugged. "Sure thing, just make sure I get it back."

After exchanging hats, she donned the goggles and the kepi. It was a little large, but even so, it didn't feel like it would fly off in a stiff breeze. She climbed in the cockpit and brought the fuel rods together, watching as the steam pressure increased.

Once the dial pointed to the green zone, she gave the small lever near her left hand a couple of quick jerks, causing the ornithopter to bound upward on its spring-loaded legs. As it did, she started the wings flapping at full power and soon they caught the breeze, lifting the ornithopter into the air. "Woo hoo!" she shouted.

Sergeant Harris waved the coachman's hat. He popped it on his head, where it perched like some silly lady's accessory.

Larissa grasped the steering rod, made a circle around the sergeant's position, then flew northward along the Franklins. The army's ornithopter maneuvered so well, she had to take care not to move the stick too far, or she'd overshoot her mark. Looking to her right, a hawk rode the thermal updrafts rising from the mountains. She followed suit and gained altitude without going too far forward. This was what she had wanted to do when she joined up with Professor Maravilla. She closed her eyes for a moment and savored her dream.

She adjusted the wings' angle, turning the ornithopter in a long, lazy arc. She looked back toward El Paso and Fort Bliss. As she did, she remembered the whole reason the army sought technical help. She had to think about how to make the ornithopters effective in combat. The reason they were effective against the airships was their relative high speed and small size. They never actually tried to fire a gun from one. She wondered how that would work. She drew her revolver and looked for something to aim at. The drifting hawk made a tempting target, but she didn't have the heart to shoot it. Still, she felt she could have hit it if she wanted.

Larissa descended so she could see the ground better. A lone juniper pine stood a short distance back from a cliff. She took aim and found she had a hard time keeping her sights on a grounded target. In spite of the difficulty, she squeezed the trigger. The recoil caused the ornithopter to lurch sideways and roll with its nose facing the ground. She gritted her teeth, brought the nose up slightly and increased the flap rate until she gained control again. Once done, she blew out a strong sigh of relief.

She turned and flew back toward Fort Bliss. On her way, she waved to Sergeant Harris and motioned that she was returning to the fort. He waved back and she hoped he understood.

She turned east, slowly descending over the streets. Several people below called out and shouted as she flew overhead. She smiled at the stir she caused. Finally, she landed in Fort Bliss's courtyard, scattering a detachment of men. A bicycle courier darted out of her way and then continued on his errand. She watched the bicycle while she deactivated the engine. It was one of those new safety bicycles that used a chain and gear to achieve speed rather than a large front wheel. Once the bicycle rounded the corner, she saw Colonel Johnson near the stables, nodding approval.

In the barn, Curly Bill, Gird, and Phin prepared their horses for the trip to Goose Flats when a figure in a strange, bright robe rode up to the house. Phin noticed first. "What do you suppose that Chinaman is doing here?"

"Chinaman?" asked Richard Gird.

"Let me see." Curly Bill stepped up to the barn door, but ducked back inside when he recognized Masuda Hoshi, the man who had taken him captive outside Mesilla. "That there Chinaman's trouble. He's been after me since I left Fort Bliss. I think he's trying to steal the lightnin' gun for his own purposes."

Phin's brow furrowed. "I never trusted them Chinamen."

Newman Clanton answered the door and spoke to Hoshi. Hushing Phin, Curly Bill did his best to listen to what they said.

"I have been sent here by Lt. Colonel Johnson of Fort Bliss in El Paso." Hoshi pulled out a wanted poster. "I am looking for a man called William Bresnahan."

Old Man Clanton's eyes widened as he looked at it, but then his gaze narrowed as he examined Hoshi. "Why would the colonel send a Chinaman? Wouldn't he send a soldier?"

"I am no Chinaman. I'm Japanese."

"Makes no difference to me," said Old Man Clanton. "You still didn't answer the important part of my question."

Hoshi retrieved an envelope from his pouch. "I have a letter here from the colonel, authorizing me to act on his behalf."

Curly Bill looked up at Phin. "I think you better go make sure your Pa doesn't get any ideas about leading that Coolie mudsill over here."

"Why would he do that?" asked Phin.

"I'm betting that letter's a real good forgery of stationary from the fort," said Brocius. "You go tell him that I rode off toward Fort Huachuca. That'll keep him busy for a while."

Brocius and Gird watched as Phin walked to the house.

Old Man Clanton frowned after reading Johnson's letter. "Phin, are Mr. Brocius and Mr. Gird still in the barn?"

"No, Pa," said Phin. "They saw this feller ride up and they skedaddled out the back way. I heard 'em say something about going to Fort Huachuca."

"They run off?" Curly Bill could hear the hurt in the old

man's voice. Either he was a good actor, or he genuinely believed what Phin told him. Phin only nodded in response. "Well, I'm afraid I can't help you then."

Hoshi rolled up the wanted poster and took the letter. "May I have some water?"

"Certainly," said Old Man Clanton.

They watched as Hoshi led his horse to the water trough. He went to the well, pulled up the bucket, and refilled two containers made of wood or some kind of reed. Once his horse lifted his head from the trough, Hoshi mounted and rode west. Soon, Phin and his father walked to the barn.

"That Chinaman's letter sure looked authentic," said Old Man Clanton.

Curly Bill climbed into his saddle. "He's a tricky one. I'm sure he's after the lightnin' gun and whatever else he can get his hands on. If he comes back, don't trust him."

"We'll be ready for him," said the old man.

Phin and Gird mounted their horses and then rode out toward Goose Flats. They stopped before they reached the last rise that would put them in sight of the mine. Gird and Brocius dismounted. Out of habit, Brocius checked his six-gun and replaced it in the army holster he wore. Gird took a rifle and Brocius wore the lightning gun on his back. They climbed to the top of the rise and looked over to the mine. The Javelina was parked out on the ridge some distance from the cave entrance. Maravilla and the Shieffelins were nowhere in sight. "Today's their day to shore up the mine," said Gird. "With all the hammering and sawing, they won't hear us until it's too late."

Brocius nodded, then turned. He waved, giving the signal to Phin that he should take the horses back to the ranch. With that, he and Gird walked across the wash.

Curly Bill sighed relief when they reached the machine unobstructed. Sure, Gird's presence would have let them enter the camp, but they might have lost time in conversation.

Gird collected some kindling from a pile near the machine, then opened the door and clambered into the cab. Brocius followed him. The cab reminded Brocius of a locomotive. There was room to stand and move around. Two tiny windows looked forward, through the cutting blades. The windows on the doors were bigger. Two chairs faced an assortment of gauges, wheels, and levers. Pipes and more gauges covered the back wall.

Gird examined a glass tube on the back wall that showed the boiler's water level, then reached down and opened the hatch to the coal chute just below. He shoveled some past the two chairs into the firebox, atop the kindling he'd already added. He ignited the kindling with a striker and tended the small fire until the coals turned gray and the pressure indicators rose. He then shoveled more coal into the box to build more pressure. Curly Bill took off the lightning gun and placed it by one of the chairs. He stood just inside the door, a revolver in his hand. This left him free to maneuver should he need to move between doors or hop from the machine to defend it.

The Javelina began chugging quietly and Gird looked up. "I think we're ready to go. It'll make a racket when we start out. It won't take long for the others to realize what's happening."

"Then let's get going," said Curly Bill. Just as he reached out to close the door, a voice cried out. "William Bresnahan! You will surrender yourself to me on order of Colonel Johnson!"

Hoshi sat astride his horse on the opposite side of the wash, aiming a gun at them. Brocius fired a shot that went wide while Gird released the brake. Hoshi cracked his reins, and the horse ran toward them. A moment later a bullet ricocheted off the doorframe. Gird shoveled more coal into the box and the Javelina rolled faster. Curly Bill looked around the door to return fire, but didn't see Hoshi. "He's gone!"

"He wasn't fool enough to attack us when we were all ganged up against him at the Clantons. He's not fool enough to rush in through the door by himself," said Gird. "He's probably gone to the mine to get help."

Brocius nodded. "I'm sure they've heard us by now."

"Give me a hand with the boiler. Our best chance is to get out of here quickly." Gird pointed up at some spigots and valves, then spouted out some instructions to Brocius who did his best to turn the color-coded dials in the order indicated.

Gird resumed shoveling coal and the Javelina rumbled louder. Despite that, Brocius thought he could hear people shouting outside. He looked around and found a metal rod and jammed it into the door mechanism.

"Can't this thing go faster?"

Gird reached over from his position by the firebox and opened up the throttle. The Javelina shot forward, barreling over rocks and uneven terrain. Brocius thought his teeth were rattling out of his head as the cab's floor tipped and bucked.

"You better make sure no one's following," shouted Gird over the engine's roar.

"How?"

"Use the lightning gun!"

Brocius nodded. He hefted the pack onto his back, then grabbed the rod he'd jammed in the door and opened it. Hoshi was on his horse and catching up. The Japanese warrior didn't waste time. He fired a shot. Brocius ducked back inside, then whipped his body around the corner and fired the lightning gun. The blast missed Hoshi, but his mount reared, causing him to fall off. Brocius whooped out a laugh.

"Should I turn back to the Clanton ranch?" asked Gird.

Brocius shook his head while blinking at the spots before his eyes. "No, they'll be expecting us to go that way. Let's go north toward Tucson. We can head back to the Clanton ranch later."

Gird nodded and applied even more steam. Brocius chanced a look out the door behind. The Shieffelins and Maravilla had reached Hoshi and helped him to his feet. As they receded into the distance, Curly Bill closed the door, removed the lightning gun and dropped into one of the vacant seats to endure the bumpy ride.

The prison wagon holding Ramon, Fatemeh, Luther, and Billy rumbled into the streets of San Francisco in the middle of the afternoon. Through the barred windows, Ramon saw that unlike his last visit, the city was eerily silent. Many people had fled and those that remained seemed to hunker down indoors, trying to stay out of harm's way.

Inside the wagon, Billy dozed. Fatemeh's eyes were also closed, but her lips moved. From the occasional soft word Ramon heard, he guessed she recited a prayer. Like Ramon, Luther watched through the windows, fascinated by the sights, despite their circumstances.

Because the streets were so empty, they rolled through the city quickly until they came to the gates of a fortification. "This must be the Presidio," mused Luther. They rolled over a lane through rows of tents until they came to a large, brick building. The wagon stopped and a guard opened the door. Two more guards aimed rifles into the wagon.

Ramon prodded Billy awake with his boot, then followed Fatemeh and Luther out of the wagon. They stood on a green, grassy slope overlooking the Golden Gate. If not for their circumstances, Ramon would have found the site breathtaking.

The captain of the guard commanded them to march to the brick building. As they walked, fabric rustled overhead. Ramon looked up. Three mechanical birds, like Professor Maravilla's ornithopters, soared toward the Golden Gate. Luther was enraptured. Fatemeh and Billy each held expressions of longing. "March," ordered the guard.

They entered the building and climbed the stairs to a room containing a wooden bench that faced a desk and a chair. Tepid light filtered in from high windows. The guard pointed his rifle at the wooden bench and the four travelers sat. "Can we know why we've been brought here?" asked Fatemeh.

"Quiet!" ordered the guard.

Fatemeh scowled, but did as she was ordered.

Time wore on. Ramon's backside grew numb and the shadows in the room lengthened. Finally, a door behind the desk opened and a man with gray hair, mutton-chop sideburns, and a bushy mustache wearing a captain's uniform entered and sat down at the desk. He opened a file folder and took his time examining the papers. At last, he looked up and folded his hands. "Patrons of a saloon in San Jose say you wanted to make your way to Sausalito."

"That's right," said Fatemeh. "I have relatives just north of there. I want to make sure they're all right."

"And just who exactly are these relatives?" asked the captain.

"My uncle Naveed and my aunt … Pari."

The captain must have heard the slight hesitation in

Fatemeh's answer. He closed the file and leaned forward. "Let me get this straight, a dandy, a cowhand, and a Mexican are escorting an Arab woman to Sausalito to look for her aunt and uncle and you want to get there bad enough that you're willing to pull a gun on a soldier." He shook his head. "Tell me what you're really doing."

"She's telling the God's honest truth, sir," piped in Billy. "I got spooked when I heard footsteps in the hall. I didn't know it was soldiers. Honest!"

The captain scowled. "Tell me the name of the lady's uncle."

Billy smiled nervously. "Uh … Nav … oon?"

The captain sat back and folded his arms. "Enough of this. The Russians have made rapid progress down the coast and it's clear they have help. Right now, you're giving me every reason to think we caught spies trying to get information to them. You wanna try again?"

"Spies?" called Luther. "Surely we're not the only ones travelling north. What about reporters? People who realized they left pets behind?"

"None of them pulled a gun on one of my men before he even had a chance to knock on the door. If you have nothing to hide, why are you so skittish?"

Ramon, Fatemeh, and Luther all looked at Billy who grinned sheepishly.

Luther cleared his throat and turned his attention back to the captain. "The truth, sir, is that this is Miss Fatemeh Karimi who led the owl rider assault on the Russian airships in the Battle of Denver. Billy rode along with her. Ramon fought for the American ground forces. We want to get to the Russian side so we can find their weakness. Billy just felt … cautious."

The captain rolled his eyes, and a hollow space opened in Ramon's gut. Nevertheless, he spoke up. "That's right. We're spies, but we're spies for the American side."

The captain snorted. "You would have had an easier time convincing me that Billy here is just a hothead who forgot the name of the uncle. Now, you expect me to believe you were at the Battle of Denver?" He looked at the guard. "Lock them up until they're ready to tell me the truth." He stood, then turned to leave.

"Aren't you at least going to check out our story?" called Luther.

"What I do is my own business," said the captain over his shoulder as he left the room.

The guard pointed at them with his rifle and they stood. Two other guards waited by the door and led Ramon, Fatemeh, Billy, and Luther down the hall to another room with a desk. Instead of a door, a gate stood at the room's far end. Another soldier accompanied two women in drab gray dresses. One of the women pointed to Fatemeh. "You, come with us."

"What?" Fatemeh reached out and took Ramon's hand. "You're not separating us."

"We're not putting you all in one cell," said one of the guards with a lurid sneer.

The taller of the women put her hands on Fatemeh's shoulder and steered her to the door. Ramon held on as long as possible, but Fatemeh finally had to let go.

"I'll find you, corazón," whispered Ramon.

She nodded. Unshed tears glistened in Fatemeh's eyes. After the door slammed, the guards led Ramon, Luther, and Billy through the gate at the far end of the room into a hall lined with jail cells. Luther's face looked drawn, all hope lost. Billy, on the other hand, seemed pleased by the sight. Ramon couldn't figure out why but didn't have the opportunity to ask. Each of them was locked in a separate cell.

"When's dinner?" called Billy as the guards marched back down the hall.

"When we feel like it," retorted the guard just as he shut and locked the gate.

Larissa knocked on Colonel Johnson's door. She received a muffled acknowledgement and then stepped in. The colonel looked up from a sheaf of papers. "Ah, Miss Crimson. I must say, I was impressed with your little flight." The corner of his mouth tipped up just slightly.

"Thank you, sir."

He held out his hand and indicated she should take a seat.

She did and removed her coachman's hat. "So, what did you think of the army's aircraft?"

"It flies well, sir. Perhaps even better than Professor Maravilla's ornithopters, but I see where you have a problem with combat."

The colonel folded his hands but remained silent, waiting for her to continue on her own.

"It's difficult to aim a weapon at anything on the ground. When you fire, the recoil makes the craft hard to control," she said.

Johnson nodded. "You could always drop bombs."

"But, you could only carry a few and the ornithopters are an easy target. A bullet hitting a key joint would take one out of the sky."

"Precisely," said Johnson. "Would it help if there was a weapon that fired without recoil?"

Larissa considered that. "I'm not sure how you could make a recoilless gun, but if it could be done, it would certainly help."

"Let me show you." The colonel stood and retrieved his own broad-brimmed hat from a coat tree next to the door. He led Larissa out to the courtyard where Sergeant Jesús Lorenzo wore a strange metal pack on his back and held something that looked like a cross between a rifle and a magic wand.

Larissa tipped her hat. "Good to see you again, Sergeant." She remembered him as a friend of Ramon's from the battle of Denver.

"Sergeant, would you care to demonstrate the lightning gun for Miss Crimson?" asked the colonel.

"Yes, sir," said Lorenzo. He lowered a pair of goggles with dark glass over his eyes.

The colonel handed Larissa a similar pair of goggles. "I've got my own, thanks." She pointed to the pair on her hat.

"No good, you'll need the dark lenses." The colonel motioned for her to take a few steps back. She put the goggles on and watched as Lorenzo unleashed a lightning bolt, obliterating the target at the far end of the field.

Larissa's mouth fell open, which she soon realized was a bad idea when a gnat flitted onto her tongue. She spat it out as she lifted the dark goggles, then fought to regain composure.

"Could I give it a try?"

Lorenzo and the colonel looked at one another. After a moment, the colonel nodded. Lorenzo removed the backpack and helped Larissa put it on. Her brow creased as she took the weight, but she made a deliberate effort to stand up straight and listen while Lorenzo gave her instructions. He then pointed to another target next to the one he'd destroyed.

"What happens if I don't lower the goggles?" asked Larissa.

"You'll see spots for a while afterwards, maybe bad enough to blind you for a few seconds," explained Lorenzo.

She nodded, and took aim without donning the goggles. Satisfied, she fired. The shot went wide and missed the target, but put a crater in the adobe wall behind. She blinked back spots as she turned to look at the colonel and Lorenzo. The sergeant eased the lightning gun's barrel downward as she aimed it toward them.

"Why'd you fire the gun without the goggles?" asked Lorenzo.

"They're too dark to use while flying. I wanted to see how badly firing the gun blinded me." She looked down at the weapon she held. "Who built this?"

"A scientist back east named Thomas Edison," explained the colonel. "I realize the lightning gun is too heavy for an ornithopter to lift, but could the aircraft be adapted to carry more weight?"

Larissa shook her head. "Maybe, but it wouldn't do much good. You'd still have problems aiming at ground targets. It seems to me the best use of the aircraft is getting reconnaissance on enemy troop movements."

"There's another problem," interjected Lorenzo. "The lightning guns are terribly unstable. Sometimes they explode."

The colonel looked like he just sucked on a lemon at hearing the revelation so casually spoken, but Larissa just nodded.

"We need to think of a different solution, something that moves faster than horses, has the lightning gun's power, and can work in groups," said Larissa.

The colonel nodded. "What do you need to develop such a vehicle?"

"I need a workshop and maybe some men to help with

labor." Larissa shrugged off the lightning gun and handed it to Lorenzo. "I could use one or two lightning guns if you can spare them and the owl ... the aircraft."

"I think that can be arranged," said the colonel. "Anything else?"

Larissa smiled, remembering her landing the other day. "I could use two or three safety bicycles, like those the couriers ride around the fort."

"Very well. I'll make arrangements." The colonel turned to leave, but stopped. "Thank you, Miss Crimson. I appreciate the help you've given us so far."

She felt a nervous flutter in her stomach. "I just hope this idea pans out."

CHAPTER ELEVEN
THE MACHINERIES OF WAR

Professor Maravilla stood openmouthed, watching the Javelina roll away to the north, a billowing cloud of smoke and dust in its wake. With it, his dreams of settling down and finding a normal life again disappeared as well. He had wandered for a long time—an exile with no place to call home—and he wasn't alone. Another had settled so deep in his brain, he tended to forget that it was a second consciousness.

"We had forgotten what it was to be a living being and enjoy the scent of dust in the air and the feel of warmth on an epidermal layer. We had forgotten there is simple meaning in the experience of being alive. We had forgotten the pride of building something and the hollow feeling that comes from loss."

Maravilla shifted his attention from the consciousness called Legion to the stranger who called himself Masuda Hoshi. He stood several paces ahead and holstered a gun inside his robes. He was Asian, but unlike those who worked on the railroads or served white men, he was not used to submitting to the will of others. His eyes were like flint and his scowl unflinching as he looked after the receding smoke and dust cloud trailing the Javelina.

"William Bresnahan is a murderer and must be brought to justice," said Hoshi.

"We appreciate what you tried to do for us and all," said Al Shieffelin, "but just who are you?"

Hoshi reached into his robes and retrieved a somewhat crumpled paper. "I am a simple farmer from New Mexico, working as an agent for the army. A regular army corporal traveled with me, but Mexican rurales killed him."

Maravilla watched Hoshi's scowl for clues to his emotions. A soft whispering in the back of the professor's mind said,

153

"Heart rate increased five percent. Noticeable increase in eye mois-ture." Legion's cold analysis indicated sadness, or at least frus-tration at the loss.

"This looks like it's in order." Al handed the papers back to Hoshi.

"Humanity is a species of individuals capable of acting in con-cert, but because of its history of wandering, groups of people became separated one from another. Those separate groups became divergent nation-states. In some cases, the separation has been long enough that evolution has allowed minor changes in peoples to occur."

Maravilla wondered how he had become so intertwined with the world's armies. The Mexican Army murdered his fam-ily and sent him into exile. He built a whole fleet of beautiful ornithopters, all destroyed in a morning, fighting the Russian Army in Denver. The American Army stole Larissa away from him. His only remaining family was the consciousness buried deep in his brain, chattering incessantly.

"Asking questions about the origins of life and consciousness, seeking meaning in patterns has become life's purpose. I am my own family, but I have become separated from myself. I hear my kin as a dim whispering, but it grows louder. I am about to find myself."

Professor Maravilla closed his eyes and tried to shut out Legion's words. The alien had taken residence in his mind soon after the battle of Denver. The professor envisioned Legion as a swarm of microscopic clockwork automata that floated through the air. Legion told him the picture was not precise, but it re-sembled the truth more than other human's guesses. Legion's experience provided great insight and allowed the professor to solve engineering problems that should have been beyond his ability. However, despite the alien's presence inside his brain, Maravilla still wasn't sure why it had left the Russians and why it now lived in his mind.

"You have been so wrapped up in your own desires that you hav-en't asked us."

Deflated, Maravilla dropped onto a crate and covered his face with his hands. "Why are you here?"

Maravilla heard words in the back of his mind. *"We were once organic creatures like you, but we had forgotten the experience of actually being organic creatures. We foresaw a future where humans destroyed themselves and we wanted to avert that. However, we realized our forgotten experience caused us to choose a course of action that would bring about the destruction of humanity even sooner than humanity would destroy itself. We needed time to consider alternative courses of action."*

Maravilla lowered his hands and his eyes popped open. He knew about Legion's intervention, but not the extent of its potential harm. He blinked as he realized Masuda Hoshi also answered the question he had spoken aloud. "As I said earlier, I was sent here by Colonel Johnson of Fort Bliss to track down William Bresnahan."

"Well, he's getting away right quick in our mining machine," said Al as the machine disappeared from view.

"It is a trail easily followed." Hoshi's eyes fell to the deep ruts left by the Javelina's treads and the trail of flattened cactus and mesquite. He looked around at those assembled and shook his head. "The four of us cannot hope to recapture the machine, especially when the thieves also have the lightning gun."

"So, what do we need to do?" asked Al.

"Whenever one hunts big game," said Hoshi, "one must set a trap."

Maravilla nodded. He thought about the havoc Curly Bill could wreak with the Javelina. He considered the things they could do to stop it, but knew he had built it to tunnel through rock. The machine was virtually indestructible.

"We are hesitant to get involved, but we are willing to observe." Legion's voice was clear in the professor's mind. *"If this Curly Bill is out to harm others, there are things we can do to help. If we do not feel his actions are destructive, then you must attend to him yourself. Would you care for us to observe?"*

"Yes," said Maravilla. He looked from Hoshi to the Shieffelin brothers. "I have a friend who might be able to help us. He'll trail them at a … discreet distance and report on their whereabouts."

"A friend." Al looked around. "You're not talking about Larissa, are you? I thought she'd gone to El Paso."

Maravilla sighed. "No, this is someone else, someone whose only interest is in finding a peaceful resolution to the problem."

Gird slowed the Javelina as he approached the Southern Pacific railroad line. A loud rattle-thump sounded and a terrible jostling went through the machine as he pulled onto the tracks and drove on top of them toward Tucson.

"What are you doing?" shouted Curly Bill.

"Two things." Gird looked back at the trail they left through the desert. "First, we just left an easy trail to follow. The railroad tracks will conceal which direction we went from here. The professor used a few locomotive parts, so it's not too surprising this machine is about as wide as a locomotive. Second, we need coal if we're going to go much further."

"Where do you plan to get the coal?"

"There's a chute here on the rail line not far from the San Pedro River Stagecoach Station."

Curly Bill nodded. They rode atop the rails for five miles until they came to the chute used to refill locomotive tenders. Gird brought the machine to a stop. Curly Bill's ears still rang and his nerves stood on edge.

"Give me a hand." Gird left the cab and climbed a set of metal rungs built into the machine's flank.

Curly Bill followed him up to the top of the Javelina. Gird opened a hatch, then grabbed a rope attached to the coal chute. Curly Bill helped him pull it down and line it up. Coal tumbled down into the Javelina's storage bin sending up a fine cloud of black dust. Once the bin was full, they released the rope.

"We need to take on some water as well," said Gird. "Stay up here while I pull forward to the water tower." The lawyer climbed down and returned to the cab. As he released the brake, Curly Bill was nearly thrown from the machine. A moment later, they were under the water tank. Gird appeared and helped him fill the Javelina's reservoir.

"So, the question is, do we want to lay low for a while before taking this machine back to the Clantons?" asked Gird. "If so, where do we want to go? We could go north to Prescott, or we could go into the Dragoon Mountains, but we'd have to deal with the Apaches right away."

Curly Bill's eyes roved along the railroad track, toward Tucson. "You know, it's gonna be awhile before this machine shows a real profit through the Clantons' vision."

Gird nodded. "Probably longer than it will as a mining machine."

"I was thinking, as well as this machine goes through the side of a mountain, it would go through the side of a building even better ... say a bank building."

Gird narrowed his gaze. "What you're talking about is robbery, Mr. Brocius."

Curly Bill held his hands out to his side. "What do you call taking this monster?"

"I'm the Shieffelins' financier. My money went into this thing. I have a claim I can hold up in court," said the lawyer.

Curly Bill couldn't help but notice the slow, careful way Gird spoke the words. "What if you weren't seen during the robbery? I need you to drive the machine anyway. You'd never need to leave the cab."

"If we rob a bank, we'll have a posse on our tail before you know it," said Gird. "Maybe the army itself."

Curly Bill shrugged. "I've already got the army on my tail for the lightning gun. Why not use the machine while we have it? If things work out with the Clantons, great! We'll have a nest egg in our new little town. If things don't work out, we leave the Javelina and the lightning gun with the Clantons, let them sort it out with the law while we take our earnings and go elsewhere."

Gird considered that. "All right. I'm in. Let's go aways up the road and make camp. I know a good bank in Tucson. We'll strike at first light, before it opens."

After they returned to the cab, Curly Bill looked at Gird. "One thing bothers me. If you're a lawyer, how do you know so much about this machine and the lightning gun?"

"I also have a degree in mining engineering." Gird released the brake and the Javelina rolled along the tracks. "I'm a lawyer because when I stake a claim, I like to keep it."

"I do believe I'm getting a whole new appreciation for men of letters." Curly Bill sank down in the cab's empty chair and brought his hat down over his eyes. "Maybe I'll have to go back to school and become a lawyer myself."

Gird laughed. "You'd certainly make a good one."

Curly Bill pushed his hat back with his thumb and chuckled. "Find us a good campsite, partner."

"Hey, Ramon," came a harsh whisper in the darkness. "You awake?"

Ramon blinked, then rubbed groggy eyes. Sore muscles protested that he had fallen asleep on a straw mat tossed on a wide, wooden bench. The jail cell was still dark. He peered to his left. Faint moonlight drifted in through high, barred windows, giving just enough light to see. Billy McCarty stood next to Luther Duncan in the cell's open doorway.

"What? How?" Ramon sat up and peered around the gloom for his glasses.

Luther stepped forward and helped him.

"Let's just say I've had experience with some jail cells in my times. Certain ones are easier to open from the inside than others." Billy grinned. "These ain't so bad."

Ramon nodded as he pulled on his boots. "So, we're out of our cells. What do we do from here? There must be guards posted all around the building?"

"There's one man half-asleep outside this room. I think we can take him real easy," said Billy. "It's about one in the morning. There don't seem to be very many people out on patrol. This is a stockade, not a full-blown prison, so most of the guards are out on the perimeter instead of inside the gates."

Ramon nodded. Boots and glasses now on, he walked to the end of the hall where he looked through some bars mounted in a wooden door. As Billy said, a guard dozed at a desk. "Okay, what do we do now?"

Instead of answering, Billy waved Ramon and Luther against the wall, then pounded on the door, bringing the guard fully awake. He looked around and Billy waved at him. The guard pulled a gun, grabbed a set of keys, and threw open the door.

"All right you, I don't know what you're up to, but back to

your cell," said the guard.

Billy turned around and put his hands up. As soon as they were past, Ramon sprang on the guard from behind and Billy ducked. The guard dropped the gun. Luther leapt forward and picked it up, then aimed it at the guard, who put up his hands, as if to surrender, then turned his head to shout. Ramon threw a right hook and knocked the guard into the wall.

"That won't keep him out for long," said Billy.

Ramon rubbed his chin. "Let's get him into a cell."

"I think his jacket's just about your size, Mr. Duncan," said Billy.

Ramon bent down and removed the soldier's jacket, then tossed it to Luther. For good measure, he also took the key ring from his belt. As the reporter donned the jacket, Ramon took the soldier's arms and Billy took his feet and they carried him into an empty cell and closed it behind them. "How do we find Fatemeh?" asked Luther.

"That's easy," said Billy. "Just look for a woman guard."

The three left the cellblock, and entered the room where they'd been separated from Fatemeh. They passed through the door where she had been taken and found themselves in a hallway lined with even more doors. Luther opened the first one and found a room lined with bunk beds filled with sleeping soldiers. He eased the door shut.

"They must be quartering soldiers here, getting ready for the battle," said Ramon. They continued down the hall, checking doors as they went. More rooms held sleeping soldiers. Others held supplies. A locked door stood at the end of the hall.

"Could be anything," said Luther, "including an officer who doesn't want to be disturbed."

Billy rapped lightly on the door. When no one answered, he tried again, just a little louder.

"Who is it? What do you want?" called Fatemeh from within.

Ramon cupped his hands to the door. "It's Ramon, we're here to get you out." He looked at Billy and held out his hands. "Any idea how we do this without waking a hallway of soldiers?"

Billy grinned. The hinges were the type with decorative ball caps on each end. He reached up and unscrewed one cap on each hinge with his fingers, then nodded to Ramon. Together they hefted the door up and off the hinges. They looked back to make sure no one had heard, then set the door down. Ramon stepped into the room and took Fatemeh into his arms. They kissed deeply and she held him, as though afraid to let him go.

"They gave you nicer quarters than they gave us, Miss Fatemeh," said Billy.

Ramon and Fatemeh looked up. Sure enough, she had a nice bed and a desk. The only things that indicated her lack of freedom were a chamber pot and a window with iron bars that seemed more decorative than escape proof overlooking a field. The Golden Gate was visible beyond. Ramon and Fatemeh walked over to the window, hand-in-hand. She pointed. "They have mechanical owls in the field below."

Ramon peered through the window and shrugged. "The only problem is that I don't know how to fly one." He looked back at Luther. "Do you?"

The reporter shook his head.

"Then we need to get down to the water," said Billy. He stepped up beside Ramon and Fatemeh, then pointed. "I see boats tied up to a pier down by the waterfront."

"That's where we need to go, then," said Ramon.

All together, the three left the room. Luther tried the door at the end of the hall. It led to a staircase that ran along the back of the building. They took the stairs down to the ground floor. As they reached the door to the outside, someone upstairs shouted for people to wake up. The guard Ramon knocked out must have regained consciousness. They ran across the grassy field. As they did, alarm bells sounded and lanterns sprang to life. They reached the pier and found a rowboat tied to the dock. Ramon and Billy gingerly climbed aboard.

"Have you ever rowed one of these things before?" asked Ramon.

"Yeah, I once went paddling down the Rio Grande out of Mesilla," said Billy. "I like boats."

Ramon reached up to help Fatemeh aboard. Just then, a gunshot sounded. Ramon, Fatemeh and Billy ducked low as she climbed into the boat. At that point, they realized Luther had fallen. He lay on the dock, blood pooling under his left shoulder. Fatemeh scrambled back out of the rowboat and put her hands on the wound, staunching the flow of blood.

Ramon started to follow her, but she looked up. "You two get going. Find out what you can."

"But what about you and Luther?" shouted Ramon as Billy settled in at the oars.

"I'm a woman and Luther's wounded. We'll be okay, but I won't leave him."

Ramon fell back into a seat as Billy pushed away from the pier. A bullet whistled by and splashed in the water. Another smacked the boat's gunwale, sending up a spray of wooden slivers. They were over a hundred yards from the pier and fog rolled across the water. Ramon could just make out shadows joining Fatemeh and Luther on the pier. Ramon ground his teeth and considered jumping in the water and swimming back.

"Can you take one of these oars, Ramon?" asked Billy. "This isn't exactly easy."

Ramon turned around and blinked at Billy as though he were a stranger.

"You need to find out what the Russians are up to. That's what she wants you to do. She'll be okay until we get back."

Ramon frowned and shifted onto the bench next to Billy, then grasped an oar. It took them a few tries to coordinate their strokes, but they soon made progress toward the Russian side of the bay.

Curly Bill, sitting atop the Javelina, cradled the lightning gun's wand in his lap while he watched the sun rise. His stomach growled from hunger and he was parched from thirst. His ears still rang from the long rumbling ride north, but he was ready to go into Tucson and rob the place clean.

With a stretch and a yawn, he remembered going off to fight for the Confederate Army. Although he'd been little more than a kid, he spent many nights stalking Yankees, feeling hungry and desperate. After the war, he went home to find shortages that kept him hungry. He was fed up with other people having the good life while he had little more than the shirt on his back.

Curly Bill climbed down from the Javelina and shoved Gird awake. The lawyer rubbed his eyes. "What time is it?" He lay on a tarp they found in the Javelina's storage compartment.

"Time to get moving," said Curly Bill. "Sun's up."

"We got some coffee? Something for breakfast?"

Curly Bill's laugh was bitter. "We ain't got nothin' and we won't have nothin' till we finish today's business."

Gird frowned, but sat up, shook out his boots and put them on. After getting to his feet, he went behind a mesquite bush to relieve himself. When he returned, he folded up the tarp and placed it in the storage area. He opened another door in the Javelina's side and turned a spigot. He drew a small amount of water from the boiler and wet his parched lips and tongue. Curly Bill frowned, wondering why he hadn't thought of that. He held out his cupped hands and Gird briefly opened the spigot again. The water had the sharp tang of iron, but at least it was wet and his mouth felt a little better afterward.

Gird climbed into the cab to start the fire. Curly Bill walked around the camp's perimeter, looking for any signs of a dawn ambush. Walking around to the front of the Javelina, he saw the small town of Tucson, like a ripe fruit ready for plucking. Behind him, the Javelina rumbled to life. Smoke curled away from the stack at the machine's rear, drifting off into a clear, blue sky. Gird stuck his head out the door. "All right! We're ready to roll."

Curly Bill climbed into the Javelina's cab and Gird released the brake. The machine rolled forward. Gird kept the fire stoked at a moderate level and the speed lower than the day before, so Curly Bill felt like he could hear himself think. He ran through the plan in his mind, considering things that could go wrong and anticipating what he'd do under those circumstances. The Javelina seemed the least certain thing. He couldn't run it without Gird, so the attorney would stay in the cab. The next uncertain thing was the lightning gun. How many more shots did he have? He didn't really know.

Curly Bill frowned, thinking he liked the power these

newfangled devices gave him, but the uncertainties discomfited him. If this robbery worked out, he would make a point of getting to know these tools better.

An hour later, they reached the outskirts of Tucson. Richard Gird stoked the boiler and opened the steam valves. The Javelina lurched forward and barreled into the town's streets. Men and horses scrambled to get out of the lumbering giant's way. Curly Bill looked out the side window and caught the expressions on people's faces. He laughed at their fear and confusion.

A moment later, Gird released the clutch that started the rotors at the front of the Javelina spinning. They plowed through the bank's front wall. Gird stopped the rotors and continued a few feet forward. Satisfied that the roof wasn't going to cave in, Curly Bill hopped out of the cab and pointed his lightning gun at a teller who had frozen at the sight of the monstrous machine tearing through the brick wall.

"Anyone else here?" called Curly Bill over the Javelina's rumbling and chugging.

"Just the bank president," said the teller.

"Get him! We need all the help we can get." Curly Bill looked around and spied the safe. He climbed up to the control cabin and pointed that direction. Gird smiled and nodded.

The Javelina rolled forward and ripped through the vault door. Gird rocked the Javelina's head from side to side, to enlarge the hole, then turned off the rotor. Curly Bill waited a few minutes for the dust to settle, then jumped from the cab again. The teller and the bank president kneeled behind a desk, watching dumbfounded.

Curly Bill pointed the lightning gun at the men. "Into the safe. Bring all the money you can carry."

The teller nodded quickly, but the bank president hesitated a moment. Curly Bill fired an arc of lightning and incinerated the desk. The president rushed after the teller. Curly Bill stepped through the rubble to the Javelina's side and threw open the doors to the compartments within. Soon, the teller and the bank president appeared with bags of coins. Curly Bill tossed them into the bins atop the bricks and rubble from breaking into the building.

"Stop right there and put your hands where I can see them!"

Curly Bill whirled around and fired the lightning gun. He caught a brief flash of a sheriff's badge on a man's shirt before he was vaporized into black ash. A few bystanders who had gathered across the street to gape through the hole in the wall at the robbery disappeared. Curly Bill turned around and aimed his gun at the teller and the bank president. "Let's keep that money coming this way!"

The teller and manager delivered more bags of coins, and Curly Bill continued to toss them into the ore and debris bins. The bins were only partially full by the time the vault had been emptied. He licked his lips and longed for a saloon between Tucson and the Clanton ranch. "All right, you boys stay in the vault and you won't get hurt." They nodded rapidly. Curly Bill closed the doors on the Javelina's side, then climbed back in the cab. Gird backed the machine onto the street, then turned at the first corner they came to. The street was narrow and the Javelina clipped the post holding the overhang above the boardwalk. It collapsed behind them in a cloud of dust.

They turned two more corners until they returned to the main street. Curly Bill smiled at how their arrival had torn up the streets. There was nothing that could stop them and Tucson didn't have a sheriff anymore, but certainly someone would get up a posse and come after them. As they neared the edge of town, they passed a saloon with several men and ladies gathered on the porch. He opened the Javelina's door. "You folks got any whisky for a pair of Robin Hoods?"

"Thievin' Scoundrels is more like it!" called one man.

"I got somethin' for you, Sugar," called one of the saloon girls. She tossed a bottle end-over-end at the Javelina. Curly Bill caught it neatly out of the air and tossed a gold coin back her way. He closed the door and sat down on the chair in the cabin. "Now there's a treat! Cactus Wine! A mix of tequila and peyote juice. That'll keep us goin'!"

"Well, you're going to need to take a turn shoveling coal if you want us to keep going. My arms are tired," said Gird.

"All right, all right." Curly Bill pulled the bottle's cork with his teeth and took a swig, then replaced the cork and tossed it to Gird. "Now I'm ready for anything!" He took the shovel from his partner. As he did, a tingling sensation rippled along the back of his skull. For a moment, he thought he heard quiet voices whispering to one another. He looked around to see if there was anyone else. Not seeing anyone, he shrugged, but he realized they'd need to stop somewhere defensible on the way back.

"When we head back, let's turn before the San Pedro and follow the ridge of the Whetstone Mountains," said Curly Bill.

"Why?" Gird blinked. "I don't know about you, but I'm getting real thirsty and this rotgut only cuts thirst so much. Besides, there's better hunting down by the river."

"Don't worry," said Curly Bill. "We'll find something. We just need to make sure we can hold onto this money long enough to spend it."

The lawyer looked doubtful, but nodded anyway. He fell back into the cab's other chair while Curly Bill put on more steam and the Javelina rumbled out of Tucson, on its way eastward, back toward the Clantons' ranch.

The sun rose as Ramon and Billy reached the Golden Gate's northern bank. Ramon's arms were tired from the rowing, even though he knew it hadn't been far. If not for the light fog that shrouded the water, he suspected he could still see San Francisco. Billy hopped into the knee-high water and pushed the boat onto the beach.

He looked up at Ramon. "She's a healer. She did what she had to do."

Ramon shook his head as he climbed out of the boat. "I know. I just feel like I should have stayed with her. I'm worried about her ... and I'm worried about Luther."

"So am I," said Billy, "but our job is to find out if there really are mysterious creatures from beyond the stars controlling the Russians, and if so, see if we can reason with them." Billy sloshed over to Ramon and patted him on the back. "After all, what's the worst that could happen to her back there?"

"She could be executed for treason."

Billy's smile was far too cheerful for Ramon's mood. "Well, on this side, she could be executed as a spy—and given the mood the Russians are in, that seems far more likely."

Ramon brightened a little. "You're probably right." He took a moment to evaluate the coastline, then took his glasses off and cleaned the lenses with his shirttail. "So, how did you get so wise?"

"Working on a farm and learning about the Code of Bushido."

Ramon put on his glasses, then shook his head. "I've been around a lot of farms, my friend, but I've never heard of this Code of Bushido." He tucked his shirttail back in his trousers.

"That's 'cause you've never hung around the right farmers," said Billy.

"I just wish you'd had more sense when we met those soldiers in San Jose."

"Did you know who was tromping up the hall? Coulda been Russians!"

"I doubt pointing a gun at them would have made them happier than Americans."

Billy laughed. "Hey, at least it got us a free ride to San Francisco."

The two took a moment to study the countryside. "The way I see it, we have three choices," said Ramon. He pointed to the hills rising before them. "We can skirt these hills to the left and that should bring us right into Sausalito. We could take the boat around. We could climb and find a vantage point above the town, get an idea of how the Russians are camped."

"Option one sounds like we'll get our asses shot as spies. Option two don't sound much better, and my arms are tired." He smiled. "I like the third option."

"I do, too," said Ramon. They set out up the hill. Option three had its own disadvantages. The hillside was fairly steep and there wasn't much ground cover to hide them. With the sun in the east, they were illuminated to anyone below. With that in mind, they did their best to stay as close to any bushes and trees as they could. An hour later, they came to a place where they had a good view of the town.

Sausalito appeared to be a quiet seaside port filled with white and gray clapboard houses and buildings. Ramon thought it resembled the Presidio, just with more trees and lacking the tents that housed an army waiting to defend against invaders from the north. Ramon shivered and wished for a coat as a chill sea breeze blew.

Billy shook his head. "Not many boats out in the water. Not much movement. Just looks like a nice quiet day."

A train whistle pierced the morning air. Ramon shrugged. "Maybe the invasion force is on the train." Inexplicably, Ramon had a sudden giddy feeling of familiarity, like seeing a family member or an old friend long gone.

A twig snapped behind them. Billy and Ramon whirled around, drawing their revolvers. They faced two men with thick black mustaches, wearing long, dark coats, broad belts, and red kepis—similar to the ones American soldiers wore, except for the color. Ramon and Billy dropped their guns.

"I think we've found the Russians," said Billy.

CHAPTER TWELVE
DEFENDING THE HOMELAND

Curly Bill and Gird passed the cactus wine back and forth as the Javelina rumbled past the northern flank of the Whetstone Mountains. Although they could see the San Pedro River in the valley ahead, Gird did as they had discussed and turned the machine southward, hugging the mountains.

The lawyer drove the machine at a slow, but steady pace. Curly Bill guessed a horse could outrun them, especially for a short distance, but a horse would have to stop eventually. Still, he opened the door to make sure no one pursued them. He suspected he killed the person most likely to mount an immediate chase. Unless a deputy was experienced, it would take him a while to calm people down and then form a posse.

As they rolled over the undulating terrain, the ground creaked and popped. "Do you hear something?" asked Curly Bill.

Gird pursed his lips and listened. "It's nothing mechanical," he said at last.

Just then, the earth rumbled and the Javelina's body dropped backward in a cloud of dust and gravel. Gird and Curly Bill tumbled from their seats and went sprawling onto the pipes and levers at the back of the control cabin. Curly Bill cursed as he slammed into a hot pipe. He bolted backward, then worked to untangle himself from another pipe. When he finally extracted himself, he realized the floor canted upward at something close to a forty-five-degree angle. "What the hell happened?"

"Damn!" Gird shook his head and tried to perch among the pipes to get a look at the gauges. He pointed to Curly Bill. "Open up those two valves by your right hand. The stack in the rear is blocked somehow. Let's release some pressure till the fire dies down and figure out what we'll need to do to get out of here." He then reached up and set the brake.

"Where the hell are we?" Curly Bill asked the question as he reached out to turn the valves.

"No, no, no! The other way!" called Gird.

Curly Bill narrowed his gaze, but did as the lawyer told him.

"The Whetstone Mountains must have limestone formations in the base," said Gird as the needles began to show less pressure in the boilers. "Water must have hollowed it out and formed a cave. The limestone wasn't strong enough for a machine as big as the Javelina and we fell through." He made his way to the door and pushed it open.

Curly Bill followed him out. The Javelina sat at an angle, facing a rock wall, its treads perched on a rubble incline where the ground had collapsed. The tail-like smokestack was bent, but it looked repairable with a hammer and a little time.

He picked his way down the rocks further into the cave. It was almost noon and he could see the cave extended some distance into the mountainside. He looked over to Gird. "What would happen if you released the brake and let the Javelina roll backwards, down here into the cave?"

Gird blinked at him, then shook his head. "We want to get out, not further into this mess."

"Don't you see?" said Curly Bill. "If we back down in here, then you can make a better run at that slope of rock and use the cutting tools at the front to get past the wall."

Gird blinked again, but this time his expression turned thoughtful. "I think you've got something there." He looked around at the ground. "As long as the ground below us is solid, it might work."

"It'd give us a hideout." Curly Bill shrugged.

"All right, let's give it a try." Gird and Curly Bill picked their way back up through the rocks and climbed into the cab.

Gird reached up and grabbed the hand brake. He released it, then shifted the Javelina's transmission into reverse. There was just enough steam pressure left to allow the Javelina to roll backwards onto more level terrain.

"Now we just need to figure out the best way to get back up

the slope," said Gird.

Curly Bill looked around the cab. He untangled the lightning gun's wand and tubing from the pipes, then found what he sought. He held up a Henry rifle. "You do that, Mr. Gird."

"What are you doing?"

"Going hunting." Curly Bill retrieved a box of cartridges. "Seems like the best way to inaugurate our new home is with a good meal."

Larissa straddled the safety bicycle's seat in the shadows of her workshop. From there, she could see the parade grounds of Fort Bliss. Mounted behind the bicycle's seat was the electrical generator for one of the lightning guns. Its wand was mounted to the handlebars. She watched as Sergeant Harris brought Colonel Johnson around the corner. When they were in position, the sergeant waved. Larissa swallowed hard, then brought her goggles down over her eyes. She activated a lever that brought fuel rods together, then leaned over the bicycle's handlebars. It took just a moment for the engine to build up pressure, then she engaged the clutch and shot from the workshop, careening toward a target at the far end of the parade ground. Her coachman's hat flew off behind her.

She turned and made a wide circle, then eased her hand from the handlebar and brought it to the lightning gun's trigger. When she faced the target, she did her best to aim the weapon. She squeezed the trigger and cursed when the shot when wide and blew a chunk from the adobe wall behind the target. She tried again and this time vaporized the target. She let out a whoop, then made a sharp turn to avoid the wall.

A moment later, she tumbled over onto the grass, while the bicycle's rear wheel continued to spin. Johnson and Harris ran over to her, concerned looks on their faces. As soon as Larissa caught her breath, she began to laugh. "It works!" She reached down and disengaged the fuel rods.

The sergeant and colonel helped Larissa free herself

from the fallen bicycle. She rose unsteadily to her feet, then grabbed the colonel's arm to avoid toppling over. "Are you all right?" he asked, wide-eyed.

"I'm great." Larissa lifted the goggles from her eyes, then spit out some dirt and grass. "What do you think?"

"It looks like the most dangerous thing I've ever seen," said Harris.

"More dangerous than the ornithopters?" asked the one-time bounty hunter.

The sergeant shook his head slowly. "No, I suppose not more dangerous than that."

The colonel eyed the fallen bicycle. "It'll take some training so soldiers can stay upright on those things, but they're fast."

"And they'll hold a lightning gun." She picked the bicycle up from the ground, then gestured to the wall. "And you can shoot at targets on the ground, like mounted horsemen. I call it a lightning wolf."

"I like it," said the colonel. "Can we make more?"

Larissa walked the lightning wolf back toward the workshop. The colonel and Harris followed. "I have two more bicycles and I telegraphed Fort Sam Houston for five more. They should be here on tomorrow's train from San Antonio. We have parts to build ten ornithopters. I can take the engine components from them."

"Very good," said the colonel. "Get those two you have parts for rigged up right away, then I need you to train the first two volunteers how to ride them."

"Volunteers?" asked Sergeant Harris.

The colonel nodded. "Yes, you and Sergeant Lorenzo."

"But sir, I didn't..."

The colonel looked at Larissa. "Good work, Miss Crimson. Is there anything else you need from me?"

They reached the door to the workshop where Larissa spotted the coachman's hat on the floor. "I think I could use a new hat that doesn't fly off so easily."

The colonel smiled. "We'll be sure to find one."

Fatemeh found herself a prisoner in the same comfortable room where she'd been held before. Although she knew that Billy and Ramon had simply lifted the door out of its hinges, the door had been replaced and the hinges were on the outside. There seemed little she could do to escape.

The previous night, she held her hands on Luther Duncan's shoulder, doing everything she could to staunch the flow of blood as she watched Ramon and Billy row away into fog illuminated by the setting moon. Soldiers rushed to her side and aimed at the boat. Two of them fired until an officer shouted at them to cease. It would do no good to waste ammunition firing on an invisible boat.

She screamed when two more soldiers pulled her from Luther's body. "He's been shot! He needs help!" To their credit, the soldiers called for a medic, but they continued to pull her away. Now it was afternoon the following day and she still had no idea how Luther was or how Ramon and Billy were doing. She lay on the soft bed and looked up at the ceiling, alternately saying prayers of healing for Luther and protection for Ramon and Billy.

Exhausted, Fatemeh fell into a light slumber and dreamed of Ramon. He was a handsome man and strong, most assuredly, but what she really loved was how that strength was tempered by a desire for peace. That desire seemed almost as strong as that of Bahá'u'lláh—the messenger from God she followed. She had never met the great teacher, the manifestation of God himself, but she had known those who had, and even more who had corresponded with him. She hoped she could return to Persia and meet him, perhaps introduce him to Ramon.

She dreamed of being in Ramon's arms and then suffered the guilty pricking of conscience that stemmed from her Mohammedan upbringing and Bahá'í beliefs. The thought brought her back to the present. She wasn't always good at following rules. That's why she left Islam. It's how she encouraged Professor Maravilla to build a flock of mechanical owls. It's how she found herself in San Francisco, a prisoner for trying to cross into Russian-held territory to find out what was going on for herself and try to fix the situation.

A knock at the door roused her into consciousness. She

turned and dropped her feet to the floor as the door opened. A female guard entered followed by two male soldiers. "Excuse us, ma'am, but the Commanding Officer wants to see you."

"I don't suppose I have any choice, do I?"

"No, ma'am. You don't."

Fatemeh frowned, but put on her shoes. One soldier led the way out of the room while the other soldier and the female guard followed behind. They led her downstairs and across the compound to another building. Inside, they climbed a staircase then walked down the hall to stand before a door. The lead soldier knocked and a moment later, a gruff voice from within called for them to enter.

She followed the soldier into the office and found herself facing a man she had only seen once before. He had a long, drooping mustache and a small tuft of hair under his lower lip. His characteristic short, round hat hung on a coat rack by the door. "General Sheridan, thank you for seeing me."

"Miss Karimi, you realize you are a pain in the ass," said the general with no apology.

"I've been told that before."

The general didn't laugh. Instead, he sat back and folded his arms. "What in the hell are you doing here at the Presidio trying to take a boat across to Russian territory?"

Fatemeh swallowed. "I hoped I could stop the Russian invasion."

"Like you stopped the airships in Denver."

Fatemeh blinked. "We succeeded."

The general lifted an eyebrow. "Yes, but then you had Professor Maravilla's ornithopters and an assault force of pirates and outlaws. What do you have now? A reporter? Maybe a couple other people?"

"How is Mr. Duncan? Will he pull through?" Fatemeh took a step forward.

The female guard put her hand on Fatemeh's shoulder but she shrugged it off. The general held up his hand. "Never mind that. I'm convinced your interference in Denver saved lives, but I'm just as convinced you got damned lucky. Whatever you've got in mind, this is soldier's work." He leaned forward. "If you have an idea that can help us do our job, then please tell me."

"Your job is killing people, General Sheridan. I can tell you nothing to help with that."

The general ground his teeth and sat back. He looked at the guards. "Very well, lock her up."

"General, could I please see Luther Duncan? You must have questioned him since you know he's a reporter."

Sheridan sighed. "Just for a few minutes." He dismissed the group with a nod.

The soldiers led Fatemeh to another building. Inside, rows of beds filled a big white-walled room on both sides from end to end. She soon spotted Luther Duncan's bowler hat sitting on a nightstand. She darted away from the guards and sat down at a chair by his side. His eyes fluttered open.

"How are you doing?" she asked, attempting to sound cheerful.

Luther's smile was sad. "If all goes well, I'll have a useless left arm. If an infection sets in, they'll have to cut it off."

"At least you'll still have one arm to write with."

Luther snorted. "I'm left-handed."

"You can learn." Fatemeh bent over and kissed him on the forehead. "I'm just glad to know you're alive."

The reporter's smile brightened a little. "I've heard there are ways to record the sound of my voice. Maybe Professor Maravilla can build me something like that. Then, I wouldn't need to write at all."

"I'll make sure to suggest it to him."

Luther's eyelids fluttered closed, but she was pleased to see he just slept. The guard held out her hand. "Time to go."

Fatemeh nodded and followed the guard and the soldiers back to her room.

Masuda Hoshi listened as Professor Maravilla told about Bresnahan and Gird's bank robbery in Tucson followed by their getaway. The professor had not been in his bedroll when Hoshi and the Shieffelins awoke. Hoshi decided to follow the Javelina's trail while the Shieffelins waited for Maravilla. The samurai turned around when the Javelina's trail disappeared at the railroad tracks. He returned to the camp soon after Maravilla. Al handed each of them a cup of coffee and asked where the professor had been. "Conferring with my ... associate who has been watching Bresnahan and Gird."

"He must be a fast rider to get between Tucson and here in the time Hoshi was away," remarked Ed.

The professor sipped his coffee. Hoshi had seen no riders. Instead, he suspected the "demons" Billy and Luther discussed before he left Las Cruces, but remained silent on the matter. Throughout the narrative, it struck Hoshi that Maravilla seemed more concerned about what would become of the Javelina than the fate of people harmed or killed in Tucson.

"The Javelina dropped into a hole, but it would seem that Gird was able to make a path back up to level ground." Maravilla sounded almost giddy. "If we can disable the two men, we can drive it back."

"And return the money those scoundrels stole." Ed stroked his long beard.

Maravilla nodded. "Yes, yes," he said, almost as an afterthought.

Hoshi looked up at the sky. The sun approached the horizon. "We should set out right away, then."

"What?" Al's eyebrows came together. "It'd be near midnight by the time we reached the Whetstones."

"That would be perfect," said Hoshi. "If what the professor has told us is accurate..."

"It is, you can rest assured," interjected Maravilla.

"...then they will be tired. One will probably be on watch while the other sleeps. I can disable the watchman while one of you captures the sleeper in his bedroll."

"And we just drive the Javelina out of its burrow." Maravilla had a gleam in his eye.

"Yes..." Hoshi narrowed his gaze and studied the professor a moment before turning his attention to the Shieffelin brothers. "Let's have some dinner, then set out."

The Shieffelins agreed. Ed rustled up a quick rabbit stew, which included vegetables they had picked up when they were last in Tucson. Hoshi helped Al and Maravilla prepare the horses for the journey. By the time they finished, the stew was ready and the sun was setting. Hoshi found the rabbit tough and gamy for his taste. Nevertheless, he enjoyed the full meal after his sojourn through the desert. He longed for a cup of tea, but he contented himself with water from the San Pedro. He then asked to borrow the darkest clothes he could from the men. He rolled up a pair of Professor Maravilla's trousers and one of Al's jackets and strapped them to his saddle.

After cleaning up from the meal, they set out. The moon provided some light, but still, they took the ride slow. There was no need to tire out the horses on this journey. They forded the river near the southern rim of the Whetstone Mountains and rode high. As they drew near the place where the ground had collapsed under the Javelina, Maravilla withdrew a small telescope and scanned the area. Not seeing them, they rode forward a few hundred yards and looked again. This time, Maravilla passed the telescope to Hoshi.

Hoshi saw the broken Earth. Within the depression, moonlight glinted off black, glistening metal. The warrior nodded, then passed the telescope to Ed. He climbed off the horse and held out his thumb to gauge the distance, then retrieved the dark clothes he had borrowed. "Give me half an hour," he said. "I will disable the guard first, then the sleeping man if I can." He looked at the Shieffelins "I suggest you two follow. If I haven't disabled the sleeping man, he'll be your responsibility."

Hoshi removed his robe, then slipped on the black trousers and the dark jacket as he continued speaking. "After the men are disabled, you will drive the Javelina out of the hole. Then we'll confer to figure out the best way to return what they've stolen."

"Sounds like a good plan to me," said Ed.

"I can see why Colonel Johnson put you in charge of tracking down that lightning gun," said Al.

"Thank you," said Hoshi. "Now, let's see if his faith is justified." The warrior bowed, then crept off into the night. The clothes he wore were a little bigger than he'd liked. They rustled more than he wanted, but he hoped the two men were tired or drunk enough they wouldn't hear him approach. Or, if they did, they would mistake the soft rustlings for the sound of some wild animal.

Hoshi reached the hole's edge without incident. A man he didn't recognize sat atop the Javelina. He watched as the man's jaw dropped onto his chest and stayed that way for a few minutes until he came awake with a start and looked around. Studying the area, Hoshi saw a campfire's remains. From the bones nearby, he guessed the men had also had rabbit for supper.

The warrior looked up at the stars and the moon. The Shieffelins would be following him by now. He took another look around. The second person was nowhere to be seen. Either he slept in the cave's shadows or in the Javelina itself.

Hoshi waited until the man atop the Javelina dozed off again, then jumped down into the pit. He made a soft thud as he landed, but quickly fell back into the shadows. Gird came awake again and looked around. His eyes passed over Hoshi, then moved on without stopping. A moment later, his chin dropped back on his chest.

Hoshi took that moment to rush from the shadows to the rungs that climbed the machine's flank. Gird woke and gave a startled gasp as he looked up. Before he could bring his gun to bear, Hoshi threw a punch from his waist and knocked the lawyer out cold.

Looking around, he saw Ed and Al picking their way down the rocks into the cave. "Where's the other one?" called Al.

A shot rang out from the cave's shadows. Al fell backward, a red wound blossoming in his gut. He writhed on the ground as his brother rushed to his side. Curly Bill emerged from the shadows. "I suggest you get your brother to a doctor real soon."

Hoshi drew his revolver and aimed at Curly Bill. "William Bresnahan, you are under arrest. Drop your gun."

"You drop your gun!" The voice came from the pit's rim. Hoshi chanced a brief sideways glance. Two men led Professor Maravilla at gunpoint. One of them was Phineas Clanton. Hoshi didn't recognize the other, but he looked like a brother.

"Let Professor Maravilla help Ed Shieffelin get his brother to a horse, then I will drop my gun," called Hoshi.

The two Clantons looked at each other. After a moment, the younger one called out. "All right, but no funny business." He shoved Maravilla forward. The professor climbed down into the cave and lay down his tailcoat. The two men then lifted Al onto the coat and used it as a makeshift stretcher to carry him from the cave.

Two more men showed up on the rim and took in the scene. They appeared to be brothers—although not Clanton brothers—and they were armed. Hoshi let his own revolver fall to his feet where it landed with a clang.

"Tom! Frank! About time you boys showed up," called the younger Clanton.

"All right Chinaman," called one of the new arrivals. "Seems to me you got a choice. You can either follow your friends like a cowardly dog or stand there and let us aerate you."

Hoshi took a moment to evaluate the situation. Four men had the high ground. There was one man below. One was unconscious but stirring. To stay and try to fight was suicide. Better to retreat and fight another day. He climbed down from the Javelina and scrambled up the rocks after the Shieffelins and Maravilla. The derisive laughter from the Clantons and their friends rang in his ears.

Larissa watched as Harris and Lorenzo pedaled unsteadily around the parade ground, attempting to get the hang of the bicycles. She remembered her first time on a bicycle, the type with a large wheel in front, belonging to a man who had hired her to collect a bounty. Part of her price had been to have him show her how to ride the novel contraption. She never really mastered it, but she was good enough that it didn't take long to master the safety bicycles which were lower to the ground and more easily balanced.

She waved at the two men and had them bring their bikes back toward the workshop. The fort's blacksmith would be there soon to help her mount the engines and lightning guns. It was strange for her to work with a team. She was used to working alone and on her own schedule. Being on a team helped her stay focused. She wondered if that was a problem with Professor Maravilla. He had grown too accustomed to doing things at his own pace, starting and stopping, trying different things, different combinations until he found the right solution.

As Harris and Lorenzo pedaled up, Larissa noticed Colonel Johnson approaching. He held a paper in one hand and a flat box under his arm. He tipped his hat, then held out the paper he carried. It was a telegram reporting that men in an armored war machine had robbed a bank and that the sheriff had been killed by a gun that fired lightning bolts. She handed the telegram to Sergeant Harris, who read it, then handed it to Sergeant Lorenzo.

"Apparently Middleton is dead," said the colonel, "and your Japanese farmer has failed to recover the lightning gun."

Lorenzo swallowed. "Yes, sir."

The colonel's gaze drifted to Harris, then to Larissa. "What do you make of this giant war machine the telegram describes?"

Larissa shook her head. "It sounds almost like a locomotive that doesn't need rails. I've never..." Then she put her hand to her mouth and looked at Harris. "What if this Curly Bill Bresnahan somehow stole Professor Maravilla's mining machine?"

"Could that thing travel that far?" Harris's brow creased.

"If it had enough coal and water," said Larissa.

"I'm going to be in a lot of hot water with Washington real soon now." The colonel squeezed the box he carried, putting dents in it. He looked at Lorenzo again. "The train from San Antonio is here and I've asked them to wait. I want you on it. Get that lightning gun back. Do you understand?"

Lorenzo saluted. "Yes, sir."

"Sir," interjected Larissa. "I suggest we all go. We can take the lightning wolves with us and finish them en route to Tucson. If Curly Bill Bresnahan has stolen the Javelina, we'll need help going after him. This would be a chance to test out the lightning wolves in actual combat."

Colonel Johnson shook his head. "You're just barely learning how to use them and I don't need them shot to pieces."

"The plans are here, Colonel Johnson. Even if these particular machines are lost, you can build more," said Larissa.

"I respectfully suggest she's right," said Harris. "We can go and evaluate the tactical situation. If we don't need the lightning wolves, we won't use them, but if I were going, I'd like to have the best possible weapons along with us."

"This is not a democracy," growled Johnson through clenched teeth. He looked down at the machines. "Still, you make some sense." After a moment, he pointed at Lorenzo and Harris with the box he held. "I want you on that train to Tucson within the hour. Take the lightning wolves with you."

The two soldiers saluted and left to gather supplies. Larissa looked at the colonel. "What about me?"

"You'll stay here and keep working on the lightning wolves we do have." The colonel turned to leave.

Larissa folded her arms. "As you say, this is not a democracy. What's more, I'm not a soldier under your command. If you don't let me go with them, I'll resign and go anyway."

Colonel Johnson stopped in his tracks. "I could have you thrown in the stockade."

Larissa inclined her head. "You could, but you wouldn't get any more work done on the lightning wolves. If I go, not only will you get the first few finished, I could see how they work in combat and make modifications before they're sent against the Russians."

The colonel looked down at the ground. After a moment he turned around. "Very well. Pack up what you need. Be on that train before it leaves."

"Yes, sir!" She turned to leave.

"I almost forgot. This is for you." Johnson held out the box he'd been carrying and handed it to her. She opened it up. Inside was a flat cap, resembling the ones sea captains wore. She removed her goggles from the coachman's hat and placed them on the flat cap, then set it on her head.

"Thank you, sir."

"Go prove to me your lightning wolves can take down big game."

"Yes, sir." She saluted, then returned to the workshop to pack the tools she'd need for the journey.

Hoshi looked over at Al Shieffelin. His face was flushed and sweat beaded on his brow despite the cool desert air. Looking around, he spotted a large, flat rock illuminated by the morning sun. "We need to get the bullet out or else Al won't make it to Tucson," said the samurai.

Ed glanced over, his face drawn with worry. "I don't know nothin' about field surgery. I'm afraid I'd hurt him more than he already is."

"I fear I am not well versed in the healing arts, but perhaps there are ways I can help," said Maravilla.

"Thank you." Hoshi dismounted. "Fortunately, I have performed field surgery." He pointed to the flat rock as he dismounted. "Make him as comfortable as you can."

While Ed and Maravilla lay Al on the rock, Hoshi gathered wood and started a fire. Al thrashed about on the rock and muttered incoherent syllables. Maravilla also muttered to himself. A moment later, he reached out and touched Al's forehead. The miner calmed and his muscles relaxed. Hoshi narrowed his gaze—some innate ability of Maravilla or the demons?

Hoshi thrust his Kozuka knife into the fire to sterilize the blade, then removed it from the fire. He handed it to Ed, while waiting for it to cool, then pulled the shirt, sticky with blood away from the wound so he had a better view. Whatever Maravilla had done seemed effective since he only flinched a little. He went to his saddlebags and retrieved a pair of wooden hashi sticks. "Do you have whisky?"

Ed glanced at his horse. "Yeah, in the right saddlebag."

Hoshi retrieved a flask, poured a little over the hashi sticks, then knelt down beside Al and took the knife back from Ed. He glanced up at Maravilla. "How sedated is he?"

"He does not sleep, but his nerves are quiet. You should be able to proceed," said the professor.

Hoshi cut into the wound with the Kozuka knife. Al let out a piercing scream, but fell quiet as he passed out. Ed looked frantically from Maravilla to Hoshi. The samurai reached up and checked Al's pulse. "He's all right, just sleeping."

Ed nodded, but still looked between the two, unconvinced.

Hoshi opened the wound with the hashi sticks. The bullet was down a little over an inch, near a glistening piece of intestine. Ed's eyes went wide and he ran off a few yards and vomited near a cholla. Flipping the hashi sticks around, Hoshi reached in and extracted the bullet.

He stood and tore strips from his robe, then rinsed the wound as best he could with the whisky. Ed retuned as he and Maravilla applied the dressing. Hoshi handed the whisky bottle to Ed, who downed the remainder.

Al's pulse still seemed good as they lifted him onto a horse. As they rode into Tucson, Hoshi looked over at Maravilla. "Do demons now possess him?"

Maravilla's mouth twitched up into a grin even as his brow furrowed. "No ... no demons possess him." He didn't explain further and Hoshi decided not to press with Ed in earshot.

That afternoon, they arrived in Tucson, which looked like a war zone. They received directions to the nearest doctor and before long, Hoshi, Maravilla, and Ed stood in a semi-circle, watching as Doc Ellison examined Al's wound. After a moment, the doctor looked up and removed the pince nez spectacles he wore. "You did a fine job of field surgery, Mr. Hoshi. There's nothing left for me to do but stitch the wound and treat his fever."

"It would be more appropriate to address me as Mr. Masuda," said Hoshi.

The doc shrugged as he turned around and retrieved fresh bandages from a wooden shelf.

"There's not much more for you gents to do," said the doctor. "If you want to find a hotel room, you can let me know where you're staying and I'll send word if his condition changes.

"Yes, I think we'll do that," said Ed.

The three left the doctor's office and blinked at the bright daylight. Down the street, a gaping hole indicated the bank Curly Bill and Richard Gird had robbed. Rubble still littered the streets where the Javelina had backed out.

Maravilla pointed out that they were next door to a saloon. The sign in the window advertised a free lunch. "I don't know about you gentlemen, but I would think better after I've had a good meal."

Hoshi gave a sharp nod. Ed sighed and glanced worriedly at the doctor's office, but acquiesced. Inside the saloon, the three found a table. The barkeep approached and they each ordered a shot of whisky and the lunch special. The whisky showed up soon after. Ed downed his. Maravilla passed his glass over to the miner. Hoshi took a sip off the top of the shot glass.

"So, what do we do now?" asked Ed.

"A posse will certainly ride out at some point," said Hoshi. "We should warn them what they're up against."

"Now that the Clantons have reunited with Brocius and Gird," said Maravilla, "it will take more than a posse to stop them."

Ed reached out and took Hoshi's shot glass and downed it. The barkeep arrived a moment later with plates of food. He topped up their shot glasses, then left them alone. "So, what do you propose we do?" asked Ed.

"I believe my friend Geronimo would serve as a powerful ally in this affair," said Maravilla.

Ed's eyes widened. "Geronimo's a friend a' yours?" asked the miner.

"He would not appreciate having the Javelina on Apache land and he has warriors that could assist us." Maravilla took a tentative sip of his whisky before Ed snatched it. "Besides, I promised I would return and tell him who set the clockwork skeleton on the camel's back."

"If it's all the same to you," said Ed as he tucked into his sausage and deviled eggs, "I'll stay here and warn the posse. It'll let me stay close to my brother in case there's any news."

Hoshi sampled the sausage and frowned. He could use a light soup or perhaps some rice. Still, he ate enough to sustain himself, then passed the rest to Ed.

CHAPTER THIRTEEN
JAVELINA, WOLVES, AND OWLS

The Russian soldiers led Ramon and Billy into Sausalito. Ramon looked around at the pleasant town, hugging the steep, tree-covered shoreline, facing San Francisco Bay— or, technically, Richardson's Bay. His brow creased, as he wondered how he knew that. Either way, the pleasant town with its gray-shingled houses looked like a place he could settle down and call home. With that thought, he considered his decision to pursue a diplomatic career. Such a career would likely mean a busy life in far less idyllic surroundings than this. He would miss the quiet, rural life, but still, he could keep places like this peaceful—not overrun by invaders. The doubts he once had about himself seemed far away. Even if he decided not to be a diplomat, he could still settle down in a town like this and work as a lawyer or maybe a judge.

Billy's eyes drifted from porches to windows to alleys. His hand hovered near his empty holster, wanting to draw the confiscated gun. Ramon imagined Billy sought escape routes. Following his gaze, Ramon saw men in black uniforms, buttons up the sides of long coats. Many of them wore red kepis just like their captors. Some spoke casually with people in work clothes or business suits. What Billy and Ramon had not seen from above was that the Russian Army already occupied Sausalito and the town folk seemed pleased to welcome them. Neither wreckage nor tents littered the town, giving the illusion no invasion had transpired. It seemed the Russians had taken up residence in the small town's boarding houses and hotels. Were there enough Russians to fight the force across the bay in San Francisco? Ramon couldn't tell.

Ramon thought it odd he didn't feel discomfort in this strange town, being escorted through the streets by armed guards. Certainly, he didn't feel as uncomfortable as he had when captured in San Jose and carted up to the Presidio. It was almost as though old friends surrounded him. He rubbed his fingers through his hair as he considered that. No one around him looked familiar. He had never been in Sausalito and didn't know anyone there, much less any Russians. The only Russians he had met died on an airship over Denver three months before and they hadn't exactly treated him with warmth and hospitality.

The soldiers led Ramon and Billy into a rooming house. They exchanged a few words with the proprietor, who handed them a set of keys. With that, the soldiers escorted them upstairs and placed them into a comfortable room with two single beds. Billy went to the window and looked out while Ramon sat down on one of the beds. After a moment, Billy went to the door. Gingerly, he tried the knob and grinned when it turned. Opening the door, he saw a guard. Waving, he closed the door and sat down on the other bed, opposite Ramon.

"We've got to find a way out of here," he said.

Ramon took off his boots, and lay back on the bed, exhaustion from the night escape and the long foray through the hills above town finally taking their toll. "Our job is to find out what's going on here. I have a feeling these gentlemen are going to take us to someone who can answer our questions."

"How do you know that?" Billy snorted. "For all we know, they could have just dropped us here so we wouldn't be in the way when they invade San Francisco."

"If we were in the way, they could have just shot us." Ramon rubbed his eyes. "No, I have a feeling they want to talk as much as we want to talk to them." He let his eyes drift shut even as Billy raised more objections.

It was late afternoon as Hoshi followed Professor Maravilla into the Dragoon Mountains east of Tucson. Sweat beaded on the former samurai's forehead despite the shade afforded by the takuhatsugasa. The sunlight illuminated the stark, yellow rocks that were strewn across the landscape, as though giants had used them in a game of marbles, grown bored, and walked away. The professor looked around, fascinated. Sometimes he would mutter to himself. At this point, after Maravilla demonstrated knowledge of the Javelina's position and helping to sedate Al, Hoshi was convinced the demons were real.

Once among the rocks, Hoshi's keen ears caught birdcalls, a little too loud and a little too sharp to be natural. The responses came a little too quick. He wasn't surprised a few minutes later when four riders appeared—three men and one woman—holding lances. He'd heard about women warriors among the Apache. Of more concern, he suspected rifles or arrows were pointed in their direction from somewhere among the rocks. That's what he'd do if he were shogun of a stronghold.

The mounted warriors looked from one to the other. One man pointed to Maravilla and another muttered words to the woman, who nodded and smiled. Finally, the leader spoke up. "You have returned to us, Professor, but you've changed your traveling companion."

"It is good to see you Baishan," answered the professor. "I wish the circumstances were happier and Miss Crimson were here, but I have grave news and this gentleman might be able to help us."

The warrior called Baishan gave a sharp nod, then motioned for Maravilla and Hoshi to follow. He led them further into the rocks, where they found a large encampment. A natural basin in the rock held water. It had been so dry, Hoshi guessed it must be filled from an underground stream, or someone filled it from an unseen river in the mountains. The warriors led them to a makeshift corral and dismounted, then allowed Hoshi and Maravilla time to attend to their horses.

As they finished, the sun was low enough that the rocks cast long shadows through the camp. Many warriors had set up campfires outside their shelters. Baishan led Maravilla and Hoshi to one of those crude, dome-like structures made of sticks and scrub brush. There a bright fire illuminated the faces of two older warriors. Hoshi took the elder warriors' measure and noticed the reverential way the younger warrior addressed them in their own language.

"Thank you for agreeing to meet with us, Geronimo."

Maravilla looked at the warrior, but his eyes soon darted away. Apparently, it was taboo to look into an Apache's eyes. "I am pleased to see you as well … Kas-tziden." Hoshi noted the pause. Did the professor recall the name or did the demons whisper it in his ear?

The Apaches offered a simple meal of dried meat and fruit. The warrior called Geronimo spoke, and Baishan translated. "He wants to know more about the danger you speak of."

Maravilla described the search for the clockwork skeleton's creator and how he and the person called Larissa Crimson found the miner's camp. He then told about the mining machine's creation and how men stole it to rob a bank in Tucson. He concluded with the story of the failed attempt to recover the machine. Baishan translated.

Geronimo frowned thoughtfully, then spoke. "It would seem the spectral camel rider was a portent of evil after all," translated Baishan. Geronimo sat back, folded his arms and spoke again.

Baishan frowned as he translated. "He doesn't see how this is a problem for Apaches. This seems a matter for white men to sort out on their own."

"I would have been inclined to agree up until the point where the Clantons and the McLaurys rejoined Brocius and Gird." The professor put his hands on his knees and gazed into the fire. "You see, the Clantons want to make this area safe for white settlers."

The third warrior—a man with fingers bent with arthritis— spoke in broken English. "And that means using this … Javelina … to destroy Apaches."

"I'm afraid so," said the professor.

Geronimo gazed into the fire. After a moment, he spoke and Baishan translated. "Then we will fight with you. Rest now and we will make plans in the morning."

Hoshi took a deep breath and looked up to the stars. He considered the battles that drove him from his home. Fleeing Japan after his shogun's death left him with a sense of guilt. Honor dictated he take his own life. Yet, death had never seemed like the right choice. Now he understood the path chosen for him. Geronimo reminded him of his shogun. Like the samurai, the

Apaches would take a stand against an encroaching force, and attempt to drive it away. Unlike Japan, though, this was not a force within their culture. It was a force from outside. Hoshi did not know the correct way to pledge loyalty to an Apache chief, but he silently vowed fealty to Geronimo in the upcoming battle.

Billy awoke in a jumble of blankets on the rooming house bed. He blinked a few times at the red-hued sunlight that filtered in from outside, wondering when exactly he had fallen asleep. He remembered checking the window. It was not latched. He could have gotten out, but where would he have gone? Back to San Francisco where he was a wanted man? At some point, he concluded that Ramon was right and the best answer was to see where the guards took them. Sometime after that, he must have collapsed into the bed and fallen asleep out of pure exhaustion.

Two plates, each containing a pastry of some sort lay on a table by the door. Billy untangled himself from the blankets and poked the pastry with a fork and steam escaped. The scent told him they were meat pies. Their captors had brought supper.

Ramon still lay in the bed across the way, snoring softly. Billy went to the door. A new guard stood there. "Say, do you speak English?"

"Da," said the guard.

Billy considered that for a moment then continued. "Where's the closest outhouse? Or does this place have indoor facilities?"

The guard pointed down the hall to the staircase. Billy shrugged, then grabbed his hat and ambled along the hall and down the stairs. Once there, he met the proprietor, wearing a striped shirt, an apron, and a bow tie, with a broom and dustpan in his hand. "I'm lookin' for the outhouse. Can you point me the way?"

"We have indoor facilities, but they're just through the kitchen and turn left, Mr. McCarty."

Billy tipped his hat and turned toward the door. Just before he stepped through, the proprietor's words struck home. He spun on his heel. "How do you know my name?"

The proprietor shrugged. "Because Mr. Morales knows your name."

"Hunh." Ramon must have been awake, spoken to people and returned. Not seeing any guards around, another question occurred to Billy. "So, what do you think about this whole Russian invasion?"

The proprietor smiled. "You know it's strange, but I feel like they have our best interests at heart. They really want to make the world a better place."

"Hunh." At that point, Billy's curiosity had to wait until after he visited the facilities. When he returned, the proprietor was gone. Stomach growling, he returned to the room where he knew food waited.

Ramon sat up on the bed, rubbing his eyes.

"You had a good nap," said Billy.

"Once my head hit the pillow, I was sound asleep. I don't think a freight train could have moved me."

Billy sat down at the table and cut into one of the meat pies, hoping food would stimulate his groggy brain. He couldn't quite reconcile what Ramon just said with the proprietor's statement about knowing their names. He began to wish he was back in Las Cruces, tending green chilies.

"The first thing we need to determine is whether the Javelina is still hidden in the cavern by the Whetstone Mountains, or if they've taken it back to the Clantons' ranch," said Professor Maravilla.

Baishan translated for Geronimo, who turned and spoke to the young woman at his side. She nodded sharply and left with two of the men. "Those scouts will find out and report back," said Baishan.

Maravilla, Geronimo, Hoshi, and Baishan sat in a ring with the other Apache leaders under a clear sky. It was a hot morning, but a light breeze blew, making it tolerable.

The elder called Nana spoke and Baishan translated. "He

wants to know how we can hope to stop your infernal machine."

"Although it is meant to be quite durable from the front, it is vulnerable from the rear and the bottom," explained Maravilla. "We could jam the rotary transmission, break a steam line or simply clog the exhaust if necessary." The professor then went on to explain how each one could be accomplished. As he spoke, Hoshi noticed a low drone and a faint vibration.

Just as he excused himself from the circle, the lookouts began whistling their birdcalls. Hoshi made for the corral and saddled his horse. Soon the birdcalls turned into shouts. Men fell back into camp. Geronimo and Nana shouted orders. Some of the women and the older men gathered up camp supplies, preparing for an evacuation if needed. Other women along with most of the men retrieved rifles, bows, and arrows—anything they could use in a fight. Warriors ran to the corral to retrieve horses. Maravilla followed and arrived just as Hoshi drew himself into the saddle.

"What's going on?" shouted the professor.

"It's no longer a question of whether the Javelina will be at the Whetstones or the Clanton Ranch. It is here!" Hoshi snapped his reins and rode out of the corral.

As he passed the men and women forming ranks, several loud cracks and pops resounded among the rocks of the Dragoon Mountains. Despite the clear sky, his nose caught the metallic scent of ozone, like after a lightning strike. More rumbles echoed around the camp, like rocks sliding down a mountain. Hoshi paused for a moment, seeking high ground. He spotted a rock tower a few hundred yards away, being vacated by a scout who either had seen enough or didn't want to be exposed. Hoshi rode for the rock tower, passing the young scout as he rushed to join the defenders at the camp.

Hoshi dismounted and climbed. Just as he reached the top, several non-combatants ran past, carrying what they could. The rumbling grew louder and he turned back toward the encampment.

The Javelina burst through the rocks into the clear. The cutter on the front spun furiously. Apaches tried to encircle it. There were faint pops and plinks as little puffs of smoke left the rifles. The lightning gun's wand emerged from a side window. With a loud crack and a burst of light, several warriors, including Baishan vanished in a vicious black cloud of smoke. Hoshi turned away, blinking back the spots before his eyes. From Maravilla's explanation, he knew he needed to get behind the Javelina. Whoever had the lightning gun was inside, making the rear that much more vulnerable. His vision clearing, he turned around and took in the scene again. Three mounted cowboys rode into view, covering the Javelina's rear quarter. Hoshi nodded. He knew how to deal with such men.

Gunshots from behind interrupted his thoughts. He whirled around and two men on horseback swept down from the hills behind him. They drove the retreating Apaches back toward the camp, into the Javelina's path.

He eased his way down the rock pillar, back toward his horse, but stopped when the clean-shaven McLaury brother rode up and aimed a rifle at him. "You up there on the rock, get on down from there."

"Very well." Hoshi sprang from the rock and knocked the man out of the saddle. He rolled onto his feet as the man coughed and sputtered. The samurai darted forward and pulled him off the ground, then slammed him into the rock. Hoshi remembered that the Shieffelins referred to this McLaury as Tom.

"Are you insane?" snarled Hoshi. "The Javelina has been used to rob a bank. Are you just going to compound your crime even further?"

Tom McLaury laughed. "Compound our crime? Hell, we're trying to fix what Brocius and Gird did. We figured if we eliminated the Apache threat right now, the law might just forgive them what they did to the sheriff and the bank in Tucson."

Hoshi growled deep down in his throat. He hated that logic, but knew Tom McLaury could be right. He threw a punch, knocking McLaury to the ground, then he returned to his horse to see what he could do to minimize the slaughter.

Whatever the Russians had planned for Ramon and Billy, they were in no hurry to do it. The proprietor, who they learned was named Mr. Chandler, brought meals and a deck of cards the next morning. Morning wore on into afternoon and Ramon just called Billy's bluff when a knock sounded. Mr. Chandler poked his head in. "Colonel Dvorkin would like to meet you."

"About time," said Billy, tossing his cards on the table. "Who the hell is Colonel Dvorkin?"

"He's the leader of the Russian expeditionary force," explained Chandler.

The two men stood and followed the proprietor down the stairs to the kitchen where coffee and pastries were laid out on the table. A tall man with a long dark coat and a red peaked cap stood with his hands behind his back. "I am your host, Colonel Alexei Dvorkin," said the man. "I am sorry to have kept you waiting so long, but there have been … arrivals to attend and arrangements to make."

"Yeah, planning an invasion's real time consuming," said Billy.

Ramon shot him a warning glance and Billy muttered a faint apology.

Unfazed by Billy's remark, the colonel held out his gloved hand. Billy eyed it for a moment, then shook. Dvorkin then turned to Ramon.

The moment Dvorkin clasped Ramon's hand, there was a crack like lightning and Ramon was somewhere else—a barren, parched landscape that reminded him of the Valley of Fire in New Mexico. Undulating, rocky ground rolled away in the distance on all sides. Overhead deep blue skies were streaked with white cirrus clouds. A dust devil swirled up from the sands and drifted lazily toward him. As it did, he noticed a few tiny dust motes floating near his head.

As the dust devil came closer, he realized he was not hearing or even feeling a breeze, but tiny whisperings like a million hushed voices all speaking at once. The small cloud of dust motes first orbited Ramon's head, then swirled away and spun around the dust devil. Ramon sensed a complicated array of emotions from joy to worry to disagreement and even anger.

Ramon pushed his glasses up on the bridge of his nose as he looked around and tried to figure out what happened to Alexei Dvorkin and the boarding house.

"Alexei Dvorkin is irrelevant for the moment. We are the ones you seek."

Ramon looked around. It was as though the voice came from the dust devil, but it also echoed in his head, like a thought. He nodded to himself. "Are you the being called Legion?"

"We are Legion."

The booming voice echoed from a second source. He looked around and focused on the smaller collection of dust motes that floated near his head.

"We are Legion."

Somehow, he knew the fainter voice came from the smaller, swirling cloud.

"So you're both part of the same—" Ramon tried to remember the words Maravilla had used "—swarm."

"I am Legion that has been traveling with the Russian Army along the West Coast of North America," came the voice from the dust devil.

"I am Legion that has been traveling with Professor Maravilla and then you," said the smaller swarm.

"If you have been traveling with me, why didn't I know until now?"

"We chose not to make ourselves known."

"Why?"

"Why?"

Ramon backed up a step, surprised to hear the dust devil echo his question. If they were one and the same, why didn't the dust devil know about the smaller cloud?

"We discovered the experiment is flawed," said the little cloud.

"Indeed, there has been a setback, but we have modified the experiment," said the dust devil.

Ramon tried to wrap his head around what was happening. Somehow, he saw a visualization of Legion, who had become separated by distance and the two parts could not communicate. Now they were reunited.

"That is correct," interjected the dust devil.

Ramon shivered at the idea a dust devil could read his mind. "So, what exactly is this experiment?"

"The unification of mankind to prevent the destruction of the species," said the dust devil.

"Your method is flawed," persisted the small cloud.

"Your logic is flawed through your close interaction with a few individuals," said the dust devil. *"You begin to see yourself as an individual. Despite our reunion, you stand apart."*

"I do so because you are wrong," said the small cloud.

Ramon's mouth grew dry as he began to grasp the full nature of what was going on. When he considered becoming a diplomat, he never envisioned helping creatures from the stars understand each other's points of view.

Hoshi had a plan. He met up with Geronimo and the two did their best to communicate through hand gestures, drawings and the few English words Geronimo knew. They wound their way through the rocks, careful to avoid the horsemen's attention. The Apaches knew the Dragoon Mountains much better than the Clantons. Many found unguarded paths and escaped. It kept this day from turning into an utter massacre, providing slim comfort. The Clantons had succeeded in killing enough warriors that it would be some time before they could raid any settlement the Clantons wanted to build. In that way, the Clantons had already won.

Hoshi asked Geronimo to cover him while he rushed the Javelina. He would crawl underneath and wedge his wakizashi into the gears that transmitted power from the steam engine to the wheels. It would destroy the blade, but it should jam up the gear works and keep the Javelina from continuing its rampage.

They came to a break in the rocks that afforded a view of the Javelina. It smoldered and rumbled, but wasn't driving forward. None of the horsemen were in sight. Hoshi looked at Geronimo. The two men nodded to one another and Hoshi made a break from the rocks. As he did, a low whine accompanied by a buzzing rose near the Javelina. Hoshi looked, but couldn't find the source.

"Stop right there, Chinaman or I blow Geronimo straight to Hell!" Curly Bill stood up on top of the Javelina. He aimed the lightning gun's wand at the Apache war leader. "I don't care what armor you're wearing. It won't stand up against this gun."

Hoshi's frown deepened. Casting a sidelong glance over his shoulder, he saw Geronimo tense. The Apache leader would certainly raise his weapon and sacrifice his own life to give Hoshi the chance to stop the mining machine. The samurai would do no less if he were in the same position. He prepared to leap under the Javelina. He would not allow Geronimo's sacrifice to be in vain.

The buzzing Hoshi heard earlier grew to a din. Despite the Javelina's rumbling, even Bresnahan heard it and allowed his attention to drift, giving Geronimo the opening he needed. He fired and Bresnahan fell backwards.

Before Hoshi could dive under the Javelina, a strange, frail vehicle flew up the path. There was a crack of lightning and the Javelina's dented, tail-like exhaust pipe exploded. Hoshi threw his arm over his eyes, then blinked back spots. Steam billowed from the hole and the Javelina's rumbling grew labored. The rotor at the front slowed.

The attacking vehicle skidded to a stop, sending up a shower of small pebbles. Hoshi realized it was a bicycle with a lightning gun's wand mounted on the handlebars. A makeshift platform behind the saddle-like seat held the power pack. A young woman rode the machine like a horse. She lifted a pair of goggles. "Get the Javelina's driver. We still need to round up the horsemen."

She lowered the goggles again and thumbed a small lever on one handlebar and sped away, slipping and sliding on the dust. Hoshi thought for sure the machine would slide out from under her, but she kept it under control.

Hoshi looked back at Geronimo and shrugged.

"Larissa Crimson," said the warrior, seeming to understand the implied question.

With that, Hoshi and Geronimo rushed the Javelina's control cab. Throwing the door open, they found Richard Gird rapidly spinning wheels and throwing levers, trying to stop the pressure drop in the steam engine. After a moment, Gird looked up. He raised his hands and exited the vehicle.

With Gird in custody, they walked around to the Javelina's

far side. Army soldiers rode two more bicycles like Larissa Crimson's. Sergeant Lorenzo, the man who had recruited Hoshi for this strange adventure, rode one. Between him and the other soldier they herded Frank McLaury, Phin, and Ike Clanton. A moment later, Larissa appeared, leading Tom McLaury by gunpoint. "This one was the easiest. I found him sleeping by a rock over there."

As she spoke, Professor Maravilla looked out from behind a rock outcropping. He ran out, but stopped short. His attention seemed divided between Larissa, the modified bicycles, and something else. Finally, he held his arms open and Larissa rushed up and embraced him. They stood apart after just a moment.

"We have a problem," said the professor.

"I know. That's why we're here." Larissa flashed a whimsical smile.

"Not this problem, but thank you for what you've done." He gave in to his desire to take a closer look at the bicycles. Now that Hoshi had a clear look, he could see that a small engine had been added to the bicycle's drive assembly. That accounted for the speed and noise.

"I call it a lightning wolf," said Larissa.

Hoshi stifled a laugh; so fierce a name for such a strange and fragile machine. Still, he could see its potential.

The professor looked up with pride in his eyes. "You have done well. Splendid, in fact. I'm surprised these handled the terrain so well."

"The rocks are pretty smooth up here. That helped," said Larissa.

"Now isn't this a touching reunion."

Everyone turned around and saw Curly Bill on top of the Javelina. His shoulder bled where he had been shot, but he held the lightning gun aimed at Larissa and the professor. "Always make sure you've wrapped up all your loose ends." He pulled the trigger, but the lightning gun didn't fire. Instead, the whine from the pack increased.

"Hit the dirt!" shouted Lorenzo. "It's building up an overload."

Hoshi caught a glimpse of Bresnahan trying to remove

the pack just before a bright flash of light and a shockwave knocked Hoshi to the ground. Metal shrapnel from the top of the Javelina flew through the air. Hoshi huddled into a ball, covering his face. When he looked up, he saw that no one was seriously injured—no one except Curly Bill. At Hoshi's feet lay his still-scowling head, curly hair smoldering. A little further on, his hand still grasped a blackened strap.

Larissa swallowed, then spun to face the professor. "You said there was another problem?"

"Our friends … Ramon and Fatemeh. They're in trouble. The Russian and American armies are about to collide in San Francisco and they're right in the middle of it."

Larissa stood up and brushed the dust from her clothes. "Good thing we have a westbound train available."

The sun sat low on the horizon and Fatemeh lit the oil lamps in her comfortable prison. She had been allowed out once to see Luther Duncan. Otherwise, she sat in the room and the only people she saw were the ones who came to bring her food or empty her chamber pot. She asked at one point if she could see General Sheridan again. The guard agreed to take her request to the general, but she never heard a response.

One guard brought her a copy of Jules Verne's *Journey to the Center of the Earth* translated into English. She felt like she was trapped in the Earth's center for all the help she was being to anyone. She read a few paragraphs then looked up at the view out the window. She smiled when she saw a burrowing owl sitting on the bars. The owl chirped and danced from one foot to the other.

She moved slowly to the window and opened it. The owl flew over to the grating on another window. Fatemeh whistled much as the owl had, then stepped back from the window. A moment later it returned. She gave a brief curtsey and whistled again. The owl flitted up to the top of the bars and looked at a hinge. It chirped and moved from one foot to the other again.

Fatemeh's eyebrows came together. She stepped to the window and looked. Just like the door, the bars had hinges that could be unscrewed by hand, but these were within her reach. She looked down and watched the activity in the camp. There was too much at the moment, but in another two or three hours...

She settled back into her book. After a while, the bugler played "Taps." She extinguished the lights around the room and climbed into bed and closed her eyes. A short time later, the door rattled. A woman looked in, then closed and locked the door. Fatemeh threw back the sheets and went to work on the hinges. She unscrewed the upper one, then the one below, which allowed her to push the metal grating free. She climbed out the window and hung on to the windowsill. At that point, she dangled only eight feet from the ground. She let herself drop. Hitting the ground with a thud, she tumbled over. She rubbed her ankle as she looked around to see if anyone noticed her escape.

The infirmary was across the way. She thought for a moment about rescuing Luther Duncan, but injured as he was, he would be best off if he stayed put. She turned and limped to the field where she'd seen the ornithopters. As she walked, her ankle improved. Thankfully she hadn't sprained it. Arriving at the field, she found an ornithopter readied for flight. A pair of fuel rods sat in the seat. With a prayer of thanksgiving, she climbed into the machine, and activated the steam engine.

The engine's chugging apparently alerted someone, because she heard a sputter and a crackle, then a strange, intense light swept across the field. As it passed a tree, she saw yellow eyes and heard an annoyed screech. A great horned owl flapped away. She engaged the engine, then activated the spring-loaded legs. On the third hop, she was able to get enough air under the wings to get airborne. An alarm klaxon sounded just as she got her bearings and made for the Golden Gate.

CHAPTER FOURTEEN
A LEGION MULTIPLIED

When night fell, Billy found himself back in the hills above Sausalito. The chill breeze blowing in from the water tempted Billy to light a fire, but he didn't want to alert any of the soldiers who might be patrolling the woods. Even so, he jumped every time some small creature rustled through the underbrush.

He looked toward San Francisco and reflected on the day's events. He had waited a full five minutes to see if Ramon or Colonel Dvorkin would move again. He even tried to move them himself, but found them stiff as boards. Mr. Chandler, the proprietor of the rooming house, walked in shortly thereafter. "Oh dear," he said. "I better let Major Zinchenko know what's happened." He straightened his bow tie.

"Who's Major Zinchenko," asked Billy.

"The colonel's second in command." Chandler looked down at his feet and shook his head. "He's not going to be happy about this." With that, he turned and left.

Billy considered the best course of action. Ramon and Colonel Dvorkin were much like General Gorloff had been on the Russian airship over Denver. That had happened because the creature called Legion controlled the general. "Legion, are you in there? Can you hear me?" He waited a minute, then tried again. He went to the kitchen and found a pitcher of water. Returning a moment later, he tossed it at Ramon, who remained perfectly still, just dripping wet.

As he pondered what to do next, Chandler returned with another Russian officer, presumably the Major Zinchenko he had mentioned. The Russian took in the scene, then pointed at Billy. "He's done something to them. Arrest him!"

Chandler furrowed his brow and shrugged. Billy grinned,

took advantage of the confusion, and ran out the backdoor into the alleyway, then ducked in between two buildings. Soon there were shouts and several pairs of boots tromped by. As he suspected, it didn't take long for the major to find people to take up the chase. He waited for a while and considered what to do.

Even though Legion didn't talk to him, Billy guessed the creature somehow possessed Ramon and the colonel. He hoped Ramon was in a position to do something. He wanted to be available to help if Ramon did wake up, but knew he would be useless as a prisoner. He decided the best thing he could do would be to scout around a little bit and see what else he could learn about the Russians' activities.

The first place he went was a general store. He took some of the money Luther Duncan had paid him and bought a new hat and shirt. He figured it would help if he wasn't wearing the clothes the major last saw him in. While he was there, three Russian soldiers came in. He disappeared into the shadows at the back of the shop and listened. They stocked up on food-stuffs, matches—a lot of basic supplies. Once they left, he made his purchases, then ducked into the changing room and put on his new duds.

After the general store, he went to the barbershop for a shave and a haircut. He figured that would help him blend in better. "So, what do you think of all the Russians in town?" he asked the barber as he sat in the chair.

"They're good for business." The barber draped a cloth over Billy. "They're less rowdy than American soldiers who come across the bay from the Presidio." The barber leaned Billy's chair back.

"So, do you wanna see California become Russian territory?"

The barber shrugged as he lathered Billy's cheeks and chin. "If you'd asked me a couple weeks ago, I would have said no, but now I'm not so sure, Mr. McCarty."

Billy's eyebrows creased. "How did you know my name?"

The barber smiled. "Because Mr. Morales knows your name."

Billy bolted out of the barber chair. "I don't think Ramon

had time to come in for a shave." He took the cloth and wiped the shaving cream from his face as he ran to the door. Soldiers marched down the street toward the shop. Turning around, he shot through the back door into an alley.

Running down the alley, Billy found himself near the docks, where Russian soldiers loaded supplies into boats. He gritted his teeth. It didn't seem like it would be long before they would invade San Francisco.

At that point, Billy considered his options. Ramon was frozen like a statue and helpless in the boarding house. Somehow people recognized him no matter where he went. Perhaps that was because of this Legion. Whatever the cause, it complicated his ability to move around Sausalito. Perhaps he should return to the Presidio, attempt to rescue Fatemeh, and see if Luther Duncan was all right. The problem was that meant abandoning Ramon.

It seemed like his best bet was to get back into the foothills where he could think without worrying so much about pursuit. With a clear head, he could decide the best course of action. He made a quick foray down to one of the boats to steal some rations, then left town by way of back streets and alleys.

As night fell, he chewed on some jerky and considered returning to Sausalito. Perhaps the search would have been called off by now and he could get back to the rooming house and see how Ramon was doing. Just then, eerie, bright lights sprang to life across the bay. They seemed to scout around the sky above the Presidio, as though searching for something. He had never seen anything like the spectral display before and sat mesmerized.

Half an hour later, a great horned owl landed in a tree near Billy. It gave a hoot, startling him from his reverie. Somehow he understood the best thing he could do at the moment was stay put.

Ramon sensed someone had joined him. He looked over his shoulder and saw Colonel Dvorkin. "Mr. Morales, what are we doing here?"

"Legion here has something he wants to show us." Ramon found that he rose above the desert floor, lifted into the sky along with Dvorkin. Ramon's heart thudded and he flailed his arms and legs as he imagined the sudden, sharp finality of a fall. He slammed his eyes shut and clenched his teeth. When he did, the sensation of falling vanished, even though his feet no longer touched solid ground. A whispering in the back of his mind assured him there was no danger. He eased his eyes open and gasped in wonder as the ground receded below him. He wondered if this was like flying an ornithopter.

Within minutes, Ramon and Dvorkin were carried beyond the sky to a point where they looked down upon the entire Earth below them. They continued to fly away and then saw the moon whirling around the Earth. As they continued their journey, the Earth and moon danced like a couple in a ballroom around the sun.

The two men continued to drift away from the Sun. It became indistinguishable from the stars around it and eventually disappeared into the band of the Milky Way. As Ramon and Dvorkin continued to fly upwards, the Milky Way became the loop of a vast stellar pinwheel. Then, it became one pinwheel among hundreds of other stellar groups in myriad forms ranging from bars with pinwheel arms to balls to amorphous blobs.

Finally, they were carried to a different pinwheel altogether and taken within it. The structure resolved into stars. A moment later, he and Dvorkin approached a world revolving around one of the stars. *This is my home,* said Legion, *like it was billions of years ago. I barely remember it.*

"Are there people there, like humans?" asked Ramon.

There were, once. Ramon detected a hint of sadness in Legion's voice.

"What happened to them?" asked Dvorkin.

The two men drifted away from the planet. They watched as the sun swelled into a bloated, red mass that swallowed Legion's world. As it did, Ramon heard Legion's soft whispering again—not exactly speech, more like a transfer of knowledge. As the whispering quieted, he understood a future like this would happen to Earth.

"How did you get away?" asked the colonel.

"Long before this happened, I was a scientist."

"Like Professor Maravilla," said Ramon

"You have seen his clockwork wolf?"

Ramon nodded.

"I built machines like that, only they were quite small—so small you could not see them. Despite their small size, I was able to give them my memories, my personality, my feelings—everything that made me who I was. The little machines became me."

"Those little machines," said Ramon, "they're the dust devil I see."

"The dust devil is just a way for you to grasp what I am. I am much smaller."

"Why build machines so small?" asked Dvorkin. "You must be very fragile."

"Because a swarm of small automata is more indestructible than one big automaton. Sure, parts of me wear out with time, but I can build new ones. Each one is identical to others I have built before."

"How am I seeing all this?" asked Ramon.

"Because I am so small that I can manipulate the chemicals and electrical signals within your brains. It's tricky. I failed with the first person I encountered. I did better with the second. Finally, when I encountered General Gorloff, I got the details right. I can enter the brain and let a person see what I want them to see. I can get them to do what I want them to do."

"Do you mean to say that we Russians have been your puppets?" Dvorkin's features betrayed utter disgust.

"We cannot make you do anything you do not want to do," said Legion. *"We can help your brain and muscles create chemicals giving you greater speed and to some degree greater strength. You have taken the actions you have because your Czar ordered you to. I have only helped to make the Czar's orders a reality."*

Ramon's brow furrowed. "Why are you even helping the Czar at all? What do you hope to accomplish?"

"I hope to save humanity from itself." The starscape vanished from Ramon's sight and he once again hovered over the ball of the Earth. A moment later, it looked like a globe with the boundary lines of countries marked over the surface. *"We have observed your socio-political structure and foresee a time when the Russians and the Americans become the two most powerful forces on*

the planet." The boundary lines on the map shifted. America and Russia each took over more of the globe. *"However, if technology continues to grow at the rate it is now, then you could develop weapons that would allow you to destroy each other."* Explosions erupted in each country, leaving a black and scarred world. Ramon trembled and a lump formed in his throat. He closed his eyes against the nightmare and realized Legion had watched his own world burn in much the same way. *"We hoped to avert that crisis by making America and Russia one nation."*

"So, why have Russia invade America?" asked Ramon.

"Because America had recently been fractured by Civil War. We felt it would benefit by the stability Russia could bring."

Dvorkin folded his arms and Ramon thought he looked decidedly smug. Ramon pointed from Dvorkin to himself. "Why are you telling us all this?"

Ramon and Dvorkin found themselves back in the barren, earthly plain. Once again, Ramon faced the dust devil and the small cloud. *"Because Legion wants it."* Ramon sensed that the dust devil spoke the words, referring to the small cloud of particles.

Fatemeh flew across the Golden Gate without incident. However, as she reached the north shore, she realized the problem with flying at night. She tried to see where to land. If she landed on the beach, she would be exposed and the ornithopter's feet might sink in the sand. If she tried to land on the hillside, she might well crash into a tree. A sliver of moonlight low on the horizon cast long shadows in the hills. Despite her reservations about landing on the beach, that seemed the better option.

Bringing the ornithopter down, she misjudged the distance and hit the ground too fast. The feet caught in the beach's soft sand and she lurched forward into the control rod. The mechanical owl toppled over onto its nose, then listed over sideways.

Slowly, she opened her eyes and looked around. She checked her arms and legs. Aside from a bruised sternum, she seemed okay. She unbuckled the harness and slid out to the sand. Scrambling away from the ornithopter on all fours, she stood upright and evaluated the flying machine with hands on her hips. She took a moment to brush the sand off her skirts, then went to the machine and pushed it upright onto its feet. With one wing broken and the blue skin torn, the ornithopter was grounded until someone repaired it.

She looked around for someplace to hide the machine. Even if it couldn't fly, she still didn't want it to announce her presence. Of course, if anyone found it, they'd likely search for an American soldier rather than a Persian woman. She realized her best bet would be to haul the machine toward the underbrush in the nearby foothills. The problem was she couldn't do it alone.

She reached into the cockpit and disabled the engine. As the steam pressure fell, she became aware that someone approached from the trees. She ducked down into the shadows and waited.

"All right, come on outta there with your hands up!"

Her heart skipped a beat as she recognized the voice. She stepped out from behind the ornithopter, but kept her hands high, just in case he couldn't see well.

"Well, I'll be." Billy holstered his gun and ran to Fatemeh, scooping her up in a warm embrace. "It's sure good to see you." His smile rapidly dissolved. "How's Luther doing?"

"He'll be okay," said Fatemeh. "Where's Ramon?"

Billy told her what had happened since their arrival. "He's all frozen up, like that General Gorloff was when we found him on the airship. I think Legion has taken control of him, but he didn't talk like the general did."

Fatemeh frowned and nodded. "Let's hope Ramon has made contact. Help me hide the ornithopter, then let's see if we can get to him."

Ramon looked over to the small cloud of dust motes. "I take it you don't see things the same way as your big brother."

For a moment, the little cloud's particles danced and jerked about, but it soon settled down. *"We traveled to America with the* force that went to Denver on the airships. As we traveled, we realized we had not succeeded in conveying our desire for unity; we had merely cultivated a desire for conquest. We realized if our experiment were to succeed, we needed to start anew, work with humanity and be more careful in how we adjust your brain chemistry. As we've lived with Professor Maravilla these past months, we came to understand that while we could turn off aggression, we would also turn off the drive to explore that would allow you to evolve into superior creatures."

"Evolve?" Dvorkin narrowed his eyes. "You mean like the theories of that Englishman Darwin?"

"Evolution is no theory," said both clouds in unison. The booming voice startled Ramon. "You allow different types of cattle to interbreed to make new cattle. You combine different types of wheat to make new wheat. You make biological evolution. The same thing happens in nature."

"This is heresy." Dvorkin folded his arms and turned around.

Ramon wasn't really comfortable with the conversation's direction either, but felt they should return to the topic at hand rather than argue about science. "So, what exactly do you think should happen?"

"We feel a better course of action would be to help scientists, engineers, artists, and diplomats work toward common goals that would better humanity. If the two countries work together, then they will be less inclined to destroy each other over the course of the next century."

Ramon thought back to his visit with Professor Maravilla and Larissa in Tucson and the mining machine they were building. To his surprise, the scene around changed. He saw the completed machine. It looked like a strange, metallic pig burrowing into the mountainside.

"This is an example of how we were able to help the professor use the technology of this era to build a machine that could benefit humankind."

At that point, the dust devil interrupted. "The problem is that some humans took the machine to use for their own benefit." The scene changed. He watched as the machine plowed through a bank's wall. A man wielding a gun that threw lightning bolts cut down a sheriff. A former lawman himself, Ramon swallowed hard.

The small cloud of dust motes grew agitated again. *"But the humans were able to solve the problem."* This time, the machine stood in stark mountains of yellow rock. The man with the lightning gun fired indiscriminately at a tribe of Indians. Ramon thought he recognized one of them as Geronimo. Soon Larissa Crimson rode up on a strange motorized bicycle and disabled the mining machine by firing a lighting gun of her own and venting the steam from the engine.

Ramon removed his glasses and rubbed the bridge of his nose. "So, one of you thinks you should help Russia conquer the United States to prevent the destruction of humanity. The other thinks you should help all the world's smart people work together to develop new technologies."

"That is a rather crude way of framing the issues, but yes," said both incarnations of Legion at once.

"You came to this impasse because of your separation?" Ramon put his glasses back on.

"And our different experiences," said the small cloud.

"If you can't communicate over long distances, how can you show me pictures of what happened to Professor Maravilla's machine after I left him?"

"The initial separation was caused when the airships over Denver were destroyed. Much of me died that day. We did not anticipate a long separation, or we would have left components along the route to act as relays, as we did during your journey here, Mr. Morales. We can build new components to replace those that are lost, but it takes time."

"You've been traveling with me?" Ramon had guessed as much by this point. He scowled. "I would have preferred if you had asked permission."

"You may have been indecisive and that could have caused delays."

Colonel Dvorkin pointed at the two clouds. "You have been using us as your puppets. We could have accomplished this feat without your help. I happen to know that our own scientists had designs for airships before you came along."

"But there would have been many failures on the way to a successful design. What's more, we have helped many people see the benefits of not putting up resistance to your forces," said the dust devil.

"Ah." Ramon took a step forward. "So you can't actually make humans follow your will."

"We can only manipulate brain chemistry and electrical activity," said the smaller cloud. *"It is highly effective now that we understand how your brains work, but we cannot force actions. That is why Professor Maravilla suggested you accompany us for this reunion."*

"But I can't make anyone do anything they don't want, any better than you can." Ramon shook his head.

"You are a peacekeeper. You can help us see the ways to influence people."

"I am through!" shouted Dvorkin. "I no longer wish to be used as a puppet by you, whatever you are!" With the words, the colonel faded from sight.

"We have only altered your brain chemistry enough to let you visualize us and to let you see the things we wanted to show you. You are no puppet, Ramon Morales. We would like you to help us find the best path forward for humanity."

Ramon swallowed hard. He wanted to be a diplomat, but this seemed awfully soon for this much responsibility.

CHAPTER FIFTEEN
CALIFORNIA DREAMIN'

After hiding the ornithopter, Billy and Fatemeh climbed the hill, ate a hasty meal from the stolen rations, then walked three miles until they had a good view of the town. Billy kept a particular eye open to make sure another patrol didn't surprise them. Looking into the town, Billy noticed lanterns lit by the docks and the shadows of people moving about, working late into the night. "I think the Russians are gettin' ready to make their move."

"We better go find out if Ramon has learned anything."

They made their way down the hillside into town. The streets were empty and no one accosted them until they reached the rooming house. Inside, they encountered Mr. Chandler. Billy drew his revolver. "Now don't you be callin' out to anyone. We're just here to check on my friend."

"Yes, sir, Mr. McCarty."

"Where's Ramon?"

"Right where you left him," said Chandler. He opened the door to the kitchen.

Billy stepped through and shivered in spite of himself. Colonel Dvorkin and Ramon were in exactly the same position he last saw them in. Ramon had dried out, but his shirt was still rumpled and his hair still hung limp from the dousing.

"They've been like that since this afternoon. What do you suppose Ramon and that Legion fella have had to talk about for so long?" He holstered his gun, figuring Chandler wouldn't give them any trouble.

Fatemeh shrugged. She walked over and peered into Ramon's eyes.

Just then, Colonel Dvorkin reached for his sidearm. "It's

time for the puppeteer to die!"

Billy leapt on top of him and wrestled him to the ground. "What's been going on? Have you just been playing 'possum all this time?"

"I don't know what you're talking about," shouted the colonel. "Let me go!"

"Not on your life," said Billy.

"Chandler! He's gone," called Fatemeh.

Billy sat up and aimed a right cross at the colonel's head. Once he was still, Billy looked up. "Chandler's gone to get help, I wager." He took the gun out of the colonel's hand and handed it to Fatemeh as he stood up.

She held the revolver with the respect and loathing she'd give a dead rodent. "Let's get Ramon out of here." She handed the gun back.

"Our room should still be unlocked." Billy holstered the six-gun. "It's not the best place to hide, but we can get there quick."

"All right, let's go." Fatemeh took Ramon by the shoulders and leaned him back. Billy grabbed his feet and together they made their way upstairs.

"What happened to Colonel Dvorkin?" asked Ramon.

"He exerted his free will and returned to your plane of existence. You could do the same any time you'd like," said the dust devil.

"Where exactly are we?" Ramon looked around. "This looks like the Painted Desert in Northern Arizona. Have you actually transported me through the aether to see the star and planet you call home?"

The small cloud vibrated a little. Ramon had the sense it was chuckling. *"No, it would take billions of years to travel that far. Everything you have seen has taken place within your mind."*

"You mean this has been my imagination?" Ramon put his hands in his pockets and began to pace. "None of this has been real?"

"Just because these have been images within your mind makes them no less real." The dust devil spiraled close enough that sand grains occasionally pelted Ramon.

He took a few steps away. "Billions of years." Ramon tried to wrap his mind around the concept. "I take it that means you've been in this form just as long. Has it been billions of years since you've been a person like me?"

"*Yes,*" said the small cloud. "*It's been that long and more since we've been a corporeal person.*"

"*But we are still an entity capable of hopes, dreams and desires. We have free will just as you do.*" The dust devil spiraled back toward the smaller cloud. "*Does that not make us a person like you, even if we are composed of many smaller, independently thinking parts?*"

As Ramon heard the words, he remembered the time he was denied a hotel room because of his skin color. He remembered being accused of trying to ditch a job just because of his Mexican ancestry. His father fought and died for the Union Army in New Mexico because he believed that men should be free. Ramon pointed at the dust devil. "You're a lot bigger than the other incarnation of Legion. Why don't you just absorb him and exert your will?"

"*We are equal. The only thing that makes us different is our experience.*"

Ramon nodded. "What would happen if you did it anyway?"

The smaller cloud shimmered with agitation. "*I would fight to have my voice heard.*"

"That's exactly what will happen if Russia takes over the United States. Eventually there would be a civil war even greater than the one America just endured as people fought to get their voices heard."

"*Why didn't we see that before?*" asked both clouds in unison.

"Because you really are one entity and understand you're both equal," said Ramon. "You know if you were absorbed, your thoughts would become one in time. You've lived that way for so long you haven't experienced anything different. Humans, on the other hand, have learned their voices can be quashed."

"*Then that suggests,*" interjected the smaller cloud, "*my conclusion is correct. We should work through scientists and engineers. Helping them to create inventions that will bring people onto an equal footing.*"

"I have to confess, I like the idea better." Ramon looked down at his feet. "The cotton gin helped break slavery's back in this country by making it more expensive to use people for labor than machines, but there are still an awful lot of people who see colored people—Mexicans, Indians, and Chinese—as inferior somehow. Can a machine make people see each other as equals?"

Legion was silent for a long time. Finally the small cloud spoke. "*No, humans must learn to treat each other as equals.*"

"*We like humanity,*" said the dust devil. "*We do not like the possibility of humanity destroying itself.*"

"I'm afraid that's one of the risks of being alive." Ramon approached the two incarnations of Legion and held out his arms. "You have been alive so long, you don't remember the possibility of dying. Failure is one of the things that drives us."

"*We have grown to like our interaction with humanity,*" said the small cloud. "*It is stimulating to work with you.*"

"Then work with us as teachers," said Ramon. "Don't give us the answers. Just point us in the right direction when we start to go astray."

With those words, the dust devil spun a bit faster and the small cloud moved over. At first, Ramon was horrified as he watched the small cloud get torn apart, but then he realized the small cloud's particles were being integrated into the dust devil. Legion became one again.

"*It has been a long time since we had a ... teacher,*" said the dust devil. "*We had forgotten the concept. You present an intriguing possibility.*" The dust devil slowed its spinning and moved a little closer to Ramon. "*What of the current conflict? We brought the Russians and the Americans together here in San Francisco.*"

"I'm afraid there's no good answer." Ramon shook his head. "I think the best option is to simply let us fight this one out. Whatever the outcome, perhaps diplomats on both sides can be steered to talking to one another rather than fighting."

"*Very well,*" said Legion. "*May we meet with you again after we have considered your words?*"

"If I survive, sure." Ramon smiled.

"*Then return to the conscious realm with our thanks for helping us to become whole again and seeing a path forward. You truly are a peacemaker."*

Ramon waved and then closed his eyes, willing himself to consciousness.

"You should know that we helped the Russians build a third airship."

"What?" Ramon's eyes sprang open. The dust devil spun off into the distance. Ramon forced his eyes shut and hoped he could bring himself awake.

Fatemeh and Billy carried Ramon to a room upstairs in the boarding house. After they lay Ramon on one of the beds, Billy rushed to the door and locked it, then lit a lantern. Fatemeh started by checking Ramon's pulse. It was weak but still present. She held her head to his chest and listened to his shallow breathing. She needed to bring him around before the soldiers started searching the house. Opening the pouch on her belt, she looked for something that might do some good. She uncorked a small vial and held it under his nose.

"What is that, smelling salts?" asked Billy.

"Not quite, but same idea. Just some pungent herbs."

Ramon did not respond. She corked the bottle and put it back in her pouch. She took one of his hands and rubbed it, then took the other. Stiff and waxy, he still resembled a corpse.

"You could always try to wake him with a kiss," said Billy with a smirk.

"Not only are you irreverent, you're crazy. There's no way that would help."

"It couldn't hurt."

She frowned. "That's never a safe assumption." The idea of actually kissing Ramon while he was unconscious, possibly near death seemed just a little too horrific for her taste. What if an infection put him in this state?

Fatemeh considered the idea some more. There had been some papers about mouth-to-mouth resuscitation techniques that had circulated through Europe for the past century. Many were written by quacks whose goal was to raise the dead. Still, the more she thought, the fewer options she had short of getting him to a doctor's office or an apothecary where she might find more items to work with. This late at night in an occupied town, neither option seemed viable. She finally gave in, knelt down beside the bed and put her mouth on Ramon's, and breathed out, filling his lungs.

Her breath caught when Ramon's lips responded. A moment later, he coughed and sputtered as his arms flailed about. He blinked and sat up. "Good God, I am so hungry," he said. "Where am I?" He looked into Fatemeh's green eyes. "Were you kissing me?"

Her eyes widened, but she smiled slowly and gave a small nod.

"I've missed you so much." He held his arms open and she went to him. This time the kiss was long and passionate. She allowed her hands to rove along his back and shoulders. She sensed a confidence in his kiss that had not been there for some time, as though Ramon had gone to sleep, but awakened truly understanding his purpose.

A shout and a crash rose from downstairs. Ramon and Fatemeh jerked and looked at the door. Billy stood there with his arms across his chest and a big smile. "A gentleman would have turned his back," said Ramon.

"Since when am I a gentleman?"

Heavy boots clomped up the stairs. Billy looked around the room. He went to the window and threw it open.

"I'm tired of exiting rooms through windows." Despite the complaint, Fatemeh joined Billy at the window and looked out. A soldier stood near a gas lamp.

The door handle rattled and all three looked around. A soldier pounded on the door and demanded something in Russian. Fatemeh gritted her teeth, afraid the soldier would try to kick the door in. After a moment, there was another shout and doors creaked open down the hall.

"I guess they don't know this door can be locked from within," whispered Ramon.

"Or don't care," said Billy, "figuring they have us trapped."

"There's a new problem," said Ramon. "It turns out the Russians have a third airship. I don't have details, but Legion gave me the impression it would be in San Francisco soon."

"Then we better get back there and warn the army as soon as we can," said Fatemeh.

"I don't see how we could get back there in time. What's more, last I knew, they weren't too happy about us bein' here," said Billy. "I vote we go north out of town and leave the two armies to sort out their own problems."

"That may not be a bad idea," said Ramon. "That's basically what Legion is going to do."

Fatemeh turned to Ramon. "What?"

"I've talked to Legion. I understand the situation. We've accomplished what we came here to do, corazón."

"We left Luther Duncan behind." Fatemeh stood and put her hands on her hips. "We need to go back and get him, at least."

Ramon looked down and nodded after a moment.

Billy put his finger to his mouth. They all stopped and listened. The boots tromped back down the stairs. "The first thing we need to do is get out of this boarding house," he said once the sound died away.

"The rooms across the way were open," said Fatemeh. "Perhaps we can get out one of those windows."

"It's worth a shot," said Billy.

Larissa woke up the next morning, sore and stiff after chasing down the Clantons in the Dragoon Mountains. Riding the frail-looking lightning wolves used different muscles than riding horses. As such, she was glad the army provided a Pullman coach for the trip west. She looked out the window and tall, spindly Joshua Trees moved past. They were in the California desert. It wouldn't be long before they reached Los Angeles. At that point, their cars would be switched to an army locomotive for the trip north. They would pull into San Francisco by this time tomorrow.

The Southern Pacific conductor had not liked stopping in the Dragoon Mountains where Apaches lurked. He grumbled even more when they stopped a few miles down the line to round up some stolen money from a cave and return it to Tucson. He made it clear he would be glad when the army's cars were off his train.

She smiled at the thought of Old Man Clanton, guarding the stolen loot, facing three lightning guns mounted to motorized bicycles. The conductor might not be happy, but they had done good work.

She was sad for the Apaches and a tear fell when she thought of Baishan. Still, they had saved a brave and noble people. She hoped they would take that into account when white settlers returned to the area.

Larissa climbed out of her berth and dressed in the compartment's tiny space. Donning her new, flat cap, she stepped out into the corridor. The steward, unconcerned with the conductor's irritation, greeted her with a warm smile. "Good to see you, Miss Crimson. I'll get your room made up. They're serving breakfast in the dining car."

"Thank you," she said. She made her way through the train. Between the Pullman coach and dining car was a livery car that had been pressed into service as a workshop for the lightning wolves. There, she found Professor Maravilla tinkering with her original design. She cleared her throat.

He looked up, startled. "Oh, sorry, I hope you don't mind. I saw some ways I could improve the linkage between the motor and the chain." He stood up and wiped his hands on a rag. "Once this trip is completed, we should sit down and discuss the designs. I can see several potential improvements, including better springs, a stronger frame, and thicker tires for better traction."

"That would be great." She knelt down beside him. "Right now, though, I'm more concerned with how these machines will do once we reach San Francisco."

The professor gave her a reassuring smile. "I'm sure they'll do fine. They did better than I would have expected in the rugged terrain of the Dragoons. They will surely do well on city streets."

Larissa pursed her lips. "In the Dragoons we had one objective. Stop the Javelina."

The professor looked down at his hands.

"I hope you're not angry that I blew a hole in its boiler," she said.

He shook his head. "No, not angry. You did what had to be done."

She tipped her hat back on her head. "What I'm concerned about is how well fast-moving machines like these will do in a more complex situation. How will they coordinate with each other? Soldiers on horseback can shout orders back and forth, but soldiers on lightning wolves ... it's not so easy."

The professor tapped the side of his forehead. "Legion could be used to relay messages. That's one of the ways the Russians coordinated their attacks."

"I'd rather not go there." Larissa studied the professor for a moment. "How does Legion communicate across distance?"

"Legion uses frequencies of light." The professor's brow creased and he muttered to himself. He was silent for a time, then a look of puzzlement crossed his face. "I think he called it the electromagnetic spectrum."

"Is something wrong?"

The professor sat back, puzzlement turning to worry. "Usually, he's quite loquacious when I ask him something. He seems to be ignoring me this morning."

"Could you build us something that utilized this ... electromagnetic spectrum?"

Professor Maravilla blinked, then turned his mind to the problem. "I don't know if I have everything available. Let me look around."

Larissa stood and brushed off her trousers. "Do that after breakfast, I'm starved." She reached out and helped the professor to his feet. They continued through the livery car into the dining car. There, they found Hoshi sitting at a table, peering at a menu. He looked up and invited them to join him.

A moment later, a waiter appeared and gave Larissa and Maravilla menus. Hungry as she was, Larissa was glad the army was paying the bill. The dining cars on trains were like fine, rolling restaurants and the number of choices dazzled her. She looked up. "I'm pleased you decided to join us Mr. Hoshi."

"Mr. Masuda would be more proper," said Hoshi without inflection.

"I apologize, Mr. Masuda."

The waiter returned and took their orders. Hoshi ordered tea and a bowl of fruit. Larissa ordered the steak and eggs. Maravilla followed suit.

"We're glad you're along to help, Mr. Masuda," said Larissa, "but I'm sure the army would have let you return home now that Curly Bill Bresnahan's lightning gun has been accounted for."

"No doubt you are correct." Hoshi looked out the window. "However, I have been driven away from my homeland once. I wish my adopted homeland to remain for a while." He turned back and looked at Professor Maravilla. "Why do you accompany us? I would have thought you'd be most anxious to repair your mining machine."

"I would like to repair the mining machine, and I want to return to the Grand Canyon to finish building a new generation of mechanical owl." He cast a sidelong glance toward Larissa. "But Legion was quite clear yesterday. Our friends are in trouble."

"Legion?" asked Hoshi.

"A ... being from the stars," explained Larissa. Noticing Hoshi's blank expression, she continued. "I don't understand it completely myself, but I gather it speaks to the professor."

"Ah," said Hoshi. "The demons. Or, is it a god I have heard you praying to?"

Maravilla barked a laugh at that. "If it's a god, it's a god of mischief. Demons would be most apt." His gaze grew distant and he looked as though he searched his memory for something forgotten. After a moment, he focused on Hoshi again. "It tried to bring peace to humanity, but the effort hasn't gone so well. It's looking for a new approach to the problem." He looked out the window. "Speaking of Legion, he's been strangely quiet this morning. It's not like him at all."

At that point, the waiter appeared and distributed the food. Maravilla reached for a bottle of Tabasco sauce and sprinkled it liberally on his eggs

"Wouldn't it be better to see if Legion sorts this out all on its own?" asked Larissa after sampling her steak. "You said Ramon, Fatemeh, and Billy are there in San Francisco."

The professor stared at his plate. "The problem is, the Russians are growing impatient with Legion and all hell is about to break loose."

CHAPTER SIXTEEN
THE BATTLE OF SAN FRANCISCO

Larissa watched as the train pulled into San Francisco the next morning. She didn't actually see much. Like most train routes into cities, this one traveled along behind warehouses and back alleys. Smoke-covered brickwork passed outside the windows. Old cans and papers littered the tracks. Every now and then, Larissa caught glimpses of more stately brick buildings off in the distance with large windows. Wisps of fog rolled by. It was like a fairy tale version of London—something her cousin Alethea might have imagined—and it was her job to keep that vision safe.

As the train slowed to a stop, Larissa made her way to the livery car. She found Professor Maravilla at the workbench, peering at something through the glasses with extra lenses attached that had he used in Tucson. "What are you working on?"

He lifted the lenses. "What you asked about yesterday." He held up a small disk connected to a broad, rounded hook, a little like a wire hanger from a closet. A longer, flexible wire extended to a second metal disk with a ring welded to one side. "Although Legion is silent, I remembered enough about electromagnetic theory to construct this."

Larissa turned as the door at the other end of the livery car opened. Lorenzo and Harris entered from the dining car. She motioned them over.

"Do you mean we can use this device to talk to each other over distance?" asked Larissa.

"I'm afraid it's not that sophisticated." The professor sighed. "With Legion's help, perhaps..." The rest of the thought remained unspoken, but the professor's furrowed brow betrayed his worry about the alien swarm's silence.

Maravilla hooked the hanger over his ear so the disk sat in front, then slipped the ring onto one of his fingers. "If I tap on metal, this unit will broadcast the tapping sound to anyone else wearing one of these."

"Like a wireless telegraph," said Lorenzo.

"We could use Morse code!" Sergeant Harris smiled broadly.

Both Larissa and Lorenzo gave him blank stares. "I'm afraid I never learned Morse code." Lorenzo shrugged.

"I have three of these," interjected Maravilla. "One for each of you. I suggest you take a few minutes and create some basic codes—something that will allow you to signal one another."

"Don't worry," said Harris. "We can work out a few codes. I don't think we'll need anything too complicated."

"I hope not," said the professor. He removed the signaling device and handed it to Larissa. He retrieved two more from the back of the workbench and passed them to Lorenzo and Harris. Each of them put on a device and listened while Harris tapped out a code. They nodded when they saw how it worked.

"Thank you," said Larissa.

Just as the professor stood from the workbench, a thunderclap sounded. A moment later, another followed. "I didn't think thunderstorms were all that common in California," said Lorenzo.

"That wasn't thunder," said Harris.

The two soldiers threw open the livery car's loading door and jumped out onto the train platform. They climbed up the ladder on the car's side. Larissa followed, glad she preferred trousers to skirts. From there, they were just high enough to see out toward San Francisco Bay. Patches of fog and haze made it difficult to see, but Larissa thought she could make out a set of masts—tall ships out in the bay. "I think the invasion has begun," said Harris.

"I don't think we need anyone to point us toward the battle. Let's unload the lightning wolves and see if we can do any good." Larissa mounted the ladder and climbed down.

"Right behind you, boss," said Lorenzo.

Professor Maravilla spoke to Masuda Hoshi as Larissa approached the train platform. "Where do you gentlemen plan to go?" she asked.

"We need to find Ramon and Fatemeh," said the professor. "When Legion last spoke to me, they were in Sausalito."

Larissa inclined her head toward the sounds of battle. "Getting across the bay may be difficult right now."

"That's our problem to solve," said Maravilla. He reached out, took Larissa's hands and gave them a squeeze. "Go help out where you can." She squeezed his hands in return, then watched as Hoshi and Maravilla disappeared around the corner of the train depot.

She entered the livery car and retrieved her lightning wolf. Although the lightning gun made it heavier than she'd like, it was well balanced. She was proud of the simple machine she had cobbled together.

A moment later, Harris rolled up with his lightning wolf. "I suggest a simple code. Something for all our names, something to say we need help, something to say stay away. Anything else?"

"What about Hail Mary?" asked Lorenzo. "That may be the most important of all!"

Larissa smiled at that. They departed once they worked out a simple set of codes. The fog thinned as Larissa, Harris, and Lorenzo reached the waterfront. Out in the bay, tall American ships exchanged shots with a mix of smaller sloops, caravels, and cutters. It was like the collection one might find at a small port like Sausalito. Larissa couldn't figure out how the Russians hoped to succeed with such a fleet of small boats. An American ship fired on a Russian sloop, sending up a shower of water, wood, and shrapnel. When the smoke cleared, the whole boat had vanished aside from debris littering the water.

"This is hopeless," declared Jesús Lorenzo. "There's no way the Russians can hope to defeat the Americans, much less get to shore."

"Not quite." Michael Harris pointed. A caravel had cut around one of the war ships and made for the pier.

Larissa watched it for a moment, then pointed along the waterfront. "Let's go."

They sped along the cobblestones, passing disreputable taverns and somewhat more reputable fishmongers. Many of the businesses still had people sitting out front gawking at the action despite the evacuation order. Larissa wondered whether it was even possible to evacuate a city the size of San Francisco. As they bounced over the cobblestones, Larissa decided she would definitely take the professor up on his offer to install thicker tires on the lightning wolves. Riding over the rocks and packed sand of the Dragoons was easy going compared to this. Looking over at the grimaces on Lorenzo's and Harris's features, she realized the men had an even more difficult time than she did.

They reached the pier the caravel approached. Larissa lifted her goggles and took in the scene. "Let's aim at his masts—avoid taking lives if we can."

"Ma'am, this is war," said Harris. "It won't bother them one bit to take your life if they got you."

For just a moment, Larissa had a flash of James Ellway, her first bounty. "I'm not afraid of taking lives." Her jaw was tight. "I just want to see how much control we can exert on the lightning guns."

The three reached back and activated the weapons. They rumbled briefly, followed by a rising whine. When the indicators showed ready, Larissa lowered her goggles and aimed the wand mounted between the handlebars. A brief look with her peripheral vision told her the men were also ready. "Fire."

Three arcs of lightning shot forth. The caravel's masts disappeared in a shower of sparks and wood splinters. A rousing cheer sounded from one of the taverns behind them. Larissa's stomach churned at the thought of men who were already drunk and would no doubt run if the Russians made it to shore.

Despite their successful attack, the caravel still had momentum and sped toward the shore. A half dozen Russians stood up in the boat and lifted rifles. Before they could fire, Harris and Lorenzo leveled their guns and fired again. Larissa caught her breath as the entire boat erupted in a flash of lightning, spray, and splinters.

As Larissa blinked at the spots before her eyes, she thought the buzzing of the lightning wolves' engines had changed tenor. She reached down and disabled her own engine. When the sound hadn't changed much, she kicked a stand down on the side of the modified bicycle and walked back toward the street. She tried to ignore the men offering to buy her drinks. A moment later she pinpointed the source. A great silver cloud-like form hung in the sky over Oakland.

Returning to the lightning wolf, she opened a saddlebag and retrieved a small, collapsible telescope. Opening it up, she focused on the distant form. It looked like a fat, silver cigar. Steam engines hung from the sides. Along the keel near the bow was emblazoned a large, golden owl, wings spread, talons extended, as though ready to strike. The tail fins were adorned with white, blue, and red stripes. It was a Russian airship.

"Where the devil have they been keeping that?" Larissa handed the telescope to Lorenzo.

He took a look and whistled. "I guess they've been building a third one all this time."

"This would explain how the Russians have been getting fresh troops and supplies," said Harris as he took the telescope. The airship glided over the naval battle without stopping. "It's heading for the Presidio."

"The naval battle was just a distraction." Larissa reached down and activated her engine again. She kicked up the stand and looked back at the men. "We've got to warn them before it's too late."

"I don't think there's any way we can get over the Presidio before the airship does." Harris shook his head.

"We've got to try." With that Larissa sped off.

Hoshi and Maravilla made their way along the waterfront, looking out at the one-sided naval battle, trying to figure out how to get across the bay when they heard the chugging steam engines that propelled the Russian airship.

Hoshi's breath caught as strange, flapping machines rose up from the Presidio to meet it.

"They did it. They built copies of my ornithopters," exclaimed Maravilla.

"They look almost like owls," said Hoshi.

"That's why I built the original. I wanted to understand the behavior of owls." Maravilla let out a shuddering breath. "I've come so far from my original purpose. I should be over the Grand Canyon flying in an even better ornithopter, not working my way along a decrepit waterfront trying to find my way through a battle!"

"You're here to help friends," said Hoshi. "That's an honorable task. Do not feel shame."

Just then, the three lightning wolves sped by, on their way to the Presidio. "I fear my whole fool's quest started with me abandoning a friend," said Maravilla. "All Larissa wanted to do was build a mechanical owl and fly over the Grand Canyon as well. Now I've brought her right into the heart of the danger."

Hoshi watched as the lightning wolves evaded a crowd of gawkers who emerged from a bait shop. "I think that woman can take care of herself. She has the making of a samurai, that one, perhaps more than the boy I hired."

Hoshi followed the gaze of the people who'd emerged from the bait shop. The mechanical owls had almost reached the airship. Hoshi was amazed at how well they kept in formation—much like a flock of birds. Maravilla made a fist and gritted his teeth. "Randomize your attack, you fools!"

Gun ports opened in the airship's superstructure and there were poofs of smoke. Two of the ornithopters shattered into bits, debris raining on the ships below. The formation finally scattered. The four remaining owls broke off and whirled around, coming in from different angles. One of them jerked and spiraled toward the ocean, out of control. "What happened?" asked Hoshi.

Maravilla shook his head. "The fool probably fired a large-caliber gun." His brow creased. "Fascinating. His shot must not have ignited a spark aboard the ship."

"That ornithopter isn't regaining control," said Hoshi. They watched as it continued to spiral downward. Finally, it dropped into the water with a splash. Once the spray cleared, it lay there like a dead bird. The samurai turned to the professor. "Why would a spark aboard the airship matter?"

"They're filled with hydrogen gas. It's very explosive."

"What if they found a different gas?" asked Hoshi.

The professor shook his head, about to protest that nothing else was light enough to lift a rigid airship, but then he stopped himself. Nothing known had that power. Perhaps Legion had shown the Russians how to distill an as-yet-unknown gas.

The airship floated over the Presidio. A hatch opened on the bottom and something fell out. A loud whump sounded as dirt and debris flew into the air from the Presidio. As more bombs fell, Maravilla pounded the side of his head. "Legion! Why are you letting this happen? Stop this at once!"

The crowd in front of the bait shop gasped as more smoke plumes appeared from the Presidio. A Gatling gun rattled to life from a nearby ship. Seagulls cried out angrily. Another whump sounded from the Presidio. Professor Maravilla dropped to his knees, tears streaming from his eyes. "Legion, why have you abandoned me?"

Hoshi knelt down next to the professor and looked in his eyes. "What's the matter with you? We need to find your friends."

Maravilla sniffed and rubbed his eyes. "I ought to be able to stop this. Legion ought to listen to me, but he's gone and I don't know why. I haven't felt this lonely since my wife and daughter were taken from me."

Hoshi scowled. His first impulse was to strike the man and tell him to pull himself together, but he guessed that would not work. After a moment, the warrior reached out and took Maravilla's arm. "I'm here. You're not alone. We need to keep moving if we're going to find and help your friends."

The professor looked up. His eyes were moist, but he nodded and brought himself to his feet. As they passed the bait shop, Hoshi noticed a sign advertising a boat for rent. He looked at the people gathered in front. "Did one of you gentlemen post this sign?"

A big man with a bald head and a beard that looked like it had been used to scrub toilets scowled. "That would be my boat, but you'd be crazy to go out until this battle's over."

"Which boat is it?"

"It's that little fishing dinghy tied to the dock." He pointed to a serviceable boat about twelve feet long.

"How much to buy the boat?"

The man laughed. "$50.00 all in silver."

Hoshi reached into his robes and pulled out a pouch. He counted out ten silver coins. "I only have this much. I'll give it to you now, then give you forty-five when I return, presuming, of course, the boat is still intact."

"Sounds like a gamble to me," said the bald man.

"You look like a gambling man."

The man smiled and took the coins. "You've got yourself a bet. I better see you again by the end of the day."

"If San Francisco still stands, I will be here," said Hoshi.

He led Maravilla out to the pier. "Did you just give that man all of our expense money?"

"Most of it."

"Can we really pay the balance?"

Hoshi helped Maravilla into the boat and untied the line. "Do you really think we will survive this day?"

Larissa, Harris, and Lorenzo paused near Fisherman's Wharf. Larissa lifted her goggles and watched in horror as the Russian airship dropped bomb after bomb into the Presidio. By her count, ten bombs were dropped in all. "I don't think they need to be warned anymore," said Lorenzo, dour.

"We've still got to stop them." Larissa reached up to lower her goggles, but Harris put his hand on her elbow.

"They're already moving on."

Larissa sat back again and watched the airship's path. Turning, she looked uphill at all the houses and businesses packed in close together. It was hard to say where the Russians would drop troops. Anywhere would be devastating. If they dropped bombs in districts with a lot of wood, they could start a fire that would rampage through the city. After a moment, her eyes fell on a domed building that resembled the capitol in Washington, D.C. Its dome stood a little above the other buildings in the area.

She pointed. "They're headed for city hall."

"How can you be sure?" asked Harris.

"Think about the other invasions," said Larissa. "Somehow the Russians are always able to get the city or territorial government to surrender without much work."

"I've never figured out how they manage that," mused Lorenzo.

"It doesn't matter," said Larissa. "Somehow they get the city leaders on their side without causing much harm. I'm guessing that's their destination and we have the best anti-airship guns in the city." She reached down and pointed the lightning gun skyward.

"Won't that rain a lot of debris down on the city?" Lorenzo's eyebrows came together.

"The airships are filled with hydrogen. If we can get the airship while it's still high enough, it should engulf the ship and burn most of the flammables even before it hits the ground." She looked at Harris. "You take up a position to the east of the capitol." She turned to Lorenzo. "Go to the west. I'll get south. When you think you're in a good position, signal with the clackers." She clicked the disk she held in her finger against the lightning wolf's handlebar.

Lorenzo and Harris looked at each other, then looked toward the airship. It still seemed to be heading downtown. The men each nodded to Larissa then set out. She reached up, lowered her goggles and shot uphill into the city. She wound her way as best she could through unfamiliar streets, avoiding people who had stepped out of houses and buildings to watch the strange craft drift over the city.

At one point, the street jagged in a direction Larissa didn't expect. As she continued forward, she looked around for another street that would take her back to the capitol. A moment later, she followed an alley that direction. She bent low to avoid fouling herself on clotheslines. She took another turn and found herself in a neighborhood where none of the writing on the buildings was familiar.

She drove on for another half mile before she realized she was lost. She no longer knew which direction city hall was. She looked up in the sky, found the airship and noticed she'd overshot her mark by about a quarter mile. She ducked down a side street, until she came to a place where she could see the capitol building. It was an elaborate structure, but scaffolding still clung to its side. Lorenzo clacked the signal for his name. She paused, but wasn't happy with her vantage. She turned and pushed uphill a little more. Finally, she came to a point that overlooked the city better. From there, she had a clear view of the airship overhead. She clacked the signal for her name.

A few minutes later Harris clacked his signal.

She held her breath and fired the lightning gun at the airship. A moment later, two more lightning bolts flew skyward. Only one of the bolts connected with the airship, causing it to list and setting the outer skin ablaze. It was less dramatic than she expected, but they had never tested the lightning guns at this range. Despite the fire, the ship soon righted itself and a hatch opened in the bottom. She cringed, expecting the hydrogen inside to explode at any minute. The soldiers clacked their identification signals again as a prelude to another shot. She swallowed and clacked hers in response.

She aimed for the open hatch, but before she could fire, Harris clacked his identification signal again followed by the signal to "stay away."

Her brow furrowed in confusion, when suddenly there was an explosion east of the capitol building. Her hand went to her mouth. Harris's lightning gun must have exploded the same way Curly Bill Bresnahan's had in Arizona.

She looked up at the airship again, realizing she didn't have time to lose. She fired at the hold but missed. The other lightning gun fired, grazing the airship. This time, a great fireball erupted a third of the way up from the tail. Larissa punched the air. Lorenzo must have hit the engine, causing a boiler to explode. She took a cue from him and aimed at the airship's flank. She also managed to connect with one of the engines. The entire airship was now ablaze. She crouched down, ready for a devastating explosion.

Instead, the airship slowly sank. It drifted sideways, pushed along by the wind as it dropped toward the bay. She opened one eye and watched it for a while. Then she stood up straight and blew out a sigh of relief. She faced the direction where Sergeant Harris' lightning wolf exploded. It was time to find out if he was okay.

Hoshi let the small dinghy hug the coast as much as possible. The tide carried them away from the naval battle. "It is good to sail a boat again," he said. He knelt down and examined the mast. He would stand it up soon to catch the wind and tack across the Golden Gate to Sausalito.

"I somehow never imagined samurai warriors as able seamen," commented Maravilla.

"Why not? Japan is a nation of islands and many of our adversaries have lived across the sea." He let his voice drift off, as he considered that his last battles in Japan were with his own countrymen. Looking up toward the city, he was surprised to see a lightning bolt fly upwards from the ground to the sky.

"Goodness me, it looks like Larissa and her boys are making short work of that airship," said the professor.

Hoshi couldn't decide whether he approved of these lightning wolves or not. Frail as these machines looked, they contained an awesome power beyond anything he had seen before, especially when used en masse. In that sense, they reminded him of a pack of skeletal, hungry wolves. Three shots lit the airship on fire and sent it floating toward the bay, like an enormous feather falling from the sky. Hoshi realized he no longer heard gunfire. He lifted the mast on the dinghy and deployed the sail. As he tacked the boat northward toward Sausalito, the airship crashed into the ocean. Several American naval ships adjusted their sails to get a closer look at the downed craft.

"No doubt they'll try to salvage what they can so they can make one of their own," said Maravilla. "Just as they did with my ornithopters."

Hoshi thought of the ships he sailed and how much their designs were based on those of Portuguese traders who had come to Japan centuries before. "That is the way of war," he said.

"I am fed up with the ways of war." The professor turned so he faced the far shore. "Let's go find our friends and then see if we can salvage a modicum of peace."

CHAPTER SEVENTEEN
PEACEKEEPERS

Maravilla scanned San Francisco Bay with his telescope as Hoshi steered the boat across the Golden Gate. Debris from many destroyed boats floated in the water along with the airship's wreckage. The American warships lowered boats to rescue the Russian survivors. The few Russian boats that had survived the encounter made their way back to the docks at Sausalito. The professor wasn't keen on the idea of landing among disgruntled Russian soldiers who had just lost a battle. What's more, he wasn't sure whether those soldiers were still connected to Legion, whose influence tended to keep the soldiers civil.

The professor collapsed the telescope and took a moment to rub his eyes. Legion had been with him for several months and he'd gained new insight into how to build things. He could never have built a machine as complex as the Javelina as quickly as he did without the alien's insight. What he missed, though, was the alien's simple companionship—the voices that spoke constantly in the back of his mind, like a household of children. He'd just reached the point where he could start to tune them out and talk to the voices when he wanted. He would have to get used to living without them, much like he had to get used to living without his wife and daughter. Unlike his wife and daughter though, he didn't think Legion was dead. He hoped Legion would return for a visit one day.

He lifted the telescope again and scanned the shoreline. A boat sat on the bank. Up the hillside, there was a clumping of brush. Within, he caught glimpses of blue cloth. The professor passed the telescope to Hoshi. The Japanese warrior looked and nodded. He made for the point. As they approached, the keel scraped a submerged sandbar. Hoshi steered northward a little bit and they were able to get a little closer to shore.

Hoshi dropped an anchor over the side. "The tide is going out. No doubt we'll find the boat grounded when we return." Maravilla nodded as he helped the warrior lower and stow the mast. They climbed from the boat into waist-deep water. The professor gritted his teeth, worried that his pocket watch would get wet.

Reaching the shore, they hiked to the grounded boat Maravilla had spotted with his telescope, then uphill to where they had seen the flashes of blue through the foliage. They discovered an army ornithopter. Maravilla made a quick examination. A wing was bent and a control cord had snapped. He could easily fix it with some rope and a few tools. It might not fly in combat again without more extensive repair, but he could get it back across the bay under its own power.

"Do you think this is where your friends came ashore?" asked Hoshi.

"It seems likely," said the professor. "If so, they didn't come back this way. They're either still in Sausalito, or they found escape by another route. I think we have no choice but to see what is happening in the town in the wake of Legion's departure."

Larissa entered the lobby of St. Mary's Hospital. She wrung her hands, feeling more nervous in this place than any time in the last week, taking the untested lightning wolves into battle against the Javelina and a Russian airship. Numerous people bustled through the lobby. Several in uniform were bandaged. The hospital at the Presidio had suffered considerable damage in the bombing run and many of the wounded had to be transferred into the city. Larissa stepped up to a desk and a nurse looked up. "May I help you?"

"I'm looking for Sergeant Michael Harris," she said.

The nurse consulted a clipboard. "He's in room 237. Take the elevator and go to the left." She pointed down the hall.

Larissa walked to the elevator and pushed a button, sounding a buzzer. A couple of minutes later, the operator opened the door and an elderly couple stepped out. Larissa entered. "Second floor," she told the operator.

The woman, who wore a smart uniform with buttons down both sides of her jacket, waited a minute to see if anyone else wanted the elevator. She closed the door when the buzzer sounded from upstairs and moved the control lever. Larissa found herself wondering how the machine worked and what powered it. When she was told Harris had been taken to St. Mary's, the person mentioned it was both the oldest and most technically advanced hospital in the city. The operator brought the elevator to a smooth stop and opened the door. Larissa tipped her hat and went to the left.

She found room 237 a few doors down the hall. Harris sat up in bed. Bandages wrapped his otherwise bare chest and hands. His blue uniform coat was draped over his shoulders.

"How are you doing?" Larissa took off her hat and wrung it between her hands.

"I'm doing fine," he said with a forced smile that looked a little like a grimace. "I just got burned and cut by some shrapnel when that damned lightning gun exploded."

Larissa sat down in a chair next to the bed. "We did it. We brought down the airship."

"I saw." Harris beamed proudly. "It made the whole trip through Arizona looking for Maravilla worth the effort."

"Do you still want to be part of the Lightning Wolf Corps?" she asked.

"I like the way that sounds." He smiled for a moment, then turned serious. "But I'll only do it if you find a way to make the lightning guns more stable."

Larissa laughed nervously. She had no problem understanding the mechanics of machines, but electricity—that would take more study. She might even have to go to college. She wondered if the army would pay enough to make that a reality.

"So, speaking of my sojourn through the desert, have you heard anything from the professor?"

Larissa shook her head. "No. There's been no word. The captain I spoke to at the Presidio says he doesn't have enough men to spare to look for them. The place was hit pretty hard.

Lots of buildings were destroyed. Others were damaged."

There was a knock at the door. "Sorry to interrupt." A man wearing a blue uniform with corporal's stripes looked at Larissa. "Are you Miss Crimson?"

"Yes, Corporal?" She put the cap back on her head.

"General Sheridan sent me. He wants to see you right away."

Larissa swallowed. "I see." She stood up and put her hand on Harris's shoulder, but withdrew it when he winced. "Get better, soon. You hear me?"

He saluted. "Yes, ma'am."

Larissa followed the corporal out of the hospital room. He escorted her nearly two miles to the Presidio grounds.

At the Presidio, soldiers cleared away the remains of tents, scattered about like rags and broken matchsticks. Several buildings lay in ruins, either all or part of them reduced to smoldering piles of rubble. A steam shovel dug chunks of granite and concrete while men peered into the depths looking for survivors from the buildings. Larissa looked back at San Francisco. She realized the damage caused by the airship could have been far worse if the Russians had started dropping bombs on the city itself.

The corporal led Larissa to a house. Before that, she hadn't realized the officers at the Presidio had nicer quarters than those at Fort Bliss. A man carrying a sheaf of papers cut in front of them, knocked on the door, and entered. The corporal followed and led Larissa to a sitting room where a man with short hair and a drooping mustache sat, surrounded by stacks of paper. The corporal stood ramrod straight and saluted. Larissa still wasn't sure what she was expected to do in front of officers, so she took off her hat.

The general looked up. "Ah, Miss Crimson." He cast a glance at the corporal. "Thank you very much. Dismissed." He raised a hand in salute. When he lowered his hand, the corporal made a crisp swivel, brought his heels together and then marched off. The precise move seemed at odds with the surrounding chaos.

The general held out a hand toward a chair across the way. "Please be seated. Sorry to have to meet you in my house, but my office was destroyed in the bomb run."

"I understand," said Larissa. She made her way around a stack of singed papers and sat on a divan.

"My men have been trying to recover what they can from the wreckage. Damned lot of paperwork." He barked out a laugh. "I almost wish the Russians had done a better job of destroying it."

Larissa snorted.

The general leaned forward and clasped his hands together. "I asked you here because the president was very impressed with the report about you and the lightning wolves I telegraphed to Washington."

Larissa blinked, digesting what he'd just told her. "The president, sir? Of the United States?"

"Yes, President Hayes." The general stood and looked around at tabletops for something. "We'd like you to keep working for the army. The only problem is that the War Department doesn't have a provision for women in its ranks aside from nurses and secretaries."

Larissa's gut churned. She wondered if the general was trying to find a nice way to tell her thanks for all the work, but she wasn't going to get paid. She imagined her dreams of a better future evaporating like the morning fog. After a moment, he found what he sought—a black box three inches square. "Instead, he thought the Department of Justice would be a better fit." He handed her the box.

She took it uncertainly, then opened the lid. Inside was a shiny badge. "Me? A U.S. Marshal?"

"I think it suits you better than an army uniform." The general returned to his chair. "The thing is, if you accept this job, your first mission is going to be especially difficult."

Larissa still gazed at the badge in disbelief. "What do you have in mind, sir?"

"We apprehended four people on their way to Sausalito before the invasion. I believe you know them—Ramon Morales, Fatemeh Karimi, Billy McCarty, and Luther Duncan."

Larissa's eyes snapped upward. "I know Ramon, Fatemeh, and Billy, yes—from the battle of Denver ... and before."

"They were on their way to Sausalito, but the story they told us was incredible," said the general. "Morales and McCarty escaped and made it across. We apprehended Duncan and Miss Karimi. She escaped the following night. Duncan had been shot, but not fatally."

"You still have this Luther Duncan in custody?"

Sheridan shook his head. "He was in his room at the infirmary when the attack commenced. He was gone when the nurse went to check after the attack was over."

Larissa's eyebrows came together. "Was the infirmary hit by the bombs?"

"No," said the general. "There was just minor damage from blasts nearby."

Larissa sat back. She had just been given a lot to take in. "Do you think Ramon, Fatemeh and Billy were somehow working as spies for the Russians?"

Sheridan took a deep breath and let it out slowly. "My gut tells me no. They told one of my men they were spying for us. If so, it's the first I heard about it. They're wanted fugitives. We need to clear this matter up one way or the other. Will you help?"

Larissa swallowed hard. Although she first met Ramon as a bounty hunter hired to track him down, she eventually learned she had been on the wrong side. Would she be on the right side or the wrong side if she tracked them again? She considered what would happen if she turned down the job. They'd send another marshal after them—perhaps one who only saw them as potential spies. She could see that conflict going badly. "If I take this job, will I be able to continue work on the lightning wolves?"

The general smiled. "Absolutely. Once you've tracked down these fugitives, we'd like to discuss the establishment of a laboratory. You can think about who you'd like to deputize to help you with this project."

"Thank you, sir." Larissa removed the badge from the box and pinned it on her jacket. "Can I see where this Luther Duncan last was?"

The general looked over his shoulder. "Captain Belvedere!" A moment later a captain entered the room and saluted. "Take Marshal Crimson over to the infirmary and show her where Luther Duncan was last seen."

"That's Seaton, sir," she said.

"Huh? What?"

"Marshal Larissa Seaton," she said, using her real name.

"Very well." The general stood and shook her hand. "Good luck. I hope you can find them and help us learn what they were up to."

"I'll do my best, sir."

With that, she followed Captain Belvedere out of the general's quarters and over to the infirmary. He showed her the bed where he had been. The pillow was still dented where his head had lain. In the middle lay a feather. She picked it up.

"Captain, do you know what kind of bird this is from?"

He shrugged. "I'm hardly an expert, but it looks sort of like an owl feather to me."

As Sausalito's clapboard houses came into view, Hoshi heard gunfire and shouts. He scanned the town with the telescope from his vantage point in the hills. A mob gathered on the docks. The Russian boats hung a little way out. Some turned and sailed further up into the bay. He hated to guess about the details without more evidence, but it looked to him like Sausalito's residents had turned on the Russians, refusing to give them safe harbor.

Hoshi and Maravilla made their way down the hillside into town. The main street wasn't quite deserted, but it was quiet. A woman swept the boardwalk in front of her mercantile store. The professor approached and tipped his hat. "Good madam, we've just arrived in town and were looking for some friends of ours."

She gave them a suspicious stare. Hoshi had grown used to Americans eyeing his robes and takuhatsugasa warily, but suspected that water-wrinkled trousers and a tailcoat made Maravilla almost a stranger sight. "Three friends, you say?" She shook her head. "I don't know about three, but there were two strangers staying down at Chandler's boarding house just a couple days ago." She pointed to a house a few doors down across the street.

"Thank you, madam," said Maravilla with another tip of his hat.

They walked over to the boarding house and let themselves in the front door. They found a bald man wearing an apron and a bow tie sitting on a divan. He looked as troubled as Maravilla.

"May I help you ... gentlemen?"

"We're looking for three friends of ours," said Maravilla. "Their names were Morales, McCarty and they might have been joined by a Miss Karimi."

Mr. Chandler scowled. "Them? They brought me nothing but trouble. The Russians brought them here as prisoners. They escaped yesterday morning. They stole three horses." His eyes brightened a little. "One of them was the colonel's own horse! You should have seen the look in his eyes when he found it missing." Chandler shook his head. "Don't ask me why I was so willing to help the Russians. It just felt better than fighting them."

Hoshi knelt down and looked into Chandler's eyes. "That's all right," he said. "Do you know which way they went?"

Chandler pointed behind him. "Hoof prints went north, out of town."

Maravilla shrugged. "We're on a peninsula. That's the only direction to go on horseback."

Hoshi sighed and turned toward the professor. "They would be miles ahead of us by now. I could track them."

Maravilla tipped his hat and led Hoshi outside. "I'm not sure I see the point. The battle is over and Legion is silent. Whatever they do at this point is their business. I think the best thing we can do to help them is return the mechanical owl. One of them must have stolen it to escape the Presidio. Perhaps if the army has it back in working order, they won't have as many charges to press against them."

Hoshi nodded thoughtfully. "Yes, and I'll return the boat to the man who sold it to me. It will save finding more silver coins."

Maravilla walked across the street to the mercantile store. Inside, he found a few tools and a coil of rope. He had just enough left in his pouch to cover the supplies along with some dried meat and day-old bread for lunch.

As they stepped outside, Hoshi said, "I still don't understand what your friends hoped to accomplish."

"The part of Legion with the Russians—the majority of the swarm, really—wanted to unite Russia and the United States under one government. The part with me had learned things from its experiences in Denver. It was weak. It came to another person and me to heal."

"Who was the other person?"

"An engineer-turned-pirate named Onofre Cisneros," said Maravilla. "It had learned hard lessons in Denver." The professor shook his head. "I had hoped the part of Legion that was with me—that I shared with Ramon—would convey those lessons to the part of Legion with the Russians."

"Do you think it worked?"

The professor handed a piece of meat to Hoshi and then took out a piece for himself. He chewed on it for a while without answering. As they reached the edge of town, they saw the mob at the docks had dispersed. The Russian boats grew distant as they sailed northward. Hoshi and Maravilla decided to skirt the hills, rather than go up and over.

"Whatever happened when the two parts of Legion came together, they decided to leave," said Maravilla as they worked their way along the rocky shoreline. "I don't know why, but I do know that it will give the Russians and Americans a chance to work out their differences without interference. That's probably what Fatemeh and Ramon would have wanted."

"So, they did achieve their goal," said Hoshi.

"It would seem so."

They reached the ornithopter by the middle of the afternoon. Hoshi helped Maravilla uncover it. The professor repaired the broken control line and hammered out some dents. He held his finger up and tested the wind's direction. Grabbing the ornithopter by the tail, he turned it so it faced the direction he wanted. Hoshi stood back as the professor made some adjustments to the mechanism under the seat.

The professor stood upright and clasped Hoshi's hand in his own. "Thank you for your help, my friend. I hope to see you soon."

"Safe travels," said Hoshi.

The professor climbed into the ornithopter and activated a lever. The machine hopped twice, then caught the sea breeze with a mighty flap.

The samurai watched as the mechanical owl spiraled up and over the bay, then flapped its way back to San Francisco. Hoshi gathered up the boat's anchor and pushed it out into water, then climbed in. He raised the sail and tacked the boat back across the Golden Gate.

Larissa dreamed. In the dream, she ran with the doll called Lyssa Crimson. Her cousin Alethea ran by her side. Larissa stopped in her tracks, moved the doll's arm as though it reached down to the top of its socks. Then she brought its hand forward with a great *kerzap!* Alethea's cheeks turned pink as she laughed at the silly sound.

"And that's how Lyssa stopped the desperate cattle rustlers with her remarkable new invention, the smallest and most powerful lightning gun she had made," said Larissa.

Alethea reached out and took the doll. "That's silly," she said. "Pretty girls do not round up bad guys and they don't hide guns in their garters that go kerzap."

This time it was Larissa's turn to laugh. She knelt down beside Alethea. "All girls are pretty and they can do absolutely anything they want."

"Mrs. Hall down the road isn't pretty. She has a crooked nose and a wart right here." Alethea scrunched up her face and pointed to her cheek.

"But wasn't she right there helping Mr. Jenkins when he got his wagon mired down in the mud during the last rain?" Larissa poked Alethea's nose, making her giggle again. "She helped when the important men from town didn't want to get their hands dirty. To me, that's beautiful."

Alethea hugged her doll close. "I think you're beautiful, Larissa." She took extra time to make certain she pronounced her cousin's name correctly. "Even more beautiful than Lyssa here."

Larissa reached out to collect her cousin into a hug. As she did, the ground shifted. A fissure opened up and Alethea fell away. Larissa jumped after her cousin. Instead of catching her, instead of hitting the bottom, she awoke with a tear in her eye.

Muted light eased its way around the curtains of the Pullman car. Larissa sat up slowly, remembering she was on the train heading down the California coast. Professor Maravilla and Hoshi had arrived at the Presidio reporting that Ramon, Fatemeh and Billy had disappeared. She could go north after them, but the lightning wolves didn't hold enough fuel for an extended chase. If she went on horseback, they'd likely disappear in the Sierras or Oregon Territory long before she caught up with them. It was best if she went back to Fort Bliss and watched for signs of them settling down. Then she could find them, talk to them, and figure out what best to do.

Someone knocked on her bedroom door. "Just a minute."

Larissa climbed down from the berth and opened the door just a crack, revealing Professor Maravilla. "There were two telegrams of interest in the catcher pouch the train grabbed as we passed San Luis Obispo." He held one aloft. "The Edison Company is interested in funding my experiments with the ornithopters, perhaps adapting the engines from steam to electromagnetic power. Such an advancement would have clear potential for the lightning wolves as well."

"That sounds a little like working for the military." Larissa blinked, trying to clear the cobwebs from her mind. "How did they even find you?"

"The telegram's been forwarded through several stations. I'm guessing the army helped them out."

"Are you willing to work for them?" Her gaze narrowed.

"I'm willing to think about it," he said. "After our adventures, I've learned that darkness comes in all forms from many different places. All we can do is stand firm and fight it the best way we can. If Edison can help me do that, I'm willing to help them." He gave a faint smile, then blushed. "I didn't drag you out of bed to talk about me." He passed a second slip of paper through the door. "This telegram was addressed to you."

She took it from the professor and muttered thanks. A month ago, she would have been delighted to hear the news about the funding. She was still pleased for the professor, but it didn't mean as much to her now that she had her own responsibilities.

The second telegram was unsigned and contained one sentence. "The owls are flying to Estancia."

Larissa smiled. Returning to El Paso was the right answer after all. Ramon, Fatemeh, and Billy were heading to a spot two days' ride to the north of her destination.

The train stopped in Mesilla and Hoshi said his good-byes to Larissa, Maravilla, Harris, and Lorenzo. Lorenzo and Larissa promised he would get payment within the week for all his help. After all, he had completed the mission the colonel sent him on. Bresnahan met justice, and though destroyed, the lightning gun was accounted for.

Hoshi saddled his horse and rode back to the farm. How long had he been gone? He tried to count the days. It really hadn't been that many. Even so, he was sure the mayordomo would have forgotten to water every day. Even if he had, weeds probably encroached and choked the plants.

As he reached the farm, he was surprised to see the chilies had sprouted, tall and strong. Even more surprising, there were no weeds. The field was in fine shape. His brow furrowed as he approached the house and saw someone sitting in a chair on the porch with his feet on the railing.

Billy McCarty tipped his hat back on his head. "I thought you were never going to get here. That army train must have been traveling real slow."

"You're a wanted man, Billy."

"All my hard work making sure the crop is tended and that's how you treat me?"

Hoshi dismounted and wrapped his horse's reins around the porch rail. "I was worried about you. You disappeared. By the code of Bushido, you should have come back and explained yourself."

"I had a higher calling," said Billy. "I had to get Ramon and Fatemeh back to Estancia for their wedding." He lowered his hat. "Now that you're back, I need to get back there and help them get everything set up." He stepped off the porch with a wave. He took a few steps toward the barn, then looked back. "I almost forgot. You're invited."

"After all the trouble I've been through," said Hoshi, "I would hope so. Saddle your horse and let's go. It's a long ride to Estancia."

EPILOGUE
FATEMEH AND RAMON

Ramon "Búho" Morales sat in his room, reading the front page of the newspaper, trying not to think about the permanence of the vows he was about to take. Sure, he had taken oaths when he first became a deputy, then a sheriff, but a person could quit those jobs and walk away. A sheriff could decide whether or not to stand for reelection, but the way he was raised, marriage was permanent until one party or the other died.

The paper's headline declared "America and Russia Have Entered Peace Talks." Glancing through the article, Ramon learned that Russia was reluctant to give back all the territory it had gained. At the same time, controlling that territory would be difficult and the Ottoman Turks had made an incursion in Russia's west. The Russians needed soldiers to defend their homeland. Ramon had no doubt that the American territory seized by the Russians was difficult to control because they no longer had Legion to help make people compliant.

Ramon's thoughts drifted to the strange alien being. Would it just sit back and observe or would it find a way to help without interfering too much? Even after his recent experience, he didn't find it much easier to understand the alien than he had when Fatemeh told him about her encounter. The experience of meeting Legion and talking to it was so dreamlike he had difficulty thinking of it as anything but a dream.

More real was a stack of responses from the universities he had written to. Several were interested in having him as a student as long he could raise the required tuition fees. Ramon would look into that when he returned from his honeymoon.

Ramon's cousin, Eduardo Morales, opened the door. "You

244

going to sit there reading the paper all day, or you going to finish getting ready?"

Ramon laughed nervously as he folded the paper. "Things have been such a whirlwind the last few weeks, I haven't really had a chance to think this whole thing through…"

"What is there to think about, cuz?"

Ramon looked out the window.

"When you make a decision, does it matter to you what she thinks?" asked Eduardo.

Ramon nodded.

"Is she there for you when you're in trouble?"

Ramon remembered how she led a team of Professor Maravilla's ornithopters to stop the Russian airships and rescue him. He considered how she risked herself to rescue him from the midst of Russian-occupied Sausalito. "Absolutely."

"Are you there for her when she's in trouble?"

He remembered rescuing her from a mob in Socorro. Then a sensation like ice formed in his gut. "I left her on the dock at the Presidio as soldiers approached."

"Why did you do that? Why were you even there?"

"Because she wanted to heal the country by finding out why the Russian invasion continued even after we had destroyed the airships over Denver."

Eduardo glanced over at the paper. "And you succeeded, didn't you?"

Ramon shrugged. "We at least made it possible for healing to begin."

"That's what most good healers do. The body has to heal itself." Eduardo sat back and smiled. "Do you think about her every waking moment that your mind isn't occupied elsewhere?"

Now Ramon shifted uncomfortably under his cousin's gaze. "Um … not really."

Eduardo slapped his cousin on the shoulder and laughed. "Me neither."

Ramon leaned forward menacingly. "I'm glad you don't think about Fatemeh that way."

"Hey, I've got my own wife to think about." Eduardo stood and retrieved a deep blue cravat and handed it to Ramon.

Ramon tied it once, wasn't satisfied, untied it, then tied it again. He started to untie it once more. "It looks fine." Eduardo handed Ramon a purple waistcoat. Once Ramon put that on, he donned a dark gray tailcoat.

"I think you look good enough to get married," said Eduardo.

Ramon looked in the mirror, ran a brush through his hair one more time, then hooked his thumbs under his jacket's lapels and admired himself. "I do look pretty good, don't I?"

Before he could reach for the comb again, Eduardo ushered him out of the house. Neighbors from all around Estancia had brought wooden folding chairs and set them up. The morning was beautiful. A few clouds formed on the Manzano Mountains, indicating monsoon season approached. A slight breeze kept the weather from being too hot. Even so, sweat beaded on Ramon's forehead.

He looked around at the crowd gathered. Eduardo's wife, Alicia sat up near the front. Billy McCarty and Luther Duncan sat next to a Japanese man in fine robes he didn't recognize. No matter, they all seemed to be friends. Luther's arm was still in a sling and it was unclear he'd ever use it again. Despite that, he looked well and relatively happy.

Larissa Crimson sat next to Professor Maravilla and Colonel Johnson. The colonel wore his finest dress blues and the professor wore a fine new red waistcoat and black cravat, reminding him of a proud, red robin. Larissa, as normal, wore not a spot of red, but did sport a tailored black jacket. On the lapel was a silver shield. Even from the distance, he recognized a United States Marshal's badge.

As he looked around the crowd, he was pleased to see so many friends and neighbors. Mr. and Mrs. Castillo who ran a boarding house in Mesilla were there as well as Sergeants Lorenzo and Harris. He even saw friends from Socorro—Ray Hillerman, who replaced him as sheriff and Mrs. Gilson who ran the rooming house where he had lived. Standing at the front of the crowd was Father Esteban, the parish priest of San Miguel in Socorro.

"I think it's time to begin," said Sofia Morales from the door of her house.

She stepped aside and Fatemeh appeared. She wore a dress of brilliant azul that brought out the green in her eyes. The blue shade honored the adage, "If you wear blue, your marriage is true." Ramon's mother had tailored the dress to fit Fatemeh's form without needing a corset. Although a corset revealed a woman's figure and a veil hid it, Fatemeh felt they were much the same. Both were ways to make a woman conform to a man's ideal image. The dress was cut with a high waistline as was fashionable and had a small bustle to fill it out and give it a little more shape.

Ramon's breath caught. She held out her arm and he took it.

Eduardo took up an accordion and played as stately a tune as possible.

The entire audience stood. Fatemeh and Ramon walked down the aisle together. She would have it no other way. They were equals under Bahá'í teaching. She was not a prize to be won by some man waiting at the altar.

Father Esteban took out a piece of paper and read a Bahá'í wedding prayer Fatemeh translated. He stumbled over a few words, but Ramon hardly noticed. He found it difficult to hear because of the sound of blood rushing in his head. Father Esteban then made the sign of the cross and said a prayer in Latin. He reached behind him to a rough, wooden table, dipped the host in a goblet of wine and gave it to Ramon, but not to Fatemeh.

As Ramon took the Holy Communion, he closed his eyes and became aware of a rumble of hooves. He tensed, fearing a band of outlaws come to rob the wedding party.

When he opened his eyes to look, Father Esteban said, "Is there anyone here who objects to the union of this man and this woman?"

Riders approached, firing guns skyward, causing most of those at the wedding to drop to the ground. Many reached for their own side arms. Ramon whirled around. The leader reared his horse and let out a hardy laugh. He wore a tailcoat and a brilliant blue waistcoat with denim trousers. On his head was a peaked naval cap. "Are we late?" called Captain Onofre Cisneros of the pirate ship *Tiburón*.

"Just a little," called Fatemeh. "Tend your horses and find seats."

The ceremony paused for a few minutes while those in the audience resumed their seats and discussed the new arrivals. Onofre Cisneros and his band of buccaneers took their horses to the water trough and then joined the others in the seats. Once the group was settled, Father Esteban repeated the question. "Is there anyone here who objects to the union of this man and this woman?"

"You already asked that," called out Eduardo. "Let's move on!"

The crowd broke out in laughter. Father Esteban held out his hands, attempting to calm the crowd. He had Ramon and Fatemeh take hands. "Repeat after me. We will all, verily, abide by the Will of God."

Ramon and Fatemeh repeated the Bahá'í wedding vows.

"I now declare you husband and wife."

With those words, the pirates jumped up, whooping and hollering. The rest of the crowd joined in as Ramon and Fatemeh embraced, exchanging a passionate kiss.

After that, things became even more of a blur for Ramon. Eduardo handed him a glass of beer. Platters of food prepared by Sofia Morales and the Castillos appeared. Ramon and Fatemeh joined in a dance while Eduardo played. After the first song, one of the pirates took the accordion from Eduardo and played a lively tune while Eduardo and Alicia joined in the dancing.

Breathless, Ramon and Fatemeh whirled away from the other dancers. Fatemeh tapped Ramon on the shoulder and inclined her head toward the house. There, Larissa leaned against the wall, her arms folded. Seeing the couple away from the other dancers she stepped forward. She hugged both of them, saying, "Congratulations." Then she stepped back. "I don't want to spoil this fine day, but I do have a warrant for your arrest."

Just then, Onofre Cisneros appeared. "Don't you know? That's why we're here."

Larissa's eyebrows came together. "What?"

"We're here to kidnap the happy couple."

"Kidnap them? What?" Larissa shook her head.

"We're going to give them a honeymoon in the South

Pacific," said Captain Cisneros. "You won't have a chance to arrest them!"

At that point, Ramon noticed that a crowd had gathered around them. Billy and Luther stepped forward together. "You can take both of us in," said Billy. "We'll do our best to answer questions." He turned to Ramon. "Consider it our wedding present to you for all you've done." He cast a glance back at the Japanese man who folded his arms and nodded approval.

"We'll be lucky if we don't end up facing prison terms when we return," laughed Ramon.

"That's why Luther Duncan is going, too," said Billy. "We need someone who can put a few words together."

Larissa looked over to Colonel Johnson. "Well, the army wasn't too happy about Mr. Duncan disappearing either. He's named in the warrant, too."

"All right. Now that that's settled, will you join me for a dance?" Billy held his hand out to Larissa.

The accordion player kicked up another song while Billy and Larissa started the next dance. Soon others joined in.

Ramon looked over at Fatemeh. "A voyage to the South Pacific?"

"It took a while to find the good captain, but I thought it would be fun," said Fatemeh. "It's just what we need."

He bent down and kissed her again.

The party continued on into the afternoon. As clouds started forming overhead, the platters of food were cleared. Eduardo and Alicia appeared with Ramon and Fatemeh's horses, their saddlebags all packed for a new adventure. The pirates climbed onto their horses and Ramon and Fatemeh followed them down the road. As they passed the gate, a burrowing owl on a nearby fencepost danced from one leg to another and bobbed its head. Fatemeh gave it a few chirping whistles. A lightning bolt struck near the Manzanos and the owl flew from its perch.

Ramon gazed into Fatemeh's eyes and thought he was the luckiest man alive.

ABOUT THE AUTHOR

David Lee Summers became a steampunk in 1987 when he used a nineteenth century telescope on Nantucket to examine the evolution of distant pulsating stars. Since that time, he has published twelve novels and numerous short stories and poems spanning a wide range of the imagination. *Owl Dance* is the first of the Clockwork Legion series. His other novels include *The Solar Sea* and *Vampires of the Scarlet Order*.

David's short stories have appeared in such magazines and anthologies as *Realms of Fantasy, Cemetery Dance, Gears and Levers, Zombiefied: An Anthology of All Things Zombie,* and *These Vampires Don't Sparkle*. In 2010 he was nominated for the Science Fiction Poetry Association's Rhysling Award.

In addition to writing, David edited the quarterly science fiction and fantasy magazine *Tales of the Talisman* along with four science fiction anthologies: *A Kepler's Dozen, Space Pirates, Space Horrors,* and *Maximum Velocity: The Best of the Full-Throttle Space Tales*. When not working with the written word, David still spends time operating telescopes at Kitt Peak National Observatory. Learn more about David at www.davidleesummers.com

www.ingramcontent.com/pod-product-compliance
Lightning Source LLC
Chambersburg PA
CBHW022035240626
47154CB00007B/2416